AF440024

FRACTURED LIES

LANTERN BEACH EXPOSURE
BOOK 1

CHRISTY BARRITT

Copyright © 2023 by Christy Barritt

All rights reserved.

No part of this book may be reproduced in any form or by any electronic or mechanical means, including information storage and retrieval systems, without written permission from the author, except for the use of brief quotations in a book review.

CHAPTER
ONE

JONAH GRAY GLANCED at his watch again.

Ganon "Gandalf" Jones was ten minutes late. It wasn't like his friend not to be on time.

Ganon was always punctual, always polite, and always knew every detail of a situation down to what seemed insignificant. When they were younger, those attributes had driven Jonah crazy.

Jonah leaned back in his wooden chair at The Nautilus Bistro, an upscale Baltimore restaurant, and let the scent of both the harbor and freshly cooked seafood waft over him. He had an amazing view of the water and boats outside as he sat near the window and waited.

He'd already downed one glass of sweet tea, and he'd finished the basket of bread the waitress had brought ten minutes ago.

What was taking his friend so long?

Ganon had called and said he needed to talk. His voice had held an urgent tone.

So Jonah had come here to meet. He hadn't planned on traveling to Maryland from Cincinnati, where he'd been working a security job. But his friend had sounded nervous. That had made Jonah even more curious about the unexpected phone call.

Jonah had promised Ganon many years ago that if he needed him, Jonah would be there. All he had to do was call. Jonah had meant the words.

He'd give it another couple of minutes, and then he'd try to contact his friend.

Jonah's mind raced as he waited. He took another sip of his refilled tea and checked his phone for any missed calls.

There were none.

He and Ganon were unlikely friends. Jonah had been a football player in high school, and Ganon a straight-A STEM student.

When the two of them had been placed in the same foster care home, they'd initially kept their distance.

It wasn't that Jonah and Ganon didn't like each other or get along. They'd simply traveled in different circles and had different interests.

But that changed during their senior year of high school when their foster parents had gotten into an argument. When things started to get physical, Jonah ran interference between them, and his foster dad had taken out his frustrations on Jonah, cornering him and throwing punches.

Ganon had intercepted and taken a couple of blows for Jonah, giving them both just enough time to flee the toxic household. Thankfully, a group home had taken them in so they could finish high school together.

The two had become lifelong friends.

Jonah had gone on to join the military, where he'd served for more than a decade.

And Ganon had gotten a full-ride scholarship and received his degree in molecular engineering at MIT. He'd later begun working as a scientist for one of the world's leading skincare and cosmetic companies.

The two didn't talk often, but Jonah liked to catch up with his friend whenever he could.

He glanced at his watch again. Ganon was fifteen minutes late. It was time to call him.

Just as Jonah pulled his phone out, Ganon stepped through the front door.

The man was tall—six foot four—with a robust belly and curly dark hair left a little too shaggy to look professional. He wore oversized, dark-rimmed glasses and ill-fitting clothes.

Style had never been Ganon's thing. But that was okay. He had more important attributes.

In fact, the sci-fi and fantasy nerd had officially changed his name to Gandalf as soon as he'd hit eighteen. Ganon was a true original and never failed to amuse Jonah with his stories and *The Lord of the Rings* fanboy antics. Ganon had even bought some kind of ring patterned from the book and had proudly worn it throughout high school and college.

He was the closest thing Jonah had to a brother.

Jonah stood, relieved to see his friend. Thankfully, all the worst-case scenarios that had raced through his mind had proven incorrect.

It was a hazard of the job. Jonah had seen so many terrible things that sometimes it was hard to stop seeing more terrible things around every corner.

But he was working on changing that outlook. After Anna's death, everything had shifted. Sometimes Jonah felt like he was living up to his name—like he was running from his potential.

Would it take a big fish swallowing him to make him see the light?

That was the question he often wrestled with.

As Ganon walked closer, Jonah noted the sweat across his friend's forehead and how his skin seemed flushed. Was Ganon getting sick? Or was something wrong?

Jonah gave Ganon a brief but forceful man hug.

As soon as they sat down across from each other, Jonah asked, "You doing okay, man?"

Ganon quickly unwrapped his silverware and used the linen napkin to dab his forehead. "It's just so hot outside."

Jonah made a face. It was unseasonably warm for February. However, temperatures in the high sixties weren't what Jonah would describe as hot.

"I'm glad you made it." Jonah decided not to press the issue. "I was getting worried about you there for a while."

"Sorry about that." Ganon paused and took a long drink of his water. In fact, he practically finished the entire goblet in one swallow. "There's been a lot going on."

"It sounds like it." Jonah shifted in his stiff wicker chair. "Do you want to talk about it now or do you want to order some food first?"

Food always made his friend feel better. Ganon especially loved comfort food.

Most wounded people found ways to soothe their pain. Eating was Ganon's.

Jonah had his own vices. He supposed everyone did.

Ganon glanced at the laminated menu in front of him. "Maybe we should order. I don't know why I'm so shaky."

He was probably just upset, Jonah mused. But he was curious as to what Ganon would be this anxious about.

His friend was usually so even-keeled. Ganon could use his logic as a weapon—to win arguments, to bring peace to tense situations, to put the arrogant in their rightful place. His intelligence had frustrated more than one social worker.

The thing was—Ganon was always right. Some people just couldn't admit it.

Jonah looked at the menu as if he didn't know what he wanted to order. He did—the crabcakes were clearly the superior choice—but he gave Ganon some time to decide and catch his breath.

Finally, Ganon seemed to gather himself and closed the menu.

Jonah motioned for the waitress—a pretty twentysomething woman who giggled a lot and threw him lingering glances—and they ordered.

Ganon asked for the chicken tenders, fries, and a soda, while Jonah ordered crabcakes with a side of hushpuppies and another sweet tea.

Their food choices were as different as their personalities.

"You're looking good." Ganon quickly glanced at Jonah. "Then again, that's not surprising. Tell me about your love life so I can vicariously live through you. You've had much more luck in that area than I have."

Jonah let out a puff of air through his nose.

He hadn't told Ganon about Anna. The two of

them were never supposed to be together. Their relationship had been off limits.

Which had made it even harder to handle when she was killed.

No one knew just how much she'd meant to Jonah. Even in her death, he hadn't been able to let anyone know how special she was—not if he'd wanted to keep his job.

He shifted in his seat and cast those thoughts aside. "No love life right now."

Ganon nodded at the pretty waitress. "She might be interested."

Jonah let out a quick, airy laugh, ready to change the subject. Certainly this wasn't why Ganon wanted to meet.

"I don't know about that," Jonah finally muttered. "How about you? Are you still dating that girl? Nancy, right?"

Ganon frowned. "She moved to California to work for Google."

"Sorry, man. But you never know when a cute little scientist might show up at your job."

Jonah didn't like scientists—other than Ganon. Probably because he'd been selected for a special assignment while in the military. One of the stipulations required him to be a lab rat.

After everything he'd been through, he no longer trusted anyone with a microscope. The scars on his back and arms reminded him every day of what those researchers put him through.

"Dating doesn't matter too much to me anyway." Ganon wiped his forehead again. "I'm basically married to my job. That's about all I can handle lately."

"Make sure you take care of yourself." Maybe that was his friend's problem. Maybe Ganon was working too much. Maybe he needed more exercise and sunlight.

"I've been trying to get some 'me' time in." Ganon raised his eyebrows and shrugged to indicate he hadn't succeeded.

"You don't seem like yourself . . ." Jonah continued to study his friend, an uneasy feeling jostling inside him.

"There's something important I need to tell you." With a quick scan of the restaurant, Ganon leaned in and lowered his voice. "Maybe I just need to get this off my chest before the anxiety kills me. You're the only person I can talk to about this."

Jonah didn't like the sound of that. "What's going on?"

Ganon leaned closer. "It's about the company I work for."

"Ocean Essence?" The international company wasn't exactly a clandestine operation. They developed beauty products and invested in fancy ads to sell their "fountain of youth" serums to the masses. Ganon was the head research and development scientist there.

In fact, the company was getting ready to open a new facility as they ventured into the marine biomedical field. That's what Ganon had told Jonah last time they'd talked, at least.

Ganon's face went a little paler. "Yes, that's right. Since I've been working there, I've noticed some things that don't seem quite on the up and up."

"Are we talking about animal testing or something?" It was the only nefarious thing Jonah could imagine a skincare company being up to.

Ganon's eyes shifted back and forth quickly—too quickly. "No, it's more than that. The board . . . they've been having all these after-hour meetings, ones not noted on the schedule. Dr. Frank Hensley, the CEO, has been asking me some weird questions."

"What kind of weird questions?" Jonah wasn't sure where his friend was going with this.

He leaned closer. "I suspect someone in the company is selling proprietary information to the competition."

Jonah tilted his head. "That doesn't sound good."

Ganon's features suddenly seemed more drawn. "I know it sounds very white collar. But the cosmetics industry is actually a cutthroat business."

Jonah shifted and took another sip of his tea. "I

guess you're going to have to spell your concerns out for me then, because I'm not following. You think this person who stole the formulas will cause trouble for you in particular? Or just the company?"

"I've been working on cutting-edge, million-dollar projects." He ran a hand over his face. "But some of the formulas aren't completed yet and clinical testing has already begun. I can't verify anything yet—"

"So this could be a liability?"

"It could be, but it's much more than that. I think I know who—" Before Ganon could finish his statement, his hand covered his chest then moved to his throat. His eyes began bulging, and his face reddened.

As alarm raced through him, Jonah stood, his chair toppling behind him. "Are you okay, man?"

Ganon only clutched his throat.

But he hadn't eaten anything. He couldn't be choking.

"Someone, call 911!" Jonah shouted as patrons around him stared.

He rushed to the other side of the table and grabbed Ganon's arm. "Is something lodged in your throat?"

Ganon shook his head.

"Then let's get you laid down." Jonah moved the chair and laid his friend on the floor.

Panic flashed in his friend's gaze. Then he reached into his pocket, pulled something out, and pressed it into Jonah's hand.

A torn piece of paper with the name *Rachel Atwood* on it.

"Ganon . . . what does this mean?" Jonah leaned closer, desperate to understand what was happening. "Who is Rachel?"

"Ki . . . killed . . ."

Jonah's muscles bristled. "Rachel Atwood did this to you?"

Before Ganon could say anything else, his friend suddenly began seizing.

"YOU SURE YOU want to do this?"

Jonah gripped his phone as he stood in his temporary bedroom and stared at the dark, ominous ocean in the distance. "I've never been more certain of anything."

"You know Vincent and Tex will have your back." Larchmont's deep voice dipped even lower. "But you're treading in dangerous territory. We don't know what these people are capable of. Be careful."

"Will do." As Jonah's jaw tightened, thunder cracked overhead.

The storm would be a doozy.

Was it a sign of things to come? He prayed that wasn't the case.

"Okay, then," Larchmont continued. "Remember to keep your eye on Rachel Atwood. She's our best suspect right now. She effortlessly moved into Ganon's position at Ocean Essence after his death. She had the most to gain."

Jonah remembered how Ganon had given him that paper with her name on it before he died.

Followed by uttering the word "killed."

Jonah's back muscles tightened.

He'd researched the woman. She appeared unassuming. But Jonah knew that sometimes the deadliest people weren't the ones who looked the most dangerous.

That was what made them even more threatening.

"The plan is already in place." Jonah continued to stare outside as lightning split the sky. "I won over her dad hook, line, and sinker. He even said I could stay at his place while he's out of town. I've got my foot in the door."

"So now you just need to befriend Rachel and see if she'll share the truth. You should be an ace at this, Romeo."

Jonah grimaced. He hated when people called him that.

He had used his looks on occasion to find out information he needed. But that was only while he'd been in the field, when life-or-death intelligence needed to be obtained.

"I don't plan on breaking her heart, if that's what

you're implying." Jonah squeezed his phone harder as Anna's picture filled his mind.

He knew all about heartbreak. He didn't want to put anyone through that.

"I only agreed to let you do this mission because it's important to you," Larchmont reminded him.

Jonah frowned at his boss's words. "I know. And I appreciate it."

Most of their jobs, they got paid for—paid handsomely. But there was no paycheck waiting at the end of this rainbow.

There would only be satisfaction in knowing that justice would be served for Ganon.

Jonah was so thankful his boss and colleagues with the Shadow Agency were onboard.

He would find out what happened to his friend if it was the last thing he did.

Because Jonah was certain that someone had murdered Ganon.

He ended his call with Larchmont and paused.

Rachel would arrive here on the island next week, and Jonah planned on getting to know her in order to find out answers. In the meantime, he'd gather as much information on the lab as he could. He'd run surveillance on it. Maybe break in to explore the facilities himself. He'd figure out where people in the company hung out, and he'd go there.

He'd already profiled Rachel, and Jonah knew

cornering her wasn't the best option for finding answers.

Instead, he needed to befriend her.

Every time the woman's image fluttered through his mind, anger churned inside him.

Ganon was a good man—a *great* man. He hadn't deserved to die the way he did.

Police claimed he had a heart attack, but Jonah knew there was more to it than that. Most likely, his friend was poisoned.

Someone must have paid off the medical examiner to cover up the truth. But Jonah had to prove that.

Something was going on at the Essence lab—something deadly—and Jonah needed to figure out what it was.

Though Ocean Essence was headquartered in New York, they had several production facilities strategically spread throughout the United States. Just last month, they completed construction of a two-story, state-of-the-art development lab on the shore of Lantern Beach. They'd brought in reputable scientists and other personnel to run the lab.

The new lab as well as Rachel Atwood had ultimately brought Jonah here.

Ganon hadn't worked at this location. He'd worked at the previous development lab in Baltimore.

Jonah had broken into the facility himself to look for answers, but he hadn't found anything. Ganon's desk—and computer—had been wiped clean.

He'd gone to Ganon's home also, but it had been the same scenario—any potential evidence was gone. Surveillance cameras on a neighbor's house had showed two men entering his residence only moments after he'd died. They'd cleaned his computer and files.

If something shady was going on at Ganon's company, then Jonah wanted to figure out exactly what that was and put an end to it.

Above him, the lights in the house flickered twice before going dark.

The wind kicked up.

Thunder shook the house as lightning flashed overhead.

The storm must have knocked out power as winds ravaged the island.

Jonah opened the sliding glass door and stepped onto a sweeping covered balcony.

Dark clouds concealed the evening sky.

It was late March and still chilly outside. Beach-goers hadn't begun to fill these beaches yet, so that should make this the perfect time to be here.

The fewer people around to question him, the better.

As Jonah stood there, a door slammed somewhere within the house.

His muscles tensed.

In his line of work, he had to be extremely careful. Especially considering the enemies he'd made—too many enemies.

Anna's image fluttered through his mind again.

He reached for the gun beneath his shirt and held it close to his side.

Then he crept into the shadows and waited to find out who the intruder was.

———

Rachel Atwood dropped her keys on the table near the front door, set her purse on top of her rolling suitcase, and flipped the light switch.

Nothing happened.

Of course.

The storm must have taken out the power.

Thankfully, it was still warm inside the house.

She stripped off her jacket, which was now soaked from the torrential rain. The storm had come quickly, and she'd hardly been able to see the road as she'd driven from the ferry to her father's house.

She would have waited out the storm before heading to Lantern Beach, but her new boss had told her she could start tomorrow instead of next week.

She'd wanted to get here as soon as possible, even if that meant starting midweek.

She had her own reasons.

She hadn't told her father yet that she'd decided to come to Lantern Beach early.

She also hadn't told him why she'd fled Colorado and the danger there.

Rachel had been desperate to get away from the nightmare. Packing up, moving, and starting a whole new life seemed like the only way to escape.

She only prayed the men who'd been threatening her didn't follow her here.

Those guys were determined to silence her.

But their intimidation wouldn't work. When it came time for the trial, she would testify against Carl Nevada, a powerful businessman who thought he was above the law.

Rachel simply had to survive until he was put behind bars permanently.

There was no place like home—and there was especially no place like Lantern Beach. Being here was just what her soul needed.

When she'd heard her company was opening a lab here—and that the coveted job she'd been longing to do had opened up—she'd applied right away.

She was only sorry that her mentor had to die in order for her to get this position.

A pang echoed in her heart at the thought.

It wasn't the way she'd seen things going. But Ganon Jones would want her to carry out what he'd started.

Releasing a sigh, she paused and glanced around the dark house, a place full of childhood memories. The historic beach house had wooden ceilings, cozy dormers, and a massive stone fireplace.

It was pretty much perfect.

Thunder clapped overhead, and she jumped before scolding herself.

Those men hadn't found her.

Not yet.

It was just the storm outside.

She pulled herself together and took a step forward. "Hello? Dad?"

Rachel had peered in the garage when she arrived and had seen a truck parked there. She assumed it was her dad's latest ride. He loved changing vehicles whenever the whim hit him.

She remembered a time growing up when that hadn't been possible. A time when putting food on the table had been a challenge.

She was glad her father could pamper himself a little now. He'd earned it.

Another clap of thunder made her jump.

She paced forward, chastising herself for acting so frightened.

Until she saw a shadow move in the distance.

"Hello?" Her voice cracked.

No answer.

Fear shot through her.

Had one of Carl's men found her? Had he followed her here?

It wasn't her father.

He would have responded when she called out.

So who was this?

She sucked in a breath.

Maybe Carl's men *had* found her.

She scooted back, her hip hitting the table near the door.

The vase behind her tumbled before falling and shattering on the hardwood floor.

She flinched at the sound.

She glanced down.

Her keys had also fallen.

It was too dark to see them.

She could run, but not without her keys.

The nearest neighbor was too far away.

Her heart continued to race as she waited for whatever would happen next.

"Who's there?" Her voice trembled.

Then the shadow stepped forward.

As lightning lit the room, a man she'd never seen before flashed into sight.

He held a gun in his hands.

Rachel drew in a breath, preparing to scream, but the man's features softened when he spotted her.

"I'm not going to hurt you." The man tucked his gun into his waistband and raised his hands. "I wasn't expecting anyone here tonight."

Was that because the man had broken in? Was he a thief who'd been looking for the right opportunity to strike?

"Who are you?" Rachel's voice quivered as she stared at the stranger.

"I'm Jonah Gray, a guest of Roman Atwood."

A guest? Since when did her dad have guests here? "Dad didn't tell me he'd invited anyone to stay."

"Dad?"

She narrowed her eyes. "I'm Roman's daughter."

The man stepped back, his voice filling with realization. "So you're Rachel. I'm sorry to scare you. But he told me you weren't coming until Monday, and I was going to be gone by then. Then the power went out and—"

"Do you always bring a gun to people's houses when you stay?" Her voice hardened as she sifted through the truth of the situation.

"I always carry." The stranger stepped closer, his striking face highlighted again by the lightning that temporarily brightened the room. "For protection."

Rachel wanted to ask more about his need for a

gun, but her focus instantly shifted. She hadn't been expecting Jonah to be so close to her own age. Someone so muscular and fit.

"Maybe we can start again," he offered, his voice dipping with apology.

"Maybe." Rachel's spine softened just slightly when she heard the diplomacy in his voice. "Where's my father?"

"You just missed him. He left before the storm hit."

She frowned. "He told me he'd be here, that he didn't have any trips planned."

"A meeting with an investor in New Jersey popped up. He expects to be back in a few days."

Rachel would call her dad later to confirm that story.

"That's good news, at least." Her frown deepened. "How do you know my dad?"

"I work for him—just on a contractual basis. But he said I could stay here, and when I saw this place . . . how could I say no?"

Rachel stared at the man and nibbled on her bottom lip. His story sounded convincing, and she didn't see any signs that the man was lying.

She supposed if she'd told her father she was coming, then he would have mentioned his guest . . .

But before she could say anything else, a new sound filled the air.

Jonah stiffened and glanced at the other side of the house. "Did you hear that?"

"It sounded like someone crying for help."

They both darted toward the back deck.

They burst through the patio doors, and the wind whipped around them as they raced toward the railing.

Another cry for help cut through the sound of the storm.

As lightning flashed, Rachel spotted a man in the ocean, flailing as he struggled to stay afloat amidst the turbulent waves.

JONAH SAW THE MAN DROWNING. Leaving his gun on the picnic table, he sprinted toward the stairs leading down to the sand.

He unbuttoned his heavy corduroy shirt as he hit the ground running.

By the time he reached the dunes, his shoes were off, and he threw them aside.

Then he ran toward the water.

Cold rain pelted his face, and thunder shook the skies.

He couldn't worry about the weather now. Not when someone's life was on the line.

As soon as he reached the shoreline, he dove into the ice-cold ocean water.

Immediately, the turbulence tugged at him.

This rescue would be even more challenging than

he'd imagined. But he'd done things like this while in the military. He simply needed to keep focused on the task at hand.

Failure wasn't an option. His former commander had drilled that fact into him.

And so far, he hadn't failed—though Commander Lewis had considered it failure when Jonah had left his position in the military. He'd practically run from it—as had Vincent and Tex.

Anger still burned through him at the thought of Lewis.

That man had no regard for human life—especially for the orphans of the world, the people who had no one to miss them. To Lewis, people like Jonah were disposable.

Jonah swam out several yards before surfacing and searching the water around him.

Where had the man gone?

As lightning flashed overhead, Jonah thought he saw the man's head bobbing, only to disappear again.

Jonah quickly stroked through the water until he reached the area.

But the man was nowhere to be seen.

He must have gone under.

Jonah dove beneath the water again.

It was too dark to see anything through the churning waves.

He'd have to search the raging ocean with his hands if he wanted to find this guy.

As Jonah reached out, his arms swept the area. Finally, his hand connected with something —someone.

A leg. Jonah was certain of it.

Using his last burst of strength, he sucked in a breath and dove one more time.

His arms found the man's waist, and Jonah pulled the guy to the surface.

Jonah sucked in a deep gulp of air before turning the man on his back and beginning the arduous process of swimming with him to shore.

The undertow worked against them, trying to drag them farther out into the ocean.

It took some work, but Jonah made it through the waves to the shoreline.

As soon as his feet hit the sand, Rachel stepped into the breaking waves. Her long brown hair swarmed around her in the wind, and her eyes were wide with fright as she stared at the lifeless man in Jonah's arms.

But instead of shrinking, she met him in the water and helped pull the man ashore.

"I called 911," she shouted over the roar of the waves, wind, and rain.

Good. Jonah hoped paramedics would be here soon.

In the meantime, he knelt next to the man and shoved a finger against the man's neck.

He didn't feel a pulse.

He frowned.

Jonah hoped he hadn't gotten to this guy mere seconds too late.

————

Rachel fought panic as she stared at the lifeless man in front of her.

The rain plastered her hair to her face, and she kept shoving wet strands out of the way.

As Jonah began doing chest compressions, she knelt on the other side of the man and tried to ignore the bitter cold of the waves as they crashed around her, jostling her back and forth.

One big wave could pull her out into that ocean. That's how strong the water was right now.

In fact, when she was a child, this very ocean had nearly claimed her life.

To this day, those memories still terrified her.

"Anything?" She stared at Jonah.

He continued doing CPR and shook his head. "No, not yet."

"Keep trying." Rachel glanced at the beach in the distance.

Were those sirens she heard over the rumble of thunder and waves?

She hoped so. First responders couldn't get here fast enough for her liking.

"I'm not sure what happened." Jonah checked the man's pulse again. "He was alive only a few minutes ago. He wasn't underwater that long. He should've made it."

Rachel's heart beat harder.

She knew what he was saying. It was too late.

This man was gone.

But Jonah kept doing chest compressions. He didn't give up.

Finally, Rachel spotted a vehicle coming up the beach, its headlights spotlighting them.

She waved the driver over and then glanced down again.

Her gaze stopped on the man's hand.

The headlights illuminated numbers that had been written haphazardly there in black ink, almost like this guy had quickly scribbled a phone number so he wouldn't forget it.

The last four digits of the number caught her eye.

4189.

Rachel's heart beat harder.

She knew those numbers.

Her boss's phone number ended in those same digits.

She'd dialed it enough times to remember.

It had to be a coincidence, right?

Or was this man somehow associated with the new lab where Rachel would be working? She'd be with a whole new team here, so there was a good chance she wouldn't recognize everyone.

If that was the case, she suddenly felt much more unsettled about starting work tomorrow.

At that thought, the man's hand opened. It had been clenched into a fist, she realized.

But something dropped from his grasp.

A small golden dolphin necklace. The chain was wrapped partly around his wrist—that had to be the only reason he hadn't lost it in the ocean.

She sucked in a breath.

A golden dolphin?

This necklace looked identical to her necklace. The one her father had given her.

The one Carl Nevada had made a comment about once.

She shuddered at the sight of it.

This couldn't be a coincidence.

If Rachel couldn't be safe here on Lantern Beach, then maybe she wouldn't be safe anywhere.

JONAH SAW Rachel's face go pale when she glanced at the man's hand.

He'd seen the numbers written there. Seen the dolphin necklace.

Did that jewelry mean something to her? Those numbers? They had to. Otherwise, why would she have that reaction?

His suspicions about her grew.

As rescue workers surrounded them, Jonah stood and tugged Rachel away so the professionals could work.

The rain that hammered them was cold, and the sharp wind made the air feel even colder.

Rachel shivered again, and Jonah wished he had a coat to give her, but he didn't. He was still soaking wet from his dip in the sea.

Little things like that could help win her friendship—which was exactly what he needed to do, no matter the contempt he felt toward the woman.

Jonah knew as he watched EMTs work on the man that it was too late.

The man had been gone before Jonah had dragged him back to shore.

But this guy's death didn't make sense.

Too many things didn't add up.

The man, who appeared to be in his thirties, wore jeans, a sweater, and socks.

How would someone end up in the ocean on a stormy night fully clothed?

Jonah knew people did crazy things all the time, so it wasn't beyond the realm of possibility that the man had decided to jump in the ocean on such a bad night.

But he doubted it.

Or perhaps the man had been walking on the beach when a wave caught him and swept him away.

But Jonah didn't think that was the case either.

There was more going on here, and he didn't like the implications forming in his mind.

At least, Rachel had arrived early.

That would help him get to the bottom of things quicker.

Working for Roman was the perfect reason to

come here to Lantern Beach without raising anyone's suspicions.

Jonah may not like scientists—other than Ganon—but he'd set his personal feelings aside for the sake of this assignment.

He'd done uncountable undercover operations before.

This one should be a breeze.

But as he remembered how Rachel hadn't backed away from helping a man in need, his thoughts faltered. The selfish, deadly image he'd developed of her clashed with a new kind and gentle image that wanted to form.

Jonah had a feeling that this wouldn't be as easy as it seemed.

———

Jonah stared at Police Chief Cassidy Chambers as she got ready to take his and Rachel's statements in the kitchen of Roman Atwood's house.

Thanks to the storm, the chief's long blonde hair had escaped from the tidy bun once holding the locks back and now fell in wet tendrils around her face. Even though she'd worn a rain slicker outside, the brutal storm had pummeled her—all of them, actually.

The woman was probably close to Jonah's age—in her early thirties—and she came across as fit, capable, and all business.

Jonah had read up on the police chief before coming here. Knowing who he might encounter on Lantern Beach was of the utmost importance. It could mean the success or failure of an operation.

The power was still out, but Rachel had found some blankets to wrap around them to keep them warm until they could shower and change.

They sat at the kitchen table, and Rachel had lit a few candles around the room so they could see.

The two of them weren't being questioned as suspects, but the police chief needed to get their statements on the incident. Jonah understood the way these things worked—and he would comply.

But what he hadn't expected was for the police chief's eyes to be so sharp and perceptive—almost as if the woman could see through him.

Jonah would definitely need to keep an eye on her and be careful around her. Otherwise, his cover would be blown and he wouldn't be able to obtain the answers he needed.

"What's your name again?" Chief Chambers carefully observed him as she held a pad of paper and pen in her hands.

"Jonah Gray."

"And why are you here in Lantern Beach? At this house?"

"Mr. Atwood hired me as a security consultant for his company and then offered to let me stay here while I'm on the island. If you need to talk to him to confirm that, I totally understand."

"I may do that." Her gaze remained curious and intense. "How long are you in town?"

"Maybe a week or so." Jonah planned to stay until he had the answers he needed.

Chief Chambers nodded slowly. "Where are you from?"

"Upstate New York. But I travel all over for my job, sometimes setting up residence in other locations in order to oversee whatever project I'm working on at the time."

"Okay then." The chief turned to Rachel. "I don't think I've met you yet either."

"Rachel Atwood. I just moved here from Colorado. My things haven't even arrived yet." She frowned and pushed a wet strand of hair out of her face.

The woman was wicked smart, with two PhDs. Jonah imagined her and Ganon chatting about science.

The two of them probably had so much to talk about. Maybe not the sci-fi/fantasy stuff that Ganon had loved. But Ganon had been the smartest person Jonah had ever known.

Jonah wondered if Rachel might have given his friend a run for his money.

Was there a conniving side beneath her sweet exterior?

His gut tightened with anger.

There had to be.

Was she the one who'd sold that unfinished but proprietary information Ganon had mentioned?

That's what Jonah needed to find out. He would eavesdrop. Examine her bank account. Watch her every move.

Because the payout from selling that information would have been worth killing over—for some people, at least.

"And how are you related to Roman Atwood?" Chief Chambers turned to Rachel.

"He's my father."

The chief's eyebrows flicked up. "And what brings you this way?"

"I just accepted a new position with Ocean Essence." Rachel rubbed her fingers together as if nervous. "When the opportunity arose to come back to my home turf, I jumped on it. My dad isn't here all the time, but he is getting older. I'd like to spend more time with him. He's had more free time since he sold his company. He's working on another startup, but as time goes by he's been slowing down somewhat."

"I've seen him around town. He walks around with some type of digital recorder and is always muttering things into it."

"That sounds like my dad." A soft smile feathered across Rachel's lips. "He says his best ideas always happen when he's least expecting it, so he keeps that recorder in his pocket."

Jonah guessed Roman and Rachel had a good relationship. He'd seen pictures of the two scattered throughout the house, and their affection seemed genuine.

Roman had a lopsided grin that consumed his narrow face. The sixty-something man had a head full of white hair, a thin build, and he wore thick round glasses. Looking at him, most people wouldn't guess he was a self-made millionaire.

But he'd remained dedicated to his family despite his success.

For a long time, Jonah had envied people who had that kind of family life. It wasn't until his mid-twenties that he'd finally accepted the fact that a close family wasn't in the cards for him.

God must have had different plans for him—or, at least, God had been able to use Jonah's harsh circumstances to make him into the person he was today.

But was Jonah who God wanted him to be?

The question had haunted him for years now, and he had no definitive answers.

How could a good and just God love and forgive someone who'd done everything Jonah had?

"THANK you both for your valiant efforts tonight." Chief Chambers closed her notepad and stood. "You risked your own life to save this man. I only wish there was a better outcome."

Jonah offered a nod, relieved her questioning was over.

"Any updates on what happened to that man?" Rachel's voice quivered as the question left her lips.

The chief frowned. "As you know, he didn't make it. But we don't know yet why he was in the ocean to begin with."

"That's what I've been wondering." Jonah rubbed his ever-tightening jaw. "Any idea who he was?"

Chief Chambers shook her head. "I've never seen the man before, and he didn't have any ID on him. But we'll be looking into his identity further. We have lots of tourists around here so there's a good chance he's from out of town."

"That makes sense," Jonah said.

Rachel licked her lips as if she wanted to say more. But she didn't. Instead, she sat huddled in the kitchen chair shivering.

Chief Chambers took a step back. "I'm sure you two want to get changed and warmed up, so I'll get out of your hair. I can see myself to the door."

"Chief . . . ?" Rachel looked up nervously.

The woman paused and turned toward her. "Yes?"

"You're not by chance related to Ty Chambers, are you?"

The police chief's eyes lit with curiosity. "I'm his wife. Do you know him?"

Rachel smiled, an almost nostalgic look in her eyes. "I spent summers here as a child, and Ty and I used to play together on the beach when he visited his granddad."

Her eyes widened. "Is that right? Well, he's here now permanently, and I'm sure he'd love to catch up sometime."

"I'd love that also. Please, tell him that I said hello."

"I'll do that."

Interesting, Jonah mused.

Rachel had a connection with the police chief.

That could make her even more valuable, depending exactly on the way things played out.

But he'd have to plan his next moves very carefully. The people he'd surrounded himself with were intelligent. They'd notice if he slipped up.

And Jonah couldn't let that happen. Not if he wanted to find Ganon's killer.

———

As soon as Chief Chambers left, Rachel glanced at Jonah and shivered. Her clothes were soaked, and her hair still clung to her skin.

There was a lot she wanted to say to this stranger. To ask him.

But not with these wet clothes on.

"Do you know where you're staying tonight?" She stood, anxious to get warm.

Jonah nodded. "Your dad showed me what room I could use before he left. It's one of the guest bedrooms on the second floor."

"Do you have everything you need?"

"I do. I always travel prepared."

"Okay, I'm staying in my old bedroom on this floor." She nodded in the direction of the room. "Right now, I'm going to take a nice long shower. Thankfully, the hot water heater is gas. It's been a long day. I left early this morning to catch my flight. Then I drove here from the Norfolk airport."

"I can imagine you're exhausted. Getting warm and dry is a good idea. You don't want to get sick."

With another lingering glance at Jonah, Rachel turned on the flashlight on her phone to guide her steps. Then she grabbed the small suitcase she'd left by the front door. She spotted the broken vase there and reminded herself to come back later to clean that up.

She paused as she stared at the broken pieces.

They were more smashed than she remembered. Almost like someone had stepped on them.

But Cassidy had come in and left through the back door. So she hadn't done that.

No, Rachel was probably overthinking things. It had been dark. The shards had been hard to see.

So why did visions of someone stepping through the front door and into this home while they were trying to rescue that man fill her mind?

She repressed a nervous laugh.

She was just paranoid. The events of the past few months were messing with her head.

After quickly grabbing her keys and casting one last glance at the mess, Rachel disappeared down the hall and into her room.

Instead of heading to the bathroom, Rachel paused and leaned against the door a moment. Her heart still raced from everything that had happened.

It seemed like this was all a bad dream she would wake up from.

But that man really had drowned out there in the ocean.

Why did he have Dr. Hensley's phone number on his hand? Was that significant?

It had to be.

And what about the dolphin necklace? Was someone trying to send a message?

She reached beneath her shirt and gripped the pendant on her own necklace as fear filled her chest.

Rachel was a scientist. She was trained to be grounded in logic. Ignoring what she'd seen tonight would be reckless.

She wasn't sure how the dead man might be connected with the lab. Perhaps when she started there tomorrow, she could ask more questions. Or perhaps the truth would come out once the police chief discovered this man's identity.

That made two dead bodies Rachel had encountered recently. Was death haunting her?

And what about this stranger in her father's house?

Something about Jonah made her curious.

Still, Rachel needed to call her dad to confirm this guy was on the up and up.

She could be too innocent at times. She knew that.

Ganon had warned her before he died not to be too trusting on the job. What had he meant by that? Rachel had thought it was just friendly advice.

But he'd had a strange emotion in his eyes, and now he was dead . . . all before they'd been able to finish their secret project.

She quickly jumped in the shower, unable to endure the chill that had claimed her body any longer.

Although the hot water warmed her skin, she was far from feeling peaceful right now.

When she stepped out of the bathroom, a towel wrapped around her, she felt a slight breeze sweeping through the room.

She glanced at the sliding glass door leading onto the deck.

It was cracked open just slightly.

Her heart pounded harder.

It hadn't been cracked earlier . . . had it?

Her pulse ratcheted even faster.

Had someone been in her room while she showered?

CHAPTER
SIX

JONAH QUICKLY SHOWERED, dressed, and then went downstairs to make a pot of tea.

It was pitch-dark outside now, only lightning offering any illumination.

The power remained out, but the gas range should still work.

He needed something warm in his system, and he was entirely too wired to sleep.

He'd just pulled a coffee mug from the cabinet when he heard a footstep behind him.

He turned and saw Rachel standing in the doorway. The room was dark, but candles still offered a soft glow to the space.

His breath caught at the sight of her.

He'd known before he came to Lantern Beach that Rachel Atwood was beautiful.

But her pictures hadn't done her justice.

She was five foot six, and her eyes were brown, big, and almost childlike with their gleam of curiosity and intelligence.

At the moment, she'd thrown on some sweatpants and a UGA sweatshirt. Her wet hair was pulled into a loose bun.

She's your enemy, he reminded himself.

But Jonah had always been a sucker for a beautiful woman. Still, he couldn't be fooled by her demure demeanor.

She paused when she spotted him as if she didn't know what to make of Jonah's presence here. Two strangers staying in the same house? It would be weird for anyone in their position—especially given the circumstances of this evening.

"I feel like I should apologize for disturbing you, but this *is* my house." Rachel shrugged, looking confused—in the most adorable way.

If enemies could be adorable.

"The last thing I want is to make you feel uncomfortable." He took a step back. "I can see if there are any other rental properties available. I'm sure there are at this time of year."

He hoped she'd refuse.

Rachel didn't say anything at first, but then her shoulders softened. "If my father invited you to stay here, then of course you're welcome. The house is

plenty big. But I do have some questions for you first
. . . just so I can put my mind at ease."

"Whatever you want to know." Jonah pointed to
the teakettle as it started to whistle. "How about
some tea first?"

"That would be great. Let me just clean up the
broken vase by the front door while you prepare the
drinks."

While she did that, Jonah poured the boiling
water into two cups. A few minutes later, the two of
them sat at the table near the window, overlooking
the ocean and the storm outside. A box of various
teas Jonah had purchased at the store earlier sat
between them.

One glance at the windblown beach, and Jonah
pictured that dead body again.

Such a shame.

And such a bad way to start his stay here.

An image of Ganon lying on the floor at that
restaurant replaced the image of the other dead man.

Ganon hadn't deserved to die like that. He was a
good man. One of the best.

Jonah hadn't wanted to draw any attention to
himself here on the island. He'd wanted to stay off
the radar.

But it looked as if that wouldn't be happening.

Maybe if he planned each of his next moves
wisely, he could somehow manage to disappear into

the background again. That was what he did best—blend in with the shadows.

That's where the Shadow Agency had gotten its name.

Since none of the operatives existed on paper, they could do jobs other people couldn't.

The concept was either brilliantly clever or game-changingly risky.

He remembered the paper Ganon had given him with Rachel's name on it.

Lava flowed through his veins at the thought of it. But, instead of showing his disgust, he took a sip of his tea and plastered on a smile.

"I heard you tell the police chief you're a security consultant. What kind?" Rachel stared at him from across the table.

"I find breaches in computer systems and fix them before hackers can weasel their way into companies," he explained. "Sometimes, these guys steal money. Other times, they obtain personal information to use for blackmail. In worst-case scenarios, they're able to get their hands on top-secret information."

"And my dad hired you?" Surprise—and concern—lilted her voice. "Why? Is there something he's not telling me?"

Her dad had started E-Maid, a company that created household products for a virtually self-cleaning house. Roman Atwood had built the multi-million-dollar company from the ground up.

He'd eventually sold that company and was now launching a new company—E-Gardener, which created similar products but for landscaping. A machine that would rake the yard for you? Many were excited about that possibility, but some kinks still needed to be worked out.

Roman was a bit of a mad scientist at times—full of disorganized but brilliant ideas. Jonah had quickly learned that. But he'd enjoyed his conversations with the man.

"I work for a lot of large organizations," Jonah explained. "Many companies like your father's hire me to make sure their bases are covered. Security issues change daily as technology rapidly advances. With all the innovations in AI technology happening recently, security is even more challenging."

Rachel stared at him a moment before nodding slowly. "I see. I just wish he'd told me. I feel like maybe he's in some type of trouble."

"Don't read too much into it," Jonah assured her. "This is standard protocol. A lot of businesses nowadays face these kinds of challenges."

Really, Rachel needed to worry about herself.

Because if she'd killed his friend, then Jonah would make sure justice was served.

Besides, poison was usually the weapon of

women. Jonah felt certain something had been slipped into his friend's drink. Ganon never went anywhere without coffee.

But his travel coffee mug had been gone from his car when Jonah had checked before leaving the restaurant that fateful day.

Probably because evidence had been inside the cup—evidence of poison.

That made Rachel fit the profile of Ganon's murderer even more.

Plus, Jonah had checked her schedule in Colorado . . . and she'd disappeared for around a week at the same time Ganon died.

Was that because Rachel had secretly come to Baltimore?

He fisted his hand out of sight.

That was his best guess.

Rachel couldn't help but think that there was more to Jonah's story.

Her dad had his own security procedures in place. While everything Jonah had told her was plausible, her father usually only took measures like this reactively—not proactively.

Rachel knew as a matter of confidentiality that Jonah wouldn't be able to share too much information with her. No doubt it would be a breach of his contract with her dad. But she would call her father tomorrow morning and ask him some pointed questions.

"Is this your first time in Lantern Beach?" Rachel asked Jonah, trying to come up with some sort of pleasant conversation.

But it didn't feel right to ignore what had happened. To ignore the dead body on the beach. To pretend death hadn't shown up on their doorstep. To try to forget those numbers on the man's hand and the dolphin necklace he'd been holding.

Both she and Jonah had a rough day here on the island.

She glanced across the table at him.

The man was handsome. Too handsome, really.

He had blond hair that swooped away from his face, perfectly even features, and startling blue eyes.

Startling? Weren't startling blue eyes only found in romance novels?

That's what she used to assume. But not after meeting Jonah.

She'd guess the man was a few years older than she was, and he talked with the ease of someone who was part businessman/part salesman.

"Yes, it's my first time here. I've heard about Lantern Beach before, and I've always wanted to come." Jonah took a sip of his peppermint tea.

The scent of his drink wafted across the table toward her and brought a brief flash of comfort and familiarity.

Peppermint tea was her dad's favorite.

She cleared her throat and pushed those thoughts aside. "And how long did you say you'd be here?"

"About a week." He paused and shifted. "Did I hear you tell the police chief that you got a job at some type of lab here on the island?"

Rachel nodded and warmed her hands around her turmeric tea. It was getting cold inside the house —but her internal chill seemed to be ever present lately. Seeing someone murdered in front of you could do that to a person.

"Yes, a developmental lab just opened here maybe a month ago," she told Jonah. "I've always loved it here on Lantern Beach, and I needed a change."

"Tell me about this lab."

"It's Ocean Essence, which I'm sure you've probably heard of. But we're branching out into the world of pharmaceutical lotions and creams that can help people at a prescription level."

"Interesting," he muttered.

"It's what I've always wanted to do, and I can't wait to start. Don't get me wrong—I've been happy to help people feel more beautiful. That's important.

But there are skin issues out there that affect people on a daily basis. If I can help them . . ."

"That sounds noble."

She shrugged. "I like to think so. I'm so excited that I came early, and I'm starting midweek instead of next Monday."

"It's nice you can return home. But I have to say this island doesn't seem like the place where someone would open a skincare and cosmetics lab."

Rachel shrugged again. "I thought it was strange also, but the lab tries to focus on keeping all their products natural, so this place will be an inspiration. Since we're a marine biomedical lab, we use many substances found in the ocean to develop our formulas."

"Such as?"

"Sea salt, for example. It's actually a wonderful exfoliator, and it's good for so many things for the skin. Algae and seaweed also. There are just so many remedies found in nature that we don't need some of these chemicals the beauty industry has been using."

"So the company doesn't use any manmade substances?"

She took a sip of her drink and let the warmth wash through her. "Oh, no, they do. But they seem to be trying to move away from that. More natural products are what consumers want anyway."

"Well, that sounds fascinating." Jonah nodded, his full attention on her.

Rachel waved a hand in the air, suddenly self-conscious. "Don't get me started talking about my job. I'm excited about this new career opportunity, and I could go on and on all day."

Why was she rambling on nervously? Rachel supposed she always did that when she was anxious.

Then again, tonight had thrown her for a loop, so maybe she shouldn't be so hard on herself.

There were enough people who wanted to bring her down without adding herself to that list.

She slowly released her breath and then glanced outside.

As she did, lightning flashed.

The silhouette of a man standing on the sand dune filled her vision.

She gasped.

"Rachel?" Jonah followed her line of sight.

But as another bolt of lightning lit the sky, the dune was empty.

The man was gone.

She let out a nervous laugh. "I guess I'm seeing things."

Was Rachel losing her mind?

Or was something very strange going on here at her father's house?

CHAPTER
SEVEN

JONAH TOOK a sip of his tea as he tried to figure out how to phrase his next question.

He wanted to know more about the lab, but asking more questions right now might raise red flags in Rachel's mind. He couldn't seem overly eager.

The thing was, he also had questions about the dead man on the beach and Rachel's reaction to seeing him. She clearly knew more than she was letting on.

Jonah gripped his mug and leaned forward just slightly, careful to keep his voice light. "I couldn't help but notice when we were outside that you almost seemed to have a flash of recognition when you saw that man's face. Did you know him?"

"No, I didn't." But Rachel's words sounded strangled, and she swallowed hard.

The motion was followed by a hiccup that seemed to make her blush.

Jonah heard the truth in her statement. Rachel didn't know who that man was. So what had caused the reaction?

"Why are you asking me that?" She studied him as if he were a specimen under a microscope.

"You looked surprised when you saw him." Jonah shrugged, trying to appear casual. "I guess I was just curious. I know it's a small island, so . . ." He shrugged again. "I don't know. I'm probably overthinking it."

"Well, it's not every day you see a dead body." She shivered.

Jonah couldn't deny those words. The sight was enough to shake anyone up.

But he still felt as if there was more to the story. Rachel was the key to finding out answers about Ganon's death. Jonah was sure of it.

Just how was she involved?

The answers waited for him here on Lantern Beach.

For years, this island had been full of mystery, from back in the time of pirates and shipwrecks.

It appeared that reputation hadn't faded. He'd read up on some of the crimes that had occurred here in recent years—including a cult and a major terrorist plot.

Those things were nothing to shake a stick at.

But Police Chief Chambers had handled everything with amazing professionalism and diligence.

As a last resort, Jonah would bring local law enforcement into his investigation. But he needed more proof that Rachel had killed his friend before he alerted the police to his theory.

He pushed down a surge of resentment and tried to carefully choose his next question for Rachel.

But before he could ask anything else, a crash sounded upstairs.

His breath caught.

Had trouble from a past job followed him here?

If so, it wouldn't be the first time.

———

Rachel's muscles tensed when she heard the crash.

That noise had come from inside the house.

She was certain of it.

What if someone had sneaked inside her house through the door in her bedroom? It had been cracked open when she'd stepped out of the shower.

But she'd nearly convinced herself her dad had left it open by accident.

Maybe she'd been wrong.

She jumped from her chair and backed up until she hit the kitchen counter.

Her gaze went to the butcher block of knives behind her.

Should she grab one?

Before she could, Jonah was already on his feet and headed toward the living room. His muscles bristled as he called over his shoulder, "Stay there."

Rachel remained frozen as Jonah disappeared from the room.

She was probably just paranoid. After everything that happened tonight, who could blame her?

First, the surprise of confronting a man with a gun. Then the brutal storm that still battered the island. Then the man Jonah had rescued from the ocean only to have him die on the way back to shore.

Rachel was wound up and on edge.

Think this through, Rachel. There was probably a logical explanation for that noise.

Maybe a window had been left open.

Maybe a gust of wind knocked a lamp over.

That was probably it. The sound was probably just a lamp that had fallen.

Or maybe a picture had fallen off the wall.

Rachel rubbed her arms as she tried to soothe herself.

But suddenly, coming home didn't seem as

welcoming as it once had. Still, she couldn't stay in Colorado.

She'd left behind a nightmare there.

Silence stretched as she listened for a sign of what was happening.

There was nothing.

Was Jonah okay?

Even though the man worked in security, was he trained to handle these kinds of conflicts? Or was he simply a keyboard warrior?

There was something about him that was mysterious and almost seemed dangerous. Just what was this guy's story?

Maybe Rachel should call the police.

She stared at that butcher block again before grabbing one of the knives. She gripped it so hard that her knuckles hurt.

If Jonah wasn't back in two minutes, she was calling 911.

Then she would check things out for herself . . . maybe.

JONAH PAUSED at the top of the stairway and glanced down the hallway at the four bedrooms waiting there.

Was someone up here?

He'd almost brought his gun downstairs with him, but he hadn't wanted to frighten Rachel. So he'd left it in his room.

That had been a mistake.

He was staying in the second bedroom down the hallway. If Jonah could slip inside and grab his Sig, he'd feel better prepared for any potential trouble. He'd retrieved the weapon from the picnic table when he'd come back to the house.

He skirted past the first bedroom.

Jonah reached his room and started to twist the doorknob when he noticed the door wasn't latched.

He'd closed it. He was certain of it.

His muscles tightened even more.

Before he could figure out his next plan of action, someone lunged at him from the shadows.

The two collided and fell on the floor.

But the man—who wore a ski mask—rammed his fist into Jonah's jaw.

As pain radiated through him, Jonah snapped into action.

He quickly flipped the man and pinned him on the floor. "Who are you, and what are you doing here?"

The man grunted as he stared up at him. "You shouldn't be here."

Then he pushed Jonah off—surprisingly strong and skilled.

Jonah slammed into the wall behind him.

The move bought the man just enough time to jump to his feet.

The intruder ran into another bedroom and disappeared.

Jonah quickly followed him.

But when he reached the room, the guy was already on the balcony. The intruder jumped over the railing and onto a sand dune below before taking off in a run.

Jonah grabbed the railing and started to follow.

Before he could, the man hopped on a four-wheeler and sped away.

Jonah knew there was no way he could catch this guy.

Besides, the bigger question was—what was the man doing here?

Had Jonah's secret identity already been compromised before he'd even started this mission?

———

That was it. Two minutes were up.

Rachel had heard the crash upstairs. Then another one. And another one.

She'd dialed 911.

Even though the operator told her to stay where she was, Rachel couldn't do that. How would she live with herself if Jonah was hurt while she was down here cowering?

That was what her ex-boyfriend had accused her of doing. Being a coward—and that was after Rachel had caught *him* cheating.

Digby Bauer had tried to turn the tables on her and make it seem like their demise as a couple was her fault.

Instead of letting his accusation bring her down, Rachel had seen his words as a challenge.

She didn't have to prove to Digby that she wasn't a coward. But she could prove it to herself.

Rachel started around the corner and into the hallway when a shadow appeared.

She gasped and thrust the knife toward the figure.

But the shadow caught her arm.

Panic raced through her.

"It's okay," someone murmured. "It's me."

That was when it registered that Jonah stood in front of her.

He gently eased the knife from her hand and led her back downstairs and into the kitchen.

He didn't let go of her arm until she was seated at the table again.

"Are you okay?" He studied her face in the candlelight.

Rachel nodded, feeling halfway numb.

Her gaze stopped on his forehead. Even in the dim light, she could see the blood that trickled from a cut there. "What happened to you?"

"A man was upstairs."

Her head began to swirl.

Someone else *had* been inside the house.

"Where is he?" Her voice trembled as she asked the question.

"He ran. He had an ATV waiting outside. The noise from the storm must have concealed the sound of its engine."

Rachel nodded, her thoughts still murky with panic. "I called 911."

"Probably a good idea."

"What was he doing up there?" Her thoughts raced as adrenaline pulsed through her.

What if it was one of Carl's men? What if he'd come here to silence her permanently?

If Rachel was dead, there would be no one to testify against him.

"I'm not sure yet," Jonah said. "I wanted to make sure you were okay before I checked things out."

"I'm . . . I'm fine . . . I guess. Just shaken up."

Jonah nodded, his concerned gaze still lingering on her.

Before they could talk more, a knock sounded at the door, and then she heard, "Police!"

Police Chief Chambers was back again.

This wasn't the way Rachel wanted to start her move to Lantern Beach.

Maybe it was a sign that coming here was a bad idea.

CHAPTER
NINE

CHIEF CHAMBERS CHECKED the house before meeting Jonah and Rachel back in the living room.

While he'd waited, Jonah had cleaned the small wound on his forehead. Then he'd started a fire. He and Rachel would need something to keep them warm tonight. The temperature outside had dropped when the storm came through, and a new chill filled the air.

Jonah waited with anticipation to hear what Chief Chambers had to say.

"It's clear." The chief's gaze turned to Rachel. "There's no sign of forced entry. Any idea who else has a house key?"

Rachel shrugged, a glassy, dazed look in her eyes. "I'm not sure. The housecleaner maybe."

"Roman gave one to me to use, of course," Jonah spoke up.

Chief Chambers nodded slowly before looking back at Rachel. "I have to say, I'm surprised your father doesn't have an alarm system hooked up. I saw all the tech gadgets in his room."

"He likes to tinker with inventions. But I remember asking him about a house alarm once. He didn't think he needed one here on the island. He has always commented on how safe Lantern Beach is." Rachel shrugged.

Something flashed in the chief's eyes, but she said nothing.

Jonah knew what she was thinking: Lantern Beach was anything but safe. Numerous newspaper articles proved it.

"I'll have someone patrol past here tonight, just to be cautious," the chief finally said. "But I'm guessing that since your house is one of the larger ones on the island that it was targeted by a potential thief who thought no one was staying here."

"Maybe we caught him before he could steal anything." Rachel held her hands near the fire as if to warm them—until they began trembling. Then she quickly shoved them into the front pocket of her oversized sweatshirt.

"Perhaps," Chief Chambers said.

"My father doesn't keep very many valuable

things here, but I suppose it depends on what they're looking for." Rachel glanced at Jonah as if seeking affirmation. "I thought most thieves today targeted people through identity theft or credit card readers."

"A lot of them do." Jonah had read up on this before coming up with his cover story. "I suppose there are still some old-fashioned criminals out there, though, who love a good breaking and entering."

"It's true," Chief Chambers said. "Not all criminals are high tech—or smart."

A few minutes later, the police chief left with a reminder to keep the doors and windows locked, and Jonah turned to Rachel.

Apprehension and exhaustion lingered in her gaze. Yet tension thrummed between them. Tension because of what had happened. Tension because they didn't know each other. Tension because of their forced proximity.

"Are you going to be able to sleep?" Jonah rested his hands casually in his pockets as he waited for her answer.

Rachel shrugged. "Probably not."

"I saw a Scrabble board over there when I was starting the fire." He nodded toward a shelf full of board games. "Any interest in a late-night game?"

His voice sounded friendly and masked the resentment and suspicions he felt toward the woman.

If there was one thing Operation Adrenaline had taught him, it was how to be a good actor.

Rachel stared at him a moment before slowly nodding, her shoulders softening just slightly. "Scrabble is actually my favorite game. That sounds perfect."

Jonah grinned.

But a flash of guilt hit him.

He already knew Scrabble was her favorite game. That was why he'd suggested it.

But he had no reason to feel guilty. If Rachel was a killer, then she deserved to be brought down.

However, in his years serving in the military, he'd discovered it was much easier to deceive someone who wasn't kind than it was to try to pull the wool over the eyes of someone who might earnestly be a good person.

That was something he'd need to contend with himself.

However, he needed to remember that Rachel Atwood might not be as innocent as she portrayed herself to be.

He couldn't be the fool here. He'd already been a fool with Anna.

If he screwed up like that again, he'd deem himself incompetent for his job.

And that wasn't an option.

As Rachel played Scrabble with Jonah, she was grateful for the distraction the game offered.

Yes, she was tired. But she needed something to get her mind off everything that had happened. Scrabble was better than lying in bed unable to sleep.

Besides, she was curious about her father's newest contract employee. She'd been watching Jonah since they'd met, and her curiosity only grew with every passing moment.

She wanted to know more about Jonah Gray. The best way to learn more was to ask more questions. That was what she did as a scientist. She developed hypotheses. Tested them. Proved whether they were true or not.

Before she could start, Jonah jumped in. "This house is pretty amazing."

"I agree. It was one of the first built here on the island, by a boat captain who was apparently very successful. It even has a widow's walk up top."

"I noticed."

"It was always one of my favorite places to go and hang out when I was here as a teenager. People have tried to buy this place from my family uncountable times. My father has always refused. This place is too special to him. Plus, it's one of the few houses on the island that actually sits on four plots of land, so it's more secluded than a lot of other properties."

"That is nice. You said you spent your summers here?" Jonah stared at his letters as if trying to form whatever word he would play next.

The Scrabble board had a little turntable so they could easily adjust the board face to whoever was at play. It was much higher quality than most Scrabble boards. In fact, Rachel had bought this one for her dad for his birthday one year. It thrilled her to use it now.

"That's right. This was a great place to spend my summers. Some of my happiest memories are here." She played IDYLLIC as her next word.

"I bet. This seems like the perfect place for a person to grow up. Not that I know much about Lantern Beach. But I hope to learn more."

The smoky, earthy scent of the fireplace drifted around Rachel, bringing her a strange comfort as happy memories filled her from her childhood. "You should try to enjoy it some while you're here. I mean, I know you've had a rough start with what happened tonight, but it's not always like that here. In fact, I remember my family used to sleep with the doors unlocked, something that was unheard of where I grew up outside of DC."

"I can only imagine. This place sounds like Mayberry."

Rachel shrugged. "I'm sure it's changed in recent years. Everything does. As much as you want to escape crime and danger, that seems an impossibility in today's climate. But Humble Beginnings, as the place is named, was as close to heaven as I could get."

Jonah glanced up at her curiously. "You mentioned you knew the police chief's husband when you were younger? Did the two of you date or something?"

Rachel let out a laugh. "Oh no. Ty was like my adopted big brother during the summer. Well, maybe I had a little crush on him for a while, but nothing over the top." She laughed again. "But he's a topnotch guy. I heard he went on to be a Navy SEAL, so I'm curious as to what he's doing now. I haven't talked to him in years."

Jonah finally played his word, REGRET, and then turned the board back to face her.

Rachel already had her next word picked out, and she hoped that it still fit on the board.

"You said you grew up in Upstate New York?" she asked as she placed her letters.

"Really, I grew up all over." He leaned back on his hands.

"Military?"

"Foster care."

Her eyebrows shot up. "Oh, I see."

"One of my foster brothers used to love this game." He nodded at the board. "At the time, I hated playing it with him. Now, I'd do anything to challenge him with some word play."

"Is that right? Maybe you can get together and play again sometime."

"Unfortunately, he passed away recently." Jonah's voice dipped lower.

Rachel's hand covered her mouth. There she went putting her foot in her mouth again.

It seemed to be a bad habit she was developing—that and being in the wrong place at the wrong time. And trusting the wrong people. And believing the best in those around her.

The list could go on and on.

"I'm so sorry," she murmured.

"Don't be. You didn't know." Jonah cast her a compassionate but tight smile.

Their conversation slowly drifted into other subjects—their favorite games, movies, and food.

Easy subjects.

Safe subjects.

Rachel was ready to play the final word and win this game.

More importantly than that, she was grateful for Jonah's presence here tonight.

She felt better knowing someone she could trust was in the house.

But could she really trust this man?

She studied his handsome face for a moment and bit back a frown.

It was too soon to really say.

Plus, considering her track record, the only smart thing to do was to remain cautious.

As he shifted in front of her, she spotted the long, jagged scar on his forearm.

She sucked in a breath.

It appeared Jonah Gray had some secrets also.

Because that scar almost looked like . . . a knife wound.

CHAPTER
TEN

CASSIDY CHAMBERS STARED at her friend
Mac MacArthur as he sat on the other side of her
desk at the police station the next morning.

"Tell Tali thank you for the cranberry-orange
scone." She resisted the urge to lick the sugary crys-
tals from her fingers. "It's really delicious. The coffee
is great too."

"They're two of many perks I get since I'm
married to the most wonderful woman in the world."
He grinned, his mature face showing gentle,
wisdom-filled wrinkles.

Cassidy let out a chuckle. "I'm so glad you're
happy. You deserve it, Mac."

She meant the words. Mac deserved all the best
things in life. He was one of her favorite people.

"Thanks." Mac crossed his ankle over his knee.

"But I'm still pinching myself and wondering if this is all real or not."

"I assure you, Tali is very real and very wonderful." The woman had opened a bookstore and coffeehouse on the island, and she and Mac had hit it off. Cassidy was thrilled for her friend and mentor.

He beamed before shifting his legs again as he seemed to switch mental gears. "So, I hear you had an eventful night."

Mac was the current Lantern Beach mayor and former police chief. He and Cassidy liked to keep each other informed about island happenings. It was only smart.

They met like this often.

"A thirtysomething man drowned in the ocean." Her smile faded as she said the words. "Doc Clemson is doing an autopsy because his death seems suspicious. It's not like this guy was out in the Atlantic taking a swim. The water's freezing in March, plus the man was fully dressed, *and* it was stormy. Why was he out there?"

Mac flipped a pencil between his fingers with the skill of a circus performer. If ADHD had been a thing when he'd been a kid, Mac would have definitely fit the criteria.

"I've seen people do foolish things in their excitement over being here." Mac made a face, making it clear what he thought of people who did idiotic things.

"Me too. But there's something about this one that makes me feel like I should dig a little deeper. Plus, I'm trying to identify this guy." Cassidy broke off another piece of her scone and popped it in her mouth.

She'd lost the extra weight since having her baby fifteen months ago, but if she kept eating like this, she would gain it all back. However, she couldn't resist these scones.

"The man had some numbers written on his hand that I'm trying to identify," she continued. "They were written with permanent marker."

"Social security?"

"It doesn't appear to be that. I've tried whatever combinations possible, but nothing seems to fit." Cassidy shifted in her seat. "He also had a necklace in his hands with a dolphin pendant on it."

"Like the ones that can be found at gift shops around here?"

"Similar but nicer. It was made of real gold. Finding it in his hand was curious." She shrugged and let out a sigh. "Maybe when I get his fingerprints back, I can ID him, and the numbers will make more sense. Doc's putting a priority on this autopsy. It looks like a drowning but . . ."

"It's always better to double-check these things."

Cassidy finished chewing and took a sip of her coffee before saying, "Then there was a break-in over at Roman's place last night."

"Roman? Roman Atwood? I've only had good interactions with the man. He's a little kooky but nice." Mac shifted in his seat. "Was Roman there when this happened?"

"No, actually, his daughter was."

Mac's gaze lifted with curiosity. "Rachel's here? I haven't seen her in years. She was always a nice girl. I remember when she started a clothing donation drive to help out a family here after their house was struck by lightning and burned down. Got the whole island involved. She was only about ten or eleven at the time."

"She's not a girl anymore. She's a woman. A scientist with a PhD, actually."

Mac let out a whistle. "Is that right? I think I'm getting old."

"She's apparently working at the new lab that Ocean Essence opened here."

Mac grunted at the mention of the business, the sound making it clear he didn't approve. "That place has me curious."

Why had the company chosen such a remote location like Lantern Beach to open their new lab? Cassidy had wondered that herself.

She was sure the company had their talking

points. But the move didn't make sense. This island didn't have the infrastructure for a company like Essence.

Logistics alone had kept other large corporations from seeking a home here, especially since supplies would have to be brought in on the ferries or offloaded from ships offshore and transported to land. It simply wasn't cost-effective.

But Lantern Beach *did* have the isolation the company might want, especially if they were trying to hide something.

Cassidy let out a sigh. "I don't know what to think about that lab either."

"It only adds about twenty-five new full-time residents here. That shouldn't change the landscape of the island."

"No, but I just think the whole thing is kind of weird. This isn't the kind of place large corporations want to set up shop. It's too far off the beaten path."

Mac shrugged but didn't disagree. "Everyone I've met who works for them seems nice enough."

"They do."

"Who wouldn't want to work on Lantern Beach if they had a choice?" He stopped playing with the pencil and set it on Cassidy's desk.

Cassidy let out a chuckle. "I can't argue with that. But I also can't help but sense another storm brewing offshore."

"If it makes you feel better, weathermen are usually wrong with their predictions."

"Let's hope that we can say the same thing about me and my crime-forecasting abilities." She took another sip of coffee, her thoughts still percolating. "There's one other thing . . ."

"What's that?"

"A man is staying at Roman's house. He says he's an invited guest, a security consultant for Roman's business."

"Okay . . ." Mac squinted as he waited for her to continue.

"The thing is, I tried to look into his background, and he doesn't have one. He's like a ghost." The lack of information about the man still bothered her.

Mac raised his eyebrows. "A ghost?"

"I know it sounds funny, but it's almost like Jonah Gray didn't exist before he came here."

"You think he's using an alias?"

Cassidy thought of her own situation. She'd moved to the island under a false identity in order to escape a dangerous gang who wanted her dead. She'd had her reasons—good reasons—for keeping her true identity under wraps.

What about Jonah? Could he say the same?

She wasn't sure.

Cassidy let out a sigh. "I really don't know. I'm going to keep him on my radar, just in case."

"Probably a good idea. Does Rachel know him?"

"I don't know the specifics, but if they don't know each other yet, they will." She locked gazes with Mac. "It turns out, they're staying at Roman's house together."

Mac raised his eyebrows. "Isn't that interesting?"

Cassidy couldn't agree more.

RACHEL WOKE up extra early to get ready for her first day on the job.

Thankfully, the power had come back on sometime during the night.

As she'd wandered the house, she'd noted that nothing seemed out of place.

She was thankful for that, especially after last night's events.

She still shuddered when she remembered the broken vase. The man she thought she'd seen on the dune. Her barely open sliding glass door. The man Jonah had fought off in the house.

That wasn't to mention that dead man Jonah had tried to rescue.

It was all too much. She felt unnerved.

Before leaving for work, Rachel stared at the steps leading to the second floor where Jonah slept.

She nibbled on her bottom lip a moment before wandering up to his room. Maybe she should tell him she was leaving. See if he needed anything.

Or was that overkill? She wasn't sure.

She reached his room and noted that his door wasn't latched.

As she started to knock, it opened just slightly.

Without realizing what she was doing, she peered inside and saw that Jonah was still sleeping. She tried not to stare and forced her gaze away.

She wouldn't wake him.

She'd simply assumed he'd be awake by now. She pegged him as an early riser.

Rachel started to walk away but, before she even took a step, Jonah muttered something.

She froze and glanced back through that crack.

"Anna . . ." he murmured.

Rachel's curiosity spiked.

Anna? Who was Anna?

Did Jonah have a girlfriend waiting for him back home? It wouldn't surprise Rachel.

A man as handsome as Jonah certainly had his pick of women.

But something about the way he'd said the name . . . his voice sounded etched with agony. The pain in his tone haunted her.

Rachel hurried away. Coming up here had been a mistake. An invasion of privacy.

She would just pretend she hadn't done this.

Now, she needed to get to work.

As she started toward the door, she passed the fireplace and reflected on her Scrabble game with Jonah last night.

It had been nice to have someone to spend time with, especially in the wake of her breakup with Digby.

She didn't know who she was angrier with over the breakup—Digby or herself. Why hadn't she been able to see what a scumbag he was? How had she been so naive?

She shook the thoughts off and climbed into her car.

She'd come here to forget about Digby, not to mentally relive the ways he'd hurt her.

Before taking off for the office, Rachel grabbed her phone and called her dad. She'd meant to do so last night, but after everything that had happened she'd gotten distracted.

His phone rang and rang before going to voicemail.

She ended the call and frowned.

She wished her dad had answered, but it wasn't entirely strange that he hadn't. He had flashes of creative genius when he liked to seclude himself to work out ideas. Was that what he was doing now?

Probably.

She wouldn't get worried.

Not yet.

Instead, she pulled out the notebook she kept in her purse and jotted down an idea she'd had last night. Every once in a while, she thought of new ingredients she wanted to try. She made notes so she could remember to do more research later.

This morning, she'd been inspired by the fish-scale wallpaper her father had in the bathroom.

Yes, fish-scale.

Seeing that had reminded her of something she read once. Apparently, fish-scale-derived collagen was effective for healing wounds. She wanted to do more research into that. Maybe that was the ingredient she and Ganon had been looking for.

For now, she put her car in Reverse and started toward her new office.

Rachel hoped she'd do a good job here . . . and that she'd make Ganon proud.

But she'd wondered if there was more to her colleague's death than people were admitting.

What if he'd been murdered?

That question had been haunting her. Especially since the last time the two of them had talked, Ganon had seemed distracted. He'd given her a cryptic warning to be careful.

Why?

Did Ganon know something she didn't?

Anxiety thrummed through Rachel at that thought.

———

Rachel observed her new workplace as Dr. Frank Hensley, the CEO of the company, gave her a tour.

Dr. Hensley wouldn't permanently be working out of this office, but he was very hands-on and had insisted on overseeing things as they got their new facility up and running. The man was in his late fifties and on the shorter side with a wiry build. He had an olive complexion and thick salt-and-pepper hair.

His personality was brisk, and everything he said and did seemed measured, like he never let down his guard.

Rachel hadn't liked the man the first time she met him. But she'd come to accept his standoffish demeanor.

The building itself was brand new and sparkling clean with only state-of-the-art equipment inside. Plus, the lab was located on a secluded part of the island and surrounded by marsh grass and the beautiful waters of the Pamlico Sound.

The facilities were simply amazing.

The administrative offices were located around the perimeter of the space and at the center were desks for clerical workers and assistants. Glass windows stretched above her, creating an atrium feel.

The lab was located upstairs, the place where the scientists experimented with various formulas they were creating. The lab was visible, thanks to the glass walls surrounding it.

On the first floor, there was also an employee lounge that came stocked with drinks and snacks, a large conference room, and a door marked "Authorized Personnel Only."

Apparently, only Dr. Hensley, Vice President of Development Lloyd Gains, and CFO Mark Williams were allowed in that space. Their badges gave them special clearance.

Rachel thought she saw a biometric scanner beside the door also. She wasn't entirely sure, but she thought it might be a retinal scanner.

They weren't joking about security here.

But she wasn't surprised. Whenever research and development were involved, trade secrets were often a target of the competition.

"Now." Dr. Hensley paused after the tour of the

facilities and turned to Rachel as they stood in the hallway. "How about we get something to eat? There are six or seven of us available, and we'd like to take you to lunch. We've got a restaurant here on the island everyone raves about. It's called The Crazy Chefette."

"Interesting name."

"From what I hear, the woman who runs it used to be a scientist."

Now *that* sounded interesting. "I'm in."

"Perfect. Let's head there now." Dr. Hensley paused. "Would you like to ride with one of us?"

"If it's okay, I'll drive myself." Rachel didn't want to be stuck in a car making awkward small talk. Nothing was more exhausting.

Strangely enough, she hadn't felt like that with Jonah last night. Why was that? Why had the man so quickly set her at ease?

"Of course. You can't miss the place. If you go back to the main road and take a left, you'll hit it right before the tourist shopping area. There's lots of pink on the building."

"Sounds good. I'm sure I can find it. In fact, I think I remember seeing it on the way in to work this morning." Rachel hadn't been able to miss the pink eccentric sign and exterior decorations.

Maybe lunch with her new colleagues would help her relax a little.

Because, so far, her time in Lantern Beach had been anything but peaceful.

But as she stepped outside to go to her car, she saw something move in the marsh in the distance.

Had that been a man?

It almost appeared as if he'd ducked as soon as she'd stepped outside and looked his way.

Tension embedded itself between her shoulder blades.

No, she must be seeing things . . . again.

Either that, or Carl's men had found her.

At that thought, she quickened her steps as she hurried toward her car.

TWENTY MINUTES LATER, Rachel was seated at The Crazy Chefette. Two tables had been shoved together to accommodate everyone from the lab who'd come for the get-to-know-you lunch.

Polka music played overhead, and the hostess—a friendly woman named Cadence—explained that they were featuring European food on their menu this month. The whole place had a quirky, fun feel— and excellent reviews by both patrons and critics.

No sooner had Rachel sat down and received her glass of ice water did she glance across the restaurant and see a familiar face in a corner booth.

Jonah.

He had a sandwich and fries in front of him and a whole folder's worth of papers spread across the table. Obviously, he was here for a working lunch.

She flushed when he looked up and saw her staring at him.

Rachel gave him a little wave, and Jonah raised his glass of tea in an air toast.

Her warm, fuzzy feelings were quickly replaced with memories of last night's events.

She hoped the break-in was just a one-time thing and that the rest of her new start here in Lantern Beach would be smooth sailing.

Then she remembered the numbers on that dead man's hand. She remembered the dolphin necklace he'd been holding.

Smooth sailing didn't seem to be on her agenda. In fact, turbulence seemed to have followed her.

When she had a chance, she planned on calling the police chief to ask if she had any updates.

Rachel watched as Jonah stood and paced toward her, looking at ease in a way that made her envy him. She struggled with social anxiety more often than she'd like to admit—though she thought she hid it well.

Today, Jonah wore respectable khakis with a blue sweater that brought out his eyes. His hair was styled away from his face, and his chiseled features looked even better under the bright lights of the restaurant.

She pressed her eyes closed, surprised by the moment of attraction that fluttered through her.

Attraction was off-limits right now, even if the

man was handsome. Besides, she'd heard him say the name "Anna." She couldn't help but wonder who the woman was and how Jonah was connected with her.

Most likely, the man was in a serious relationship.

"Rachel . . . good to see you." He paused near her chair and smiled.

"You too, Jonah." She glanced at the people surrounding her. "These are my new coworkers." Thankfully, she was good at remembering names, and she introduced everyone before explaining, "Jonah is working for my father."

Jonah flashed another easy grin at the group. "It's a pleasure to meet you. I hope you all plan on trying the peach and grilled cheese sandwiches."

"That's exactly what I was going to recommend." Dr. Hensley closed his menu and observed Jonah a moment. "What was it that you said you did again?"

"I'm a security consultant." Jonah casually rested his hands in his pockets. "I look for security breaches in computer systems. So if you're ever looking to up your security measures, I'm your guy."

Rachel observed him another moment as he talked.

Something about him had been bothering her, and just then she realized what it was.

Jonah seemed more like a hands-on guy than someone who sat behind a computer. He was fit and quick on his feet. She'd met plenty of tech guys in her life, and Jonah wasn't like any of them.

She scolded herself for relying on stereotypes. But sometimes, stereotypes were stereotypes for a reason. She needed to be discerning.

"We'll keep that in mind." But Dr. Hensley's voice didn't show much interest.

With another nod at Rachel, Jonah moseyed back to his table to finish his lunch.

Rachel realized she'd much rather be eating with Jonah than her new colleagues . . . that thought deeply surprised her.

Then she remembered that scar on his arm.

Remembered the danger that seemed to be lingering close.

Until she knew what was going on, it was better not to trust anyone.

———

Being hired by Ocean Essence?

Wouldn't that be ideal?

But Jonah knew that wasn't likely to happen. Still, he had to make whatever connections he could.

The question was: was Rachel a lion or was she being thrown into the lion's den?

At the thought of her, another rush of resentment filled him.

He pictured her killing his friend, getting away with it, and now stepping into Ganon's former role at the lab. All while seeming so innocent and unassuming.

She was still the only one he'd discovered that had motive, means, and opportunity.

Motive? His job.

Means? Jonah felt certain Ganon was poisoned. As a scientist, Rachel would know how to do that.

Opportunity? That one was a little tougher since she was in Colorado. But she could be working with someone.

He didn't think everyone at Essence was corrupt. But he needed to figure out who might be. Were Ganon's suspicions right? Had someone stolen proprietary information?

If so, did Dr. Hensley know about the theft? Ganon said the man had been asking questions.

How had Ganon found out?

Jonah had so many unanswered questions, and no one at the company wanted to talk to him. Thankfully, the people he'd questioned weren't here now or they would recognize him. He'd chosen carefully whom he'd spoken with.

Also, the company had to have many, many formulas that were kept under lock and key. Which one might have been stolen? Had a corporate spy come in to swipe it?

There was still so much he didn't know.

Jonah needed an insider at the company who might provide answers to him.

His gaze drifted to Rachel again. If she wasn't the killer, maybe she would help him.

However, as soon as she learned about his deceit, she would want nothing to do with him. He had no doubt about that.

Besides, she was still his number one suspect. He had to keep that in mind. His ultimate goal was to see her behind bars if she was guilty.

But who was that man inside the house last night? Was it an enemy from one of the past assignments he'd done?

Or was someone targeting Rachel? Did someone else suspect her also?

The questions made Jonah's head pound. His headaches came at the worst possible times.

He blamed them on Commander Lewis and those drugs Jonah had been forced to take.

His stomach knotted at the memories.

As he took a bite of one of his fries, his phone rang.

An unknown number filled his screen.

Jonah stared at his device a moment before deciding to answer. But he felt cautious as he said, "This is Jonah."

Silence stretched on the crackling line until finally

someone said, "This is Walter. Walter Adams."

Jonah sat up straighter at the familiar name. He glanced at the table full of Essence employees, careful not to say the man's name aloud.

Walter was a former employee at Ocean Essence whom Jonah had tried to get in touch with multiple times. The man had been Ganon's research assistant.

But Walter had brushed Jonah off every time he'd approached. Nothing Jonah said could get through to the man.

Had something changed?

"What's going on?" Jonah asked, keeping one eye on the table of Essence employees.

"I . . . I think I'm ready to talk." The man's voice quivered. "Someone needs to say it."

"Say what?" Jonah kept his voice low, not wanting to draw attention to the conversation.

"I can't tell you now," Walter whispered. "It's not a good time."

"Name the time and place, and I'll be there."

"I can't meet face-to-face. It's too risky. I called you on a burner. No one should be able to trace me."

"Okay. Then when will you be able to talk?" Jonah didn't want to miss this opportunity.

"Tonight at six. I'll call you. Okay?"

"That sounds great." As Jonah ended the call, his heart raced.

Could this be the lead he was looking for?

That would be an answer to prayer.

He glanced at Rachel, wondering again what she might know.

His whole life had taught him not to trust people.

Getting close was always a mistake.

Always.

But if he didn't get close to her, he might not find the answers he needed.

For that reason, he'd romance the enemy—even if he hated himself for doing so.

CHAPTER
THIRTEEN

RACHEL FINISHED her grilled cheese and peach sandwich. The meal had been delicious, just as everyone had said.

She even had a chance to meet Lisa Dillinger, the owner of the restaurant. The woman seemed like someone Rachel could be friends with. They had a lot in common since Lisa used to be a chemist before turning those talents to the kitchen.

Rachel could definitely see herself becoming a regular at this place.

A surge of hope flooded her.

Maybe things weren't as bad as she'd thought. Maybe she truly could leave behind what had happened back in Colorado and start fresh.

Maybe she could even be happy again.

Her smile slipped.

Unless Carl's guys had followed her.

Unless they'd killed that man on the beach and broken into her house.

Then there was the dolphin necklace . . .

That couldn't be just a coincidence, could it?

Her lungs tightened at the memories until she felt as if she couldn't breathe.

It was too soon to feel hope. There were still too many unknowns.

As everyone at the table stood and prepared to leave, Rachel fished her keys and cell phone from her purse, and then pulled her bag over her shoulder.

She stole one last glance at Jonah before stepping toward the door.

He waved as he gathered his papers, appearing ready to leave soon also. "Good to see you."

"It's always nice to see you." Rachel cringed as the words left her lips.

Always nice to see you? Couldn't she just have said, *Good to see you too?*

She pressed her eyes closed as she fought embarrassment.

As her coworkers headed to their cars, Rachel strolled toward hers, which she'd parked around the side of the building.

She paused on the sidewalk and called her father one more time.

But, just as this morning, his phone rang and rang and rang.

When his voicemail picked up, Rachel left him a message to contact her. Then she ended the call and slid the phone into the slender pocket of her black pencil skirt and gripped her keys.

An unsettled feeling jostled inside her.

Why wouldn't her father answer?

Rachel paused, letting the chilly breeze wash over her.

Get a grip, Rachel. He's probably fine. Everything is just messing with your mind.

But was it? Or was that her naivety speaking?

As soon as she shut her eyes, she heard footsteps rushing toward her.

Just as she turned toward the sound, a man in a baseball cap shoved her against the wall and grabbed her purse from her shoulder.

She tumbled to the ground as he shoved her again.

She swallowed back a scream as she watched the man disappear.

What had just happened?

———

Jonah came around the corner in time to see Rachel on the ground. A bloody knee peeked out from beneath her skirt.

He rushed toward her. "Are you okay?"

Her eyes were wide with fright.

She hadn't just fallen, had she? Someone had done this to her.

"I . . ." Rachel raised her hand and pointed toward a figure running away in the distance. "He stole my purse."

Jonah rose, anger bristling inside him as he spotted the thief darting toward some houses behind the restaurant.

Without asking any more questions, he took off.

He was a fast runner. Maybe he could catch this guy.

However, the man had a decent head start.

The thief reached the houses in the distance and cut between some rental properties.

Jonah followed.

Cutting to the left, the man slipped between another set of houses.

As Jonah followed in that same direction, he paused in an empty lot between two towering beach houses.

The man had disappeared.

Jonah's muscles bristled.

Where had he gone?

Had he slipped inside one of the houses around him? Or was he hiding, waiting to strike?

Jonah needed to be careful.

His muscles tightened even more as he glanced around.

He slowly made his way forward, searching around him for any telltale signs or movements.

He saw nothing except the breeze swaying the shrubby trees.

He continued between the houses, keeping his eyes wide open as he paced the area, hoping to catch sight of the man or a clue about where he had disappeared.

There was nothing.

Wherever the man had gone, he was stealthy.

Jonah's jaw tightened as he admitted defeat.

Finally, he headed back toward Rachel. Even though she might be his enemy, he hoped she was okay. She'd looked truly shaken.

There was nothing he hated more than to see a woman frightened.

As he remembered her bloody knee, anger surged through him.

Rachel stood now, and two of her coworkers had gathered around her.

A small trickle of blood ran down her knee, and her hair was tousled. But otherwise, she appeared fine.

At least, Jonah could be thankful for that.

"I'm sorry." He paused and pretended to catch his breath. He needed to make himself appear more winded than he actually felt in order not to break cover. "But the guy got away. I was hoping to track him down."

"It's probably better you didn't." Rachel stared up at him with concern in her eyes. "You never know nowadays. He could have had a gun or a knife on him."

Before Jonah could ask more questions, Chief Chambers pulled up in her SUV. In mere seconds, she'd hopped out and met them.

She glanced back and forth between Jonah and Rachel before her gaze stopped on Rachel. "This is quite the welcome to the island you've received. I assure you that things aren't always like this around here."

"I should hope not." Rachel let out a nervous laugh.

As Rachel began to give Cassidy her statement, Jonah couldn't help but wonder if someone else was targeting Rachel also.

But if so, why? Did someone else suspect she'd stolen that information? Had someone from Essence hired their own agent to find out if she was guilty?

Jonah wasn't sure.

But he didn't like the scenarios playing out in his head.

They would only complicate things, and Jonah liked things to be simple.

In his line of work, that rarely happened.

RACHEL SAT at her new desk at the lab and tried to maintain her composure.

She had an office, so at least she could have some privacy. She'd be working partly in here and partly in the lab.

But she'd be lying if she didn't admit she was shaken after what had happened today.

Who wouldn't be?

When she got back to work, she'd escaped to the bathroom to clean up the scrape on her leg and run a brush through her hair. Then Dr. Hensley had given her permission to take the time to call and cancel her credit cards.

Thankfully, Rachel still had her phone where she had saved the information on each of those cards. But calling the bank and going through that process had been time-consuming and emotionally draining.

Then her conscience had gotten the best of her. She'd slipped outside and called Police Chief Chambers.

It had been silly not to tell the police chief about the numbers Rachel had seen on that dead man's hand. About how the dolphin necklace matched hers.

The police chief answered on the first ring.

"I'm not sure why I didn't tell you earlier, and I'm not sure this is even relevant," Rachel started.

"Why don't you let me be the judge of that?"

Rachel glanced around to make sure no one was near. They weren't.

Then, in a quiet voice, she said, "The man Jonah rescued from the ocean yesterday . . ."

"What about him?"

"He had four numbers written on his hand."

"I'm familiar with those numbers."

Rachel nibbled on her lips before saying, "Those numbers match the last four digits of my boss's phone number."

The chief stayed quiet a moment before speaking. "I see."

"And the necklace in the man's hand . . . I have one like it that my father gave me."

"Is that right?"

"I didn't tell you earlier because I thought . . . it

was a coincidence. I didn't want to make waves with my new position. I don't know. But it's been bugging me, so I wanted to let you know."

"I'm glad you did. Is there anyone who might want to hurt you?"

Rachel frowned again before diving into the story about Carl Nevada and what had happened in Colorado.

"Telling me was the right thing to do. Now, I can keep my eyes open for any more trouble."

"I'd appreciate that."

"In the meantime, I may have to talk to your boss about his phone number. But I'll try to keep your name out of it."

"I appreciate that as well. Thank you." Rachel ended the call, leaned back in her chair, and sighed.

At least, she'd gotten that off her chest. Now, she just needed to wait and see what the police chief came up with.

However, Rachel still had other secrets she couldn't bring herself to share . . . even if her life depended on it.

———

Rachel had a difficult time concentrating for the rest of the afternoon and mostly spent her time getting acquainted with her office and new job description.

She'd also been set up with her new ID badge and computer passwords. She'd had a brief meeting with the dermatologist she'd be working with—a woman named Noelle Purdy.

Noelle had seemed nice, and Rachel looked forward to getting to know her more.

Hopefully, tomorrow she could come in and hit the ground running.

Finally, when the workday ended, she told her new colleagues goodbye and headed back to her dad's house.

She couldn't wait to unwind.

As soon as she walked into the house, the scent of garlic and onions greeted her.

Her eyes narrowed. What was Jonah cooking?

It smelled delicious. She hadn't realized how hungry she was until now.

She wandered through the house until she reached the kitchen. There she saw Jonah with an apron on, cooking what appeared to be some type of shrimp dish. The smell of garlic and Old Bay mingled with the scents of the peppers and onions.

"The Best of You" by the Foo Fighters played on Jonah's phone, and he sang along exuberantly as if giving a concert to an invisible audience.

Rachel leaned in the doorway as she watched a moment.

The man certainly was intriguing. But the last

thing she needed right now was to be captivated by any man. Her last relationship had been a disaster, and she needed to keep that at the forefront of her mind.

Men complicated things. End of story.

Plus, there was Carl Nevada. She couldn't relax until he was behind bars permanently.

Jonah looked up and did a double take when he saw her standing there.

Then he grinned, not looking the least bit bothered that she'd heard him singing.

"Hey there. Want to sing along with me?" He held out his spoon as if it were a microphone.

"It's tempting but . . . I think I'll pass this time." Rachel nodded at the pan in front of him. "Whatever you're cooking smells good."

He shrugged as he continued to cook the shrimp. "I have enough for two. Would you like to join me?"

Her grumbling stomach begged her to say yes. "I don't want to impose."

"Don't be ridiculous. This is your house. How could you possibly be imposing?"

Rachel chuckled at his playful tone. "Well . . . there is *that*."

The fact was, Rachel had always been better in a lab than she was with people. Selena, her best friend back in Colorado, was one of those people who knew how to act in every social situation, and she never seemed awkward. Rachel had always envied her friend for that.

But Rachel would rather have a good book and a crackling fire on a quiet night, than to go out and be forced to interact with people.

Digby had said that made her boring.

But certainly, someone was out there who appreciated Rachel as she was without wanting to change her . . . right?

Besides, Digby wasn't exactly a shining example of her ideal man. Her ideal man wouldn't cheat on her—multiple times, at that.

Apparently, others had known about his shenanigans—but not her. No one had taken the opportunity to warn her. Not even her so-called friends. She'd had no idea until she walked in on him with another woman after returning early from a business trip.

He'd been the head of sales for Ocean Essence, so plenty of people knew him. Plenty of people knew about his escapades.

She'd been the woman at the office that people had simply felt sorry for. The brilliant but naive scientist who couldn't see what was right in front of her.

A few minutes later, Jonah placed the food on the table with a flourish and then helped Rachel with her chair.

"A gentleman too?" she said. "You must have been raised right."

"If foster care counts, then yes."

Her eyes widened as remorse filled her. "You're right. I'm sorry. You mentioned that last night, but I forgot."

"No apologies necessary." Jonah sat across from her, appearing unfazed. "I turned out okay . . . at least, that's what people tell me."

"Was it hard growing up in the system? Or were you placed with a good family?"

Rachel wasn't sure if she should ask those questions, but she wanted to know more about Jonah and his background—especially if they were going to live in the same house for the next week or so.

"I was placed with nine different families over the years. Some were better than others." He carefully spread a napkin in his lap.

Rachel couldn't even imagine. "That sounds rough. If you don't mind me asking . . . what happened to your parents?"

"My dad left before I was born. My mom died in a car accident when I was six. She didn't have any other family, so the state took me into custody."

"I'm . . . sorry." She shifted. "One of my friends at Essence was in foster care, and he used to tell me stories about how he was treated. It made me so angry."

"Oh, yeah? Whatever happened to him?"

Rachel felt tension thrumming inside her. "He died not long ago. I . . . I miss him. I didn't see him often, but the world lost a great person that day."

Rachel didn't ask Jonah any more questions about his childhood. Jonah would share more if he wanted. Right now, he had a somewhat stunned expression on his face.

But her heart welled with compassion for the man.

His upbringing couldn't have been easy.

For a moment, she regretted her earlier suspicion of him.

Wasn't everyone just trying to make a living? Doing their best?

That's what she'd like to think, at least.

Before she could dwell on the thought too long, the lights above her flickered and then went off.

She sucked in a breath.

Tonight, it wasn't storming outside.

Had someone cut the electricity?

BEFORE RACHEL COULD PANIC, the lights came on again.

She released the breath she held.

"I'm sure that probably happens all the time here on an island like this," Jonah assured her. "It can't be easy running electricity to such a remote location."

"You're probably right." She let out a nervous laugh.

As Rachel and Jonah sat across from each other at the kitchen table, she felt that twinge of awkwardness again as she wondered how to start the rest of the dinner conversation.

But the awkwardness didn't last long because Jonah spoke instead. "Is it okay if I pray?"

"That sounds wonderful." Prayer was something Rachel had abandoned sometime in college when she'd been taught that science had all the answers. But lately, she'd wondered if that was really true.

Because science wasn't always right. Science had let her down also. Scientific organizations often endorsed theories as absolute truth—only to have those very theories later proven incorrect.

Science got it wrong at times because science was overseen by people. Flawed people.

Her mom, for example.

Doctors had said she was fine. Perfectly healthy.

In truth, cancer was killing her.

Rachel's dad had begged doctors to listen to their concerns. But no one had seemed interested.

Only two weeks later, her mom had died. Her diagnoses had come too late.

Rachel had been devastated by the loss.

A shiver raced through her at the memory.

As Jonah said, "Amen," she glanced up, another rush of gratitude filling her.

Maybe Jonah being here was an answer to prayer, something she never thought she'd say. But he'd been a real lifesaver so far—on more than one occasion.

Still, what was he hiding? How had he gotten that scar on his arm?

And really . . . his timing here was uncanny.

She'd be wise to keep her guard up.

"How did the rest of your day go?" Jonah started as he plated the garlic shrimp over some linguini.

"Uneventful," she said. "No news from Cassidy about my purse yet."

"I'm sorry to hear that. I'm assuming this guy was just trying to steal your credit cards."

"There really wasn't much else in there. Just the normal things and my old leather-bound notebook that I carry everywhere with me."

Jonah raised his eyebrows. "Do you think someone stole your purse for the notebook?"

Rachel laughed at the thought. "I doubt anyone cares about the silly ideas I scribble there."

He tilted his head. "What kind of ideas?"

"Nothing too noteworthy. I have some special projects I work on in my own time. On occasion, I jot down formulas or ingredients I'd like to try at the lab, so I don't forget them. It's nothing too earth-shattering."

"Well, I think it sounds fascinating. I'm sure those formulas might be worth some big money."

She waved a hand in the air. "Maybe. But I don't care much about money—not that I want people to cheat me, mind you. But I'm just as happy now as I was when I was a child growing up with very little. Money isn't an indicator of happiness."

Something flickered in his eyes. Surprise maybe.

"Sounds like wise words," he murmured.

"I've seen my friends chase careers and nearly kill themselves trying to get ahead. Innovation is more important to me. I want the work I do to help people. That's why I took this new job."

Jonah stared at her, an unreadable look in his gaze before he nodded. "Sounds like you're truly one of a kind."

She smiled before taking a bite of her shrimp. The creamy, spicy sauce hit the spot. "This is amazing."

"Thanks. I learned in high school that cooking was a great stress reliever for me. My best friend and I used to experiment with different recipes when we got together."

"Sounds like a nice tradition."

"It was." A new tension filled his voice.

Rachel wondered if his best friend was the foster brother Jonah had mentioned losing.

She didn't ask.

Instead, Rachel sensed she needed to change the subject. "So how was your day? I mean . . . besides eating a grilled cheese and peach sandwich and chasing after a purse snatcher?"

"It was calm after that. I can't complain."

Before they could talk anymore, Rachel's phone rang.

She looked at the caller ID. "It's Chief Chambers."

Rachel braced herself for whatever the police chief might have to say.

Jonah tried not to show too much interest as Rachel answered the phone. But he was curious about why the police chief was calling.

Rachel put the phone on speaker and let Chief Chambers know that Jonah was here also and listening.

"I just wanted to let you know that we ran the prints on our dead man Jonah pulled out of the water, and we have a name," Chief Chambers started.

Jonah straightened as he listened, his pulse quickening.

"Does the name Travis Metcalf sound familiar?" the chief asked.

Rachel twisted her lips in a frown before shaking her head. "I can't say it does. Is he associated with the lab?"

"We're not sure yet. We're still looking into all the details. I mostly wanted to find out if the name was familiar."

"I'm sorry." Rachel frowned as she shook her head. "I wish I could be of more help. But I didn't recognize him or his name."

Chief Chambers thanked her.

As Rachel ended the call, she looked at Jonah. "I wonder who that Travis Metcalf guy is."

"I have no idea." Jonah shrugged, reminding himself to look casual. "I have a lot of questions about him and what he was doing out in the ocean during the storm. Something doesn't add up for me."

"I agree." Rachel frowned again.

Jonah glanced at his watch.

It was five minutes until six.

Walter should be calling him at any time now.

Jonah hated to eat and run—he didn't want to make a bad impression with Rachel—but he needed to know what this guy had to say. To know if Walter might have the answers Jonah had been looking for.

Besides, his conclusions about Rachel felt as if they were shifting—and he couldn't let that happen. But what if he'd been wrong about her? The woman didn't appear to have a devious bone in her body.

Besides, if she was the one responsible for Ganon's death, then why had someone broken into her place? Stolen her purse?

The pieces weren't fitting in his mind.

He'd tried to deny the fact.

He wanted someone to blame.

But he didn't want to waste time looking in the wrong direction either.

Because that would mean the real bad guy might get off scot-free.

He stood and flashed his most apologetic grin. "I'm sorry, but I promised a potential client that I'd take their call at six. Would you mind excusing me a few minutes?"

Rachel waved off his apology. "Of course. Go ahead. Do whatever you need to do."

With another nod at her, Jonah excused himself.

As he walked upstairs, he replayed the conversation he'd had with Rachel, still struggling with how valid his initial conclusions might be.

Ganon. She'd been talking about Ganon during dinner.

She'd said the world had lost a wonderful man.

And she seemed truly grieved over his death.

She didn't have anything to do with his murder, did she? Jonah was investigating the wrong person. He suddenly felt certain of it.

A surprising sense of relief washed over him at the realization.

He wanted to believe there were still some good people left in this world.

However, if Rachel was innocent, then he needed to change his focus to someone else—someone who might truly be guilty.

He prayed this conversation with Walter held the answers he needed.

AS RACHEL PUT the leftovers away and cleaned the kitchen, she wondered about Jonah's phone call. Wondered about his job and what he was doing here.

He'd given the security consultant explanation, but she still didn't have a clear picture of his purpose here on Lantern Beach. He could do this kind of job anywhere. Why come here to look into a computer network? And what was with the paperwork he'd brought with him to lunch?

Still, if her father had hired Jonah, then the man was obviously here for a good reason. Her dad was no fool, but he *could* be absent-minded. He had more ideas than he did organization and common sense sometimes.

Thankfully, he usually surrounded himself with people who balanced him out and kept him on track.

Speaking of her dad . . . Rachel frowned.

She pulled her phone from her pocket and glanced at the screen one more time, making sure she hadn't missed any calls.

It was just so strange that she hadn't heard from her dad yet.

Then again, he *had* hired a security consultant. Maybe something was going on that he hadn't told her about.

Her stomach twisted in knots at the thought.

She shoved the phone back into her pocket and washed another plate.

Had something happened to him?

Rachel had to consider that maybe her father was in danger.

She didn't want to think in worst-case scenarios, but her mind kept heading in that direction.

Maybe she should have asked her dad more pointed questions when she last talked to him. But that had been a week ago, and she'd had no idea she'd find herself in these circumstances.

As she washed the dishes, her thoughts drifted again to the dead man and to her stolen purse. Were these things somehow linked with what had happened in Colorado?

She knew coincidences weren't likely—though they did happen at times.

But as a scientist, she'd learned to follow the evidence, and the dolphin indicated she was somehow connected with the man's appearance on the island.

She frowned.

Her start here in Lantern Beach hadn't gone as she'd planned.

Was this the new beginning she'd been searching for?

Was it possible to run away from her problems?

Rachel considered herself a logical person.

For that reason, she knew the answer to that question was a resounding no.

———

Six o'clock came and went, and Walter didn't call.

Finally, after staring at his phone for ten minutes, Jonah dialed the number Walter had contacted him from earlier.

But the line rang once and then died.

What had happened? Had someone gotten to Walter before Jonah had a chance to talk to him?

If so, that would mean that someone knew Walter was going to spill the truth.

Jonah paced his room as he tried to work out his thoughts.

Was someone at Essence paranoid that others

knew about the formulas being sold? Were they silencing anyone who threatened to expose them?

That was hard to say.

The bad feeling in Jonah's gut grew stronger and stronger by the moment.

As his phone rang, his breath caught. Walter?

But when he looked at the screen, he saw it was Larchmont.

He sighed before answering. He'd end the call if Walter called.

Jonah had never met Alan Larchmont face-to-face. He only knew the man was former military himself and that he'd purposefully chosen Jonah and his friends for the Shadow Agency.

Jonah understood the man's need to keep his identity under wraps, but he wished he knew more about the man.

Apparently, Larchmont was independently wealthy. He'd funded some of their assignments himself, while others were paid for by clients.

What they did wasn't always cheap. Sometimes they needed helicopters or other expensive equipment and resources.

Larchmont was always quick to provide for them.

"What's the update?" Larchmont barked.

"Nothing yet." Jonah gave him a quick rundown on what had happened since he arrived.

"And your target?"

Rachel's image flashed in his mind, and regret filled him. "I don't think she was involved in Ganon's death."

Jonah couldn't believe he was admitting that out loud. He'd been so sure she was guilty.

But his gut told him that wasn't the case.

"What?" Larchmont's voice rose. "Why do you say that?"

His earlier conversation with Rachel flashed back to him. "She's not interested in money. And she seems like a terrible liar, not like the type who's capable of stealing or killing. I don't think she could hurt a fly."

"That doesn't mean anything. Maybe she didn't do it for the money. Maybe she needed Ganon's position at the company for some other purpose."

"She's a smart woman. She could have gotten her new position on her own right." Jonah meant the words. If he were to be honest, Rachel had done nothing but impress him since he'd arrived.

He hadn't planned on liking her. But he did.

"We're just following the evidence here." Larchmont's gruff voice pulled Jonah from his thoughts.

Irritation pinched at his spine. "I realize that, but answers aren't always easy to find."

"You have a week. Rachel's our best lead. You need to work her. Turn on that charm of yours. Find those answers and wrap this up. Vincent could use your help on his assignment in Montana."

Jonah pressed his eyes closed. "Yes, sir."

Feeling a new tension between his shoulders, Jonah shoved his phone into his pocket and made his way back to the kitchen.

Why had Ganon given him that paper with Rachel's name on it?

What if it wasn't because she'd killed him . . . but because she was next on the list of those who would be killed?

———

Rachel was washing dishes when Jonah walked into the kitchen.

She was a sight to see. Lithe, demure, gracious, and smart. He'd noticed she was sometimes unsure of herself—at least in social situations. But she covered her anxiety well.

Jonah wanted to know more about her.

He snapped from his thoughts.

Not more *about her* about her.

He wanted to know if she had a devious side—just like Larchmont had reminded him.

How was it possible that the woman had taken him by surprise as she did?

Jonah was hardly ever surprised by people. His survival skills relied on his ability to read people.

Yet his intelligence and instincts seemed to clash inside him now.

"You didn't have to do dishes." Jonah stepped closer, noting the lemony scent of the dish soap as it floated around him. "It's the least I can do since your father is letting me stay here."

"It's no problem." Rachel smiled as she rinsed a plate. "This was always the rule that my mom and dad had growing up. One person cooked, and the other cleaned. It just seems like a fair trade-off."

"Sounds like they were a wise couple." A moment of longing washed through him.

He'd always wanted the ideal family that he'd never had growing up.

When that hadn't seemed possible, he'd gone in the opposite direction. He'd been a lone wolf. The guy without anything to hold him back.

An expendable.

"They were great together," Rachel continued, a faraway look in her gaze. "I miss my mom every day. I know my dad does also."

"If you don't mind me asking, what happened?" Jonah softened his voice. He knew about loss. Knew how much it hurt.

Even if he didn't know if he could trust Rachel, he

still understood grief—especially the grief of losing a mother.

"She died of cancer two years ago," Rachel continued.

"I'm sorry to hear that. I imagine that must have been tough."

"It was." She sucked in a breath as if pulling herself together. Then she drained the sink and wiped her hands on a towel near the stove. "Listen, I need to attend to a little business. I canceled my debit and credit cards, but I still need to figure out a way to access some money until I get my new ones."

"If there's anything I can do, let me know. I'd be happy to loan you some cash."

"I hope I don't have to take you up on that, but I appreciate the offer."

As Rachel started to breeze past him, Jonah called her name. "If you're up for it, Scrabble tonight?"

A grin spread across her face. "Scrabble sounds perfect."

It would give them another chance to bond . . . and maybe another chance for him to find more answers.

RACHEL'S EYES widened as Jonah played WHIZBANG for seventy-six points. "Clever . . ."

"What can I say? I'm more than a pretty face." Dry humor filled his voice, and he winked playfully.

Rachel laughed, thankful for the blithe moment in the middle of the otherwise stressful start to her stay here.

She hadn't expected to enjoy this game so much. Or Jonah. Or doing something so simple.

As she contemplated what word to play next, she stole another glance at her temporary housemate.

Just as they'd done last night, they had started a fire in the fireplace—this time, not so much out of necessity as much as for atmosphere. They sat on the floor in front of the fire with the coffee table between them, drinking tea as they played.

Jonah's face somehow looked even more handsome as the firelight flickered across his features.

She cleared her ever-tightening throat and shook away the thoughts.

Men were nothing but trouble. She was better off being married to her job than she was being tied to any man.

"So, how's your job for my father going?" she started instead, figuring it was a safer subject.

Jonah nodded slowly. "It's coming along. I've found several areas of vulnerability in your dad's online network. By the time I finish my evaluation, his security should be stronger than Fort Knox."

"I'm sure he'll like hearing that."

"I hope so."

At the mention of her dad, she glanced at her phone.

Still no callback.

She frowned.

Her shoulders tensed when she felt Jonah studying her.

"Is everything okay?" he asked.

Rachel flattened her lips and nodded. "I hope so. It's just that I've been trying to reach my father all day, and he hasn't picked up."

Jonah's eyes narrowed. "I take it that's unusual?"

"It is. He's a busy man, but he usually makes himself available for me."

"It's probably nothing," Jonah said. "Maybe he's just been wrapped up in that meeting with the potential investor all day."

"That's probably it." But Rachel sounded unconvinced, even to her own ears.

Probably because she didn't believe her own words. Her dad would have at least shot her a text back.

Jonah grabbed his phone. "Let me see if he'll answer my call. Not that I think he would do that for me and not you, but this is business, so . . ."

"It's worth a shot." Rachel felt a nudge of hope.

She watched as Jonah dialed her father's number, and then she held her breath.

She wasn't sure if she would be irritated or relieved if her dad answered.

Probably both.

However, the phone rang and rang and rang.

But her dad didn't pick up.

The bad feeling in her gut churned stronger.

"Maybe he misplaced his phone," Jonah offered with an apologetic frown.

It was sweet of him to try to think of possible excuses. Rachel supposed his reason could be true.

But her gut told her it wasn't.

Something was wrong.

Even worse—what if something had happened to her dad? Could Carl have gotten to him?

Fear pounded through her at the thought.

———

Jonah and Rachel played Scrabble for the next two hours until Rachel finally won.

Then they said good night and headed for their bedrooms to turn in for the evening.

But Jonah wasn't ready to sleep yet.

Instead, he paced his room as his thoughts raced.

He wasn't usually one to enjoy playing board games, but he'd found himself having more fun than he'd expected with Rachel.

The woman had surprised him.

Before he'd met her, he'd had an idea of what she might be like. Uptight. Type A. Someone who loved to talk about science.

In a way those things were true. But she was so much more than that. A little shy, with a smile that felt more like a reward. Intelligent. Caring.

This investigation would be so much easier if she was mean and nasty.

But that wasn't the case. Jonah didn't want to deceive her anymore, despite what Larchmont had said.

But maybe he wasn't thinking clearly.

What if he spilled everything to her? His real

reason for being here. What he was investigating. His past.

Maybe she could help him.

Jonah shook his head as he snapped himself from those musings.

Where had that thought even come from? Was he losing his touch?

Sharing too much would be the death of this investigation.

Plus, he remembered the look on Rachel's face when she'd seen the dead man on the beach. She also had secrets.

His jaw tightened.

Besides, when Rachel found out his true intentions, the easy banter and friendly conversation they had now would disappear.

Did Jonah want to risk that so soon?

It would be foolish to throw this whole investigation away just because Jonah had the beginnings of some feelings for the woman.

If the two of them had the potential for a long-lasting relationship—and it was way too early to surmise that—then things might be different. But whatever was brewing between them was just a flash in the pan.

Jonah didn't plan on staying here in Lantern Beach. Besides, they hardly knew each other, and he needed to keep that fact in the forefront of his mind.

Mostly, he needed to remember that she may have killed his best friend.

Yet the more he got to know Rachel, the less likely that seemed.

His attraction to the woman was an unexpected hurdle, one he wasn't supposed to have to leap over.

He walked toward the window to stare out at the ocean.

Unlike last night, tonight was clear, and a half-moon illuminated some of the waves.

It was such a beautiful sight. Jonah had always considered himself more of a mountain person. But being in Lantern Beach made him wonder if he could become more of a beach person. Something about the rhythm of the waves felt calming.

As he stared at the water, movement at the edge of the dune caught his eye.

He did a double take when he saw a man standing there facing the house.

Jonah bristled.

Was this the same man who'd broken in last night? The guy who had stolen Rachel's purse?

He didn't know.

Jonah still hadn't put everything together, and he didn't know if this man worked for Essence or if he was someone else entirely.

So what was that man doing?

The man clearly didn't see him. The lights in Jonah's bedroom were off.

That could work to his advantage.

Jonah needed to see if he could take this guy by surprise and find out some answers.

CHAPTER
EIGHTEEN

He didn't want to alarm Rachel. But he *did* check all the doors before he went outside, to confirm they were locked. That fact brought him a small amount of comfort.

Then he quietly walked out the front door and around the side of the house. The sand silenced his footsteps.

Jonah remained low.

He wanted to get as close as possible to this guy before making his presence known.

Climbing to the other side of the sand dune, he paused behind some sea oats to get another glance at the man.

But the guy was nowhere to be seen.

Jonah's back muscles tightened.

He scanned the beach around him. But the darkness concealed so much—maybe too much.

The guy couldn't have just disappeared into thin air. He'd gone somewhere.

Closer to the house?

Jonah didn't like the thought of that.

His muscles remained tense as he searched the area around him for any signs of the man.

But he was nowhere in sight.

One thing was clear: whoever was behind this was a professional.

Normal people couldn't make themselves a ghost like this.

A ghost . . . ?

His breath caught. Could this have something to do with Jonah's former position in the military?

The people involved with Operation Adrenaline were trained. They would know how to escape, to cover up their crimes.

His heart pounded harder.

Jonah thought he'd walked away. That he'd left that life behind and started over.

But what if that wasn't the case?

What if it wasn't possible to have a normal life after Operation Adrenaline?

His stomach churned as he slipped back inside the house.

This could change everything.

He now needed to be more on guard than ever.

———

Rachel sat on her bed and stared at the phone in her hands.

She'd tried her father yet again.

There was still no answer.

Her concern grew stronger by the moment.

Something was definitely wrong.

Otherwise, he'd be returning her calls.

But what should she do about it? Talk to Cassidy? Call the police in New Jersey? Maybe they could stop by his place and do a wellness check?

She wasn't sure. But she had to do *something*. Her father might need help.

In fact . . . what if the incidents that had occurred on the island since she'd arrived were somehow related to his disappearance?

Too much was happening, and Rachel wasn't sure how anything was related to the other.

The dead man on the beach.

The numbers written on his hand and the dolphin necklace.

The break-in.

Her purse being stolen.

Her head began to pound.

Nothing made sense.

Moving to Lantern Beach for this job had seemed like a once in a lifetime opportunity.

She was supposed to have a fresh start. She was supposed to get away from her trouble.

But maybe that had been wishful thinking.

Maybe there was no escape.

As if to confirm that thought, her phone buzzed.

She'd gotten a text.

Was it her dad?

Her hopes fell when she glanced at the screen.

She squinted, not recognizing the number.

But the message was loud and clear:

> Don't trust Jonah Gray. He's not who you think.

Her pulse quickened.

What did that mean?

She swallowed hard.

What if . . . she hardly wanted to think the thought.

But she couldn't ignore it.

What if Carl Nevada had hired Jonah to come here and keep an eye on her?

What if Jonah Gray wasn't who he claimed to be?

Her lungs tightened until she could hardly breathe.

CHAPTER
NINETEEN

"I'VE GOT AN UPDATE FOR YOU," Doc Clemson's voice came over the phone line.

Cassidy sat up straighter in her chair at the police station as she sipped her morning coffee. "I'd love an update."

"It's about the man who died in the ocean."

That was what she'd been hoping.

Just last night, Cassidy had found out the guy's name. Travis Metcalf. He was from Minnesota. Thirty-two. Single.

She'd yet to get in contact with his relatives, so Cassidy still wasn't sure why he'd been on Lantern Beach or even where he'd been staying while here.

Having a cause of death could help answer a lot of questions.

"Jonah and Rachel heard the man calling for help

and saw him floundering in the ocean before he died, so it's no surprise I found water in his lungs," Doc continued. "Drowning is *officially* his cause of death."

"Officially?" Cassidy leaned back as she waited for Doc's response.

"In cases like this, I always do a screening to see if anything from the ocean could have contributed to a person's death," Doc said. "It turns out he had c. fleckeri venom proteins in his system."

"What exactly is that?" Cassidy didn't want to make any assumptions.

"It's a poisonous venom found in the box jelly-fish, one of the most dangerous and deadly animals in the ocean."

She sat up straighter. "Do we have that kind of jellyfish here in Lantern Beach?"

"Here's where it gets interesting—no, we don't. And, usually, people who die from these jellyfish stings have marks on their skin. There were none on our victim."

"Curious."

"It's my belief that this man ingested the poiso-nous venom instead."

"What?" Cassidy mulled over that revelation. "Where would a person get a venom like that to ingest?"

"I'm not sure, but . . . a biomedical lab might be the first place I'd look."

Her breath caught. Ocean Essence.

"Good to know." Cassidy tried to visualize what might have happened. Even if he had been poisoned . . . "Why was he in the ocean, though?"

"Just a theory but . . . what if he was running from someone?"

Cassidy shifted in her seat as she considered his words. "And he ran into the ocean?"

"Maybe the killer poisoned him and then forced him into the water to make his death look like a drowning. Or the man could've escaped from the killer and run down the beach to try and get help, when a wave caught him and sucked him in. You and I both know that's happened before. It was storming, and the swells were coming in at twenty-five to thirty feet."

Cassidy chewed on the theory a moment.

Rough surf *could* easily knock someone down and carry them out to sea.

She wasn't sure what the truth was, however. Not without more information.

At least, now she had a direction to look for answers.

But Cassidy couldn't help but wonder if this man's death and the crimes happening surrounding Rachel Atwood were somehow connected . . .

RACHEL SAT at her desk the next morning, watching orientation videos that all new Ocean Essence employees had to go through when they started working there. The onboarding process gave the background of the company and everything they did.

She knew most of this already, but Hensley had said it was still part of their "company process" for these types of job changes so she listened the best she could.

However, she was having trouble focusing.

She had too much on her mind—especially after that text she'd received last night.

Don't trust Jonah Gray. He's not who you think.

Who had sent her that message? And why? Was

someone simply trying to turn Rachel against Jonah? Or was there truth to those words?

Rachel didn't know. No matter what angle she tried to come at the text from, she only ended at confusion.

She leaned back in her chair and sighed. Maybe she needed to think about something else.

Like the fact that this morning Dr. Hensley had invited her to a company social tomorrow night at his place.

The gathering would give Rachel the opportunity to get better acquainted with some of the key employees here.

She knew she needed everyone's support if she wanted to convince her team here that she should use their time and resources toward finding a cure for vitiligo.

Vitiligo was a skin condition that caused loss of pigmentation in patches. It occurred when the cells that produced melanin died or stopped functioning, and it affected people of all skin types.

She had personal reasons for the research she wanted to do.

So Rachel needed to make a good impression.

As she sat at her desk, her gaze drifted from the computer where the videos played. Instead, she stared at the door on the side of the building. The one with the "Authorized Personnel Only" sign attached.

She understood that top-secret formulas needed to be kept somewhere under lock and key. So it didn't surprise her that there was a place off-limits to most employees.

What had surprised her was just how large the room was. Not that she had been inside. But she'd seen the outside of this building, so she knew the approximate dimensions of the room.

The room was big enough to store a lot of research files.

Dr. Hensley and Lloyd had been in and out of the room on several occasions.

It seemed odd.

A room where secret formulas were kept seemed like one that would need to be accessed every so often, but not several times a day.

Add that to the retinal scanner. That kind of security seemed like overkill for a cosmetics company.

Rachel was probably overthinking this. She was tired and hadn't gotten much sleep last night. She'd had too much on her mind.

Mostly . . . could she trust the man who was staying at her father's house? The one who sang while he cooked and enjoyed playing Scrabble with her?

Jonah had seemed too good to be true.

Maybe he was.

When her phone rang, she jumped and glanced at the screen, hoping it was her dad.

It wasn't.

Instead, it was Selena.

She hit Pause on her video and glanced at the time.

Rachel was supposed to get a twenty-minute break every couple of hours. So she would take that now.

She grabbed her phone and then stepped outside for a moment.

She hadn't talked to Selena since she'd left Colorado, and Rachel wanted to make sure everything was okay. Then she'd tell her friend she would call her later.

But when she answered the call, Selena's voice was anything but conversational.

"Rachel . . . Carl Nevada was just released from jail."

Her lungs froze. "What? How can that be possible?"

"A judge reviewed his case. One of the prosecutors dropped the criminal charges against Nevada."

"What . . . ? How . . . ?"

"I heard new evidence was found leading the police to re-examine things. That led them to another guy, someone named Rick Reynolds. They questioned him, and he confessed to the murder."

"But I saw it happen . . ."

"I know." Selena's voice dipped. "I'm not sure what the truth behind it all is. But I wanted to let you know. Rachel . . . what if he comes after you?"

Everything around Rachel began to spin.

That was the question Rachel was hoping to never have to ask herself.

———

Jonah had spent the last couple of hours looking for security breaches in Roman's company and writing reports on how to solve the issues.

He had some knowledge of cybercrime, and he was fairly good on the computer. However, Vincent had to walk him through some of the technical details.

When Jonah finished doing that, he took a break and rubbed his eyes.

Then he glanced back at his computer one more time.

Out of curiosity, he typed Rachel's name.

Several mentions of her popped up. Awards she'd received from the scientific community. An article about how she was the valedictorian of her class at Stanford. Pictures of her cozied up to a man—Digby Bauer, the head of sales for Ocean Essence.

Jonah already knew some of that information.

He'd done his research before coming here. But now he saw everything in a new light.

Rachel was now single. What had happened between her and Digby? Why had she given up her old job to come here? What kinds of secrets did those beautiful brown eyes of hers harbor?

He needed to figure out how to proceed, especially since Larchmont had instructed Jonah to keep investigating Rachel. Jonah didn't believe that she was involved. But if not Rachel, then who?

If he shifted his focus, he needed to figure out who to shift it to.

Dr. Hensley seemed as if he might be a good choice. But he was the CEO of Ocean Essence. Why would the CEO sell his own formulas to the competition?

It didn't make sense.

As he stared at Rachel's picture, his phone rang, startling him from the moment.

It was Vincent.

"Hey, Vincent," Jonah started. "What's going on?"

"I've been looking into the whereabouts of Roman Atwood. You said he left Lantern Beach the day before yesterday, right?"

"That's correct. We've been trying to reach him and haven't been able to get in touch with him. It's unlike him not to answer his phone."

"I tried to track his cell phone, but it went offline Thursday morning."

Jonah sucked in a breath. He didn't like the sound of that. "The last known location of the cell phone was New Jersey. I checked that myself."

"That's right," Vincent confirmed. "I sent someone past his residence, and no one appeared to be there. I also tried to get in touch with him at the office, but his secretary said he was on vacation."

"I know he told his employees he'd be in Lantern Beach, but he decided at the last minute to meet with an investor." Jonah rubbed his neck as his muscles there tightened. "That's what he told me."

"I can't tell you where this guy is. I ran his credit cards through the system, and they haven't been used in the past thirty-six hours."

That didn't sound good either. Jonah's gut tightened. "I need you to keep looking into this. I'm afraid something may have happened to him."

"I'll see what else I can find out."

Jonah didn't get any indications when he'd talked to Roman that the man was about to run or that anything was wrong.

But maybe he'd dig more deeply into some of Roman's personal information on this computer and see if he could find out anything.

Either way, a bad feeling rumbled in his gut.

"One other thing," Vincent said. "In case you

haven't heard, Walter was in a car accident. Ran off the road and hit a tree. He died upon impact."

"What?" Jonah sat up straighter. "I hadn't heard."

"Happened last night."

His thoughts raced. "Were there any signs of foul play?"

"Nope. But that doesn't mean there wasn't any involved."

Jonah leaned back and frowned as he processed the update.

Clearly, more was going on here than met the eye.

Jonah had come here to investigate Ganon's death. But it appeared Jonah had gotten himself tangled in something far more complicated . . . and deadlier than a single murder.

NEAR LUNCHTIME, Rachel rose from her desk, ready to stretch her legs. Plus, she had a question for Dr. Hensley.

As she reached his office and started to knock, his voice carried from inside. He was talking to someone, though she couldn't identify the other voice.

"She can't find out about this." Hensley's voice sounded gravelly and low as he said the words.

"No, she can't. But she *can* help us without knowing the truth."

"That's why we brought her onboard."

"Can you trust her?"

"I think so," Hensley said. "She wears rose-colored glasses. That will work to our advantage."

"We can hope."

Rachel's breath caught. Were they talking about her?

If so, why? Why exactly had they brought her onboard?

Unease churned inside her.

"Did you hear about Walter?" Hensley continued.

Walter? Were they talking about Walter Adams? He'd been Ganon's research assistant. Rachel had met him once.

"I did. It's a shame he was in that car accident."

"He died."

Rachel held back a gasp.

"We'll need to tell everyone here eventually," the other guy said.

"They're still not over Ganon's death. I can't imagine how they'll handle this. Two tragic deaths within a month?" There was a pause. "It's unbelievable."

As footsteps headed toward the door, Rachel hurried back to her desk, trying to ignore the tremble in her hands.

What had that conversation been about?

Did Dr. Hensley have ulterior motives for bringing her here?

Or was she reading too much into this?

And the fact that both Walter and Ganon were dead was alarming, to say the least. What if Ganon truly had been murdered as she'd theorized?

Before she could think about it too long, her phone rang.

It was Kari Moody, the receptionist. "Ms. Atwood."

"Yes?" Rachel's gaze flickered to Hensley's office as Lloyd stepped out.

Lloyd? She hadn't guessed it was him inside. Surprise washed through her. The painfully thin man was a bit of a know-it-all.

Did he look nervous? His gaze shifted around the office and perspiration covered his forehead. Yes, those seemed like classic signs of anxiety.

"You have someone here to see you," Kari said.

Rachel sat up straighter. "Who is that?"

"Police Chief Cassidy Chambers. She said she has an update for you."

An update? Maybe she would finally get some resolution. Or was that hoping for too much?

Sometimes, answers didn't make things better. Sometimes answers confirmed a person's worst fears.

But she couldn't think like that. Besides, whatever it was, she needed to face it.

"Great," Rachel said before swallowing hard. "I'll be right there."

She stood, grateful for a reason to get away from her desk.

She stepped out into the reception area and

spotted the police chief studying some company awards displayed on the wall near the chairs there.

Rachel pointed to the exterior door. "Why don't we head out here since it's a nice day? I could use some fresh air."

"That sounds great."

They stepped outside and walked to an observation deck built to look over the marsh and the Pamlico Sound. The decaying scent of the marsh drifted around them, and the reeds brushed together in the wind.

After being inside most of the day, Rachel welcomed the change in atmosphere.

"I'm sorry to bother you at work, but I was heading out this way anyway." Chief Chambers handed Rachel a paper bag.

Rachel peered inside and saw her purse.

Her breath caught. "You found it?"

Chief Chambers nodded. "It was in a field between some houses not far from The Crazy Chefette. I did look through it, and it appears your wallet is missing, and I believe you said you had a notebook inside. That's gone also. Anything else that's been stolen, you'll have to tell me yourself."

Rachel quickly rifled through her bag. "Thankfully I cleaned it out before moving here, so there's not much else worth stealing in here."

"I assume you've already canceled your credit cards?"

Rachel nodded. "I did. New ones are on their way to me."

"That's good." Chief Chambers tilted her head compassionately.

As a chilly breeze swept over them, Rachel pulled her cardigan closer. "Any leads on who took my things?"

Chief Chambers frowned, seeming unbothered by the chill in the air. "Unfortunately, there's not. We haven't had any other reports on the island of something like this happening. I'm not sure if there's a tie between this and the person who broke into your house. But it does appear you're being targeted."

Rachel quickly nodded. "Yes, it does."

"We'll keep looking into this." Chief Chambers offered an affirmative nod. "In the meantime, I thought I'd let you know that I talked to Dr. Hensley this morning."

Her heart beat harder. "And?"

"He said he doesn't recognize Travis Metcalf. But he acted a little squirmy. I'm going to keep my eye on him."

"Sounds wise."

"I didn't mention your name, just to let you know. He shouldn't have any idea you were the one who mentioned those numbers to me."

"Thank you." A measure of relief filled her.

"And one last thing. It turns out the dead man on the beach was poisoned with the venom of the box jellyfish."

Rachel's head began to spin. "What?"

Chief Chambers squinted. "I take it you've heard of it?"

"A friend of mine was working on an acne skin cream that used a very small amount of it as one of the ingredients. Other ingredients neutralized the harmful aspects of the venom so that only the beneficial aspects remained."

Rachel's mind raced.

Had Ganon also been poisoned with jellyfish venom? No, that was a crazy thought. He'd had a heart attack . . .

She shoved the thought aside, unsure how to make sense of this new revelation.

"I'd like to talk to this friend," Chief Chambers said.

Rachel frowned. "Unfortunately, Ganon died about a month ago. He had a heart attack."

"Is there anyone here at the lab who worked with him? I'm assuming this guy worked for Ocean Essence."

"He did. But I just heard that his research assistant also died—in a car accident."

Chief Chambers' eyes narrowed with cynicism.

"Is that right?"

A chill washed over Rachel as more theories tried to materialize in her mind.

A tremble raked through her.

Finally, she cleared her throat. "I can ask around and see if anyone else knows something."

"I don't want to put you in the crossfire of this, just in case there's a connection."

"I'll be discreet."

"I don't know what's going on." The chief's jaw tightened with worry. "If you ask questions, please be careful."

"I'll do my best."

"In the meantime, if you think of anything else, please let me know."

Rachel gripped the bag with her purse inside. "I will."

Chief Chambers paused before walking away. "Ty and I were wondering if you'd be interested in coming over to have dinner with us tonight."

Rachel's heart lifted at the thought of seeing her childhood friend again. "That would be great. I'd love to catch up with Ty—and to get to know you better also."

"Good. I'm glad to hear that." Chief Chambers rattled off the address. "Does 6:30 work?"

"That sounds perfect."

"Feel free to bring someone with you if you'd

like." She gave Rachel a pointed look.

Jonah's face drifted into Rachel's mind.

Would that be weird to ask him? After all, he was her father's employee. Just because he was staying in the house, that didn't mean the two of them had anything more than a casual relationship.

Plus, there was that text. Should Rachel give any credence to the warning? Or was someone simply messing with her mind?

Her head pulsed at the thought.

Was there anyone out there she could truly trust? Anyone beside her father—who appeared to be missing?

Sometimes, it didn't feel like it.

Finally, Rachel looked up at the police chief and shrugged. "Maybe. Do I need to tell you now?"

"Nope, we'll have enough food either way. So come alone or come with someone. We just look forward to having you."

Rachel nodded. "Thank you."

Maybe this dinner would give her something to look forward to. With everything that had happened, she needed a little time to relax.

But would she really be able to let down her guard?

At that thought, her phone buzzed.

Her heart leapt into her throat when she saw the message there.

It was from her dad.

> I'm okay. Sorry to make you worry.
> Been caught up in some work stuff.
> I'll call you soon. Love you, Baby
> Bear.

Baby Bear . . . that had been her dad's nickname for her when she was a child.

At least, she'd heard back from him.

So why did a bad feeling still linger in her gut?

———

Jonah was thrilled that Rachel had asked him to accompany her to dinner tonight at the police chief's house.

He needed to get to know more people on this island if he was going to find out more information. However, he knew the truth: law enforcement could usually sniff out other law enforcement.

Not that he'd officially been law enforcement—not with the covert operations he'd done. But if anyone could see through him, it would be Police Chief Chambers.

When Rachel had invited him to the dinner, he'd said yes. Then he'd volunteered to drive to the Chambers' tonight—because he was a gentleman, of course. But Rachel hadn't complained.

He and Rachel had made small talk on the way there. A few minutes later, they pulled up to a house on the other end of the island. The place looked like it had recently been renovated.

The cottage had white board and batten covering it. Six colorful Caribbean-inspired cabanas sat behind the place. Jonah wondered if they had something to do with the nonprofit Ty Chambers had started to help veterans.

As soon as they stepped out of the car, a golden retriever with the name "Kujo" on his collar greeted them with a sniff and a wagging tail. Rachel and Jonah offered him a few pats on the head.

They climbed the wooden steps to the front door, Kujo following.

As they reached the screened-in porch surrounding the house, the door opened and a smiling, much more casual-looking police chief greeted them, a child on her hip. The chief's wavy blonde hair flowed over her shoulders, and she wore jeans with a dark-blue pullover.

"Welcome, welcome!" Chief Chambers grinned. "I'm so glad you both came."

"Thank you for asking, Chief Chambers," Rachel said.

"Please, call me Cassidy."

"Cassidy then." Rachel nodded.

Jonah held up the bouquet of wildflowers he'd

picked up at the store earlier. "Yes, thank you for inviting us."

"Well, you didn't have to bring anything, but thank you." Cassidy sniffed them and leaned them toward her daughter. But the girl tried to grab the buds and pull them from the stems. "They're beautiful, despite the Great Destroyer's efforts to smash them."

Rachel leaned toward the child and smiled. "Who is this?"

"This is Faith. She's fifteen months old and curious about everything—just like her mom. That's what my husband says, at least."

"She's beautiful." Rachel glowed as she said the words, the way some women did around children.

Her body language around the child indicated she'd make a great mom one day. She was warm and friendly and caring.

Jonah shoved that thought aside, unsure where it had come from.

He couldn't let down his guard. Not if he wanted to survive. Feelings would only get him in trouble.

"Thank you. We think so too." Cassidy practically beamed as she said the words. "All right, now come on inside so you can see Ty."

As soon as they stepped into the house, the smell of garlic and basil, along with a faint floral scent—a candle maybe—greeted them.

"Ty Chambers?" Rachel's voice rose with warm excitement.

A man wearing a black "Kiss the Cook" apron stood over the stove. He turned toward them and grinned. The next instant, he rounded the kitchen island and pulled Rachel into a hug.

"Rachel Atwood. It's been a long time. I couldn't believe it when I heard you were back on the island."

"I know." Rachel grinned up at him. "But I couldn't pass up this opportunity to come back here. I have so many good memories of this place."

"Hopefully, you'll build a lot more." His gaze drifted behind her to Jonah, and he stepped forward, extending his hand. "Ty Chambers."

Jonah had already read up on the man. Former Navy SEAL. Currently ran a nonprofit called Hope House. Cofounder of a security organization called Blackout, which was headquartered here on the island.

"Jonah Gray." He offered a friendly smile. "Thank you for having me."

"Of course. Why don't you guys grab something to drink, and we can sit down for a few minutes while dinner finishes cooking?" He nodded toward a variety of drinks set up on the kitchen counter.

They did just that and situated themselves in a cozy living room.

Jonah felt a pang of longing that surprised him.

Everything about this moment seemed so normal. So warm and inviting.

For a moment, he imagined what it might be like to put down some roots. To start a family. To be grounded in a community.

But that was something that would never happen for him.

Not after everything he'd seen.

Jonah frowned.

And especially not after everything he'd done.

RACHEL TOOK a bite of her tilefish. It had been cooked in a tomato sauce with garlic, peppers, and onions. It tasted delicious, as did the Italian salad and roasted potatoes that were served alongside the seafood.

She was so glad she'd agreed to come tonight.

Catching up with Ty and getting to know Cassidy was just what her soul needed in the middle of everything else going on. Cassidy had taken Faith to Ty's parents' house for the evening—apparently, they lived seasonally at the cottage next door.

"So tell me about this lab you're working for," Cassidy started, taking a sip of her water. "Everyone on the island was surprised Ocean Essence wanted to open here."

"It doesn't seem typical now, does it? But Essence

wanted to open their new research facility on the island because their products are based on the ocean. So, what better place to develop these products than being by the ocean itself?" Rachel shrugged and took a sip of her lemonade.

"How does it work when you develop a new product?" Jonah asked. "I imagine if it was a part of a pharmaceutical company that there would be a lot of oversight by the government or the FDA, including random inspections. Is it the same for a beauty and skin care company?"

"There's a lot of oversight," Rachel said. "The Modernization of Cosmetics Regulation Act of 2022 put a lot more compliance rules on the industry. There are now facility checks, more labeling requirements. It's become highly regulated."

"I guess that makes me feel better about the products I use." Cassidy nodded before taking another sip of her water.

"It should. It's very important that people in my line of work are responsible for what products we put out there for people to use. In my new position, I'll be heading up a new line of dermatology products that Essence would like to produce."

After a momentary pause, Ty turned to Jonah. "How about you? Cassidy tells me you work in security. How did you get into that field?"

Jonah swallowed before answering. He didn't

want to give too much information away, but he needed to keep as close to the truth as possible.

"I was in the military for more than a decade. When I got out, I was looking for something I could do that would build upon the skillset I already had. I was offered a job with a security company, and I said yes. The rest, as they say, is history."

Ty shifted. "Interesting. I own a security business as well—along with my friend, Colton Locke."

"Oh yeah? What's it called?" Jonah already knew, but he couldn't let on to that.

"Blackout."

"I've heard of it. You hire former special forces, right?"

Ty nodded. "That's right. We're up to twenty full-time operatives right now, plus support staff."

"That's impressive. It sounds like we have something in common."

"What company do you work for?"

"The Shadow Agency."

Ty twisted his neck. "Never heard of them."

"We're pretty new. We do a variety of security work—but it's mostly on the technology end of things." He used the real name of the company, knowing Ty wouldn't find out anything about them online. Their jobs were all by word of mouth.

He hoped that wasn't a mistake.

"I see," Ty muttered.

Based on the way Ty studied him, Jonah couldn't help but wonder if Ty also suspected there was more to Jonah than he'd admitted.

———

After dinner, Cassidy and Ty suggested they go to the beach for a bonfire and s'mores.

Jonah thought that sounded nice.

Despite the fact he was here to find answers and work, having a moment of downtime might be the refreshment his soul needed.

So much had happened in the past several months. Anna had died. He'd left the military. Joined up with his friends to become part of the Shadow Agency.

Jonah supposed his childhood should have prepared him for turbulent times.

But it seemed as if that turbulence had never faded.

The moments of peace in his life were few and far between.

Now here he was.

Hopefully this would be one of those peaceful times.

It was a perfect night for the bonfire. Cassidy and Ty told stories about their Bible study group. Apparently, Lisa Dillinger of The Crazy Chefette fame and her husband—a police officer—were part of it. Then they invited Rachel and him to church on Sunday.

As much as Jonah wanted to relax and let down his guard, he couldn't help himself from scanning everything around him, looking for any signs of trouble. He didn't see anything—not yet.

He hated to be on edge, but how could he not? A lot was on the line here. Too much.

He sensed Cassidy studying him and reminded himself to look more casual.

The woman was sharp, and he couldn't blow his cover. If people knew why he was really here, it would hinder his chances of finding answers. He couldn't let that happen.

Cassidy's phone vibrated, and she pulled it from her pocket. Her eyes narrowed as she talked to the person on the other line.

Jonah tried not to appear too curious about whatever the call concerned. But after everything that happened, he couldn't help but wonder if this phone call tied in with any of the crimes that had occurred since he'd come to the island.

As she ended the call, Cassidy rose and brushed the sand from her jeans. "Sorry to cut this short, but that was Paige, my dispatcher. An alarm is going off at the Ocean Essence office. I'd like to check it out myself."

Rachel stood also. "What? I'll go with you."

No way was Jonah staying here while they checked this out. "I can drive her."

"You guys go," Ty said. "I'll get everything cleaned up here. We'll have to take a raincheck on the bonfire and s'mores."

RACHEL AND JONAH had to wait outside in the darkness while Cassidy and another officer checked things out inside Ocean Essence.

Dr. Hensley had shown up to let the police inside. He now waited outside with Rachel and Jonah. The man looked beside himself as he paced, his motions jerky and his back stiff.

"Do you know what's going on?" Dr. Hensley finally stopped and turned to Rachel. "The police chief didn't give me any details."

"I have no idea." Rachel shivered and wrapped her arms across her chest as an evening wind brushed over them. "We were having dinner with Cassidy when she got the call. That's why Jonah and I are here."

Dr. Hensley's gaze flickered to Jonah before he

looked back at the front door and frowned. "Is there a reason we can't go inside?"

"I'm just doing what Cassidy said," Rachel told him. "I assume she needs to check it out and make sure there's not an intruder inside. If so, it could be dangerous."

Dr. Hensley's frown deepened.

Finally, several minutes later, Cassidy stepped back out with her officer.

"You can come inside now." She motioned for them to come toward her. "From what I can tell, I only saw one thing that might have been disturbed. Someone's desk. Maybe you can tell me whose it is."

They followed her into the building.

Rachel's eyes widened when she saw her office had been ransacked. Drawers had been left open. Papers were strewn on the floor. Her computer screen was smashed.

She gasped. "Why would someone go through my things? I hardly even brought anything here to the office with me. Just my favorite pens and a jar of mints I like to keep on my desk. I haven't been here long enough to have anything of significance."

Cassidy turned to her. "Someone broke into your home. Stole your purse. And now someone went through your desk? You're definitely being targeted."

Rachel felt her throat tighten. She quickly neutralized her expression. She couldn't show any signs that there was any truth in Cassidy's words.

She rubbed her arms, suddenly feeling chilled. "I don't like this."

Cassidy stepped closer and lowered her voice. "I need to do some more digging about that situation we talked about . . ."

Rachel's pulse quickened. She was grateful Cassidy hadn't offered any more details.

That text about Jonah had shaken her up more than she thought.

She hadn't told Jonah about it yet.

She didn't want him to know—not until she knew for sure that she could trust him.

———

Jonah watched Rachel's reaction. Listened to her hiccup.

Was that her tell? Did she hiccup when she was upset?

Maybe.

Because there was definitely something she wasn't telling them.

Had she had some type of trouble in Colorado?

He'd done his research, and he hadn't seen anything obvious. But plenty could have happened that wouldn't have been available on the internet.

Would she ever trust him enough to share what that was?

Questions spun in his mind.

As Rachel and Cassidy talked, he glanced around the first-floor office area.

He was finally getting a look at the inside of this facility.

It was nice. State of the art. Clean.

But his gaze stopped on the door across the way that was marked "Authorized Personnel Only."

Were there answers inside that room? Was whatever project Ganon was working on filed somewhere in there? Had the information that had been stolen been stored in that room? If that was the case, then only someone with clearance could have taken it.

Was that a biometric scanner on the wall beside the door?

He was beginning to think finding answers would be impossible.

Jonah pulled his gaze away as he felt someone watching him.

Dr. Hensley stood in the doorway of his office. He didn't bother to hide the fact that he was studying Jonah.

Jonah offered a nod and a quick smile, trying to set the man at ease.

The last thing he wanted was to be on Hensley's radar.

But Jonah realized that on top of finding out the truth, he now felt the compelling need to protect Rachel from whatever was going on.

His desire for justice for Ganon clashed with his need to keep Rachel safe. His boss had warned him to stay on task.

But at the end of the day, Jonah only had his own instincts to trust.

Plus, why was there a new aloofness toward him from Rachel? She seemed more standoffish than she had earlier. Had something happened?

He didn't know.

Jonah thought he had time to find answers. But, based on the way these crimes were escalating, he was beginning to think otherwise.

TWENTY-FOUR

RACHEL FELT a rush of relief when she arrived back at her dad's house.

Jonah had insisted she remain near the front door while he checked the place out. She appreciated his protectiveness, especially in the wake of everything that had happened. Though she was all for being a strong woman, it felt good to have someone watching out for her.

Despite Jonah's instructions, Rachel wandered to her father's bedroom—Jonah had already cleared it and it was on the first floor.

She paused inside, her heart lodging in her throat at the sight.

It was messy and disorganized, just as she'd suspected. He had several gadgets out that he'd been tinkering with—including some kind of glasses and what appeared to be an automatic sandwich maker.

Her dad had always had a bit of a mad scientist vibe.

Seeing his room made her miss him even more.

Though he'd texted her earlier, her gut told her something still wasn't right.

Jonah appeared a few minutes later and confirmed that everything was safe.

"What a night, huh?" Rachel let out a sigh.

Jonah nodded, concern still staining his gaze. Even his body language showed an edge of protectiveness. He leaned toward her, his shoulders remaining tense and his gaze continuing to scan the place.

But could she trust him? She remembered the message she'd gotten on her phone.

What if Jonah was one of Carl's friends?

"You can say that again," he finally replied. "Our whole time here in Lantern Beach has been crazy, for that matter."

"That's right. I didn't realize that you were going to be such an answer to prayer when I walked into the house and discovered my father was letting you stay here." A flush of embarrassment swept through Rachel when she realized how her words might have sounded.

Rachel hoped Jonah didn't take them the wrong way.

Something flashed in his eyes. But as quickly as the emotion appeared, it disappeared.

"Things tend to work out the way they should, don't they?" he murmured.

"Yes, they do." Rachel let out a sigh, grateful he wasn't bothered by her words, and then she stepped farther inside.

She'd be wise to remember that she needed to keep her distance from Jonah. She didn't truly know that much about him. She couldn't trust him too easily—as a matter of self-preservation.

She glanced at him again as they both stood in the room's entryway.

Should she just excuse herself and go to her room? Would she even be able to sleep right now after everything that had happened?

She hadn't even had a chance to clean up her desk at Essence. She'd have to do that sometime before she could do any more work. For now, Cassidy wanted to leave it—just in case anything else popped up.

"Scrabble?" Jonah raised his eyebrows with exaggerated hope.

Rachel grinned. "I was hoping you might ask."

Thirty minutes later, they'd both changed into comfortable clothes, the fireplace warmed the room, and the game stretched in front of them. Jonah had even made turmeric and cinnamon tea for her, just the way she liked it.

"Any plans for tomorrow?" Jonah asked as he stared at his letters.

"There's actually a party for Essence at Dr. Hensley's house."

"Is that right? That sounds nice."

She shrugged. "Maybe. I've never been one who's much in favor of get-togethers of these sorts. I'd much rather go out with a couple of good friends and have heart-to-heart conversations, rather than rubbing elbows with numerous people at the job and putting up pretenses."

"I can understand that. But I'm sure you'll do great."

Rachel's smile slipped. "I hope so."

"Everything okay?"

A shiver raked down her spine. "I guess I'm still shaken after everything that's happened."

He shifted across from her. "I know this is really none of my business. And you don't have to listen to a word I'm saying because you don't really know me that well. But you might not want to go anywhere on this island alone for a while. At least, until Cassidy is able to find some answers."

She understood what he was saying. But what if *he* was the threat?

Rachel's gaze rushed to meet his. "You think I'm still in danger?"

"I don't see any signs that the person behind this is backing off. And if that's the case . . ." Jonah shrugged, not finishing the statement.

He didn't have to. Rachel knew what he was getting at.

"Then they're going to keep looking. In fact, whatever they're looking for, they may not find the answers without me." She shivered again.

Jonah didn't deny her words.

Rachel swallowed quickly, knowing she needed to ask Jonah about the party before she talked herself out of it. "Say, any chance you want to go to the party with me tomorrow night? I'd feel better if I had a plus one. But I understand if that's weird also. I'm not trying to make you uncomfortable—"

"I'd feel a lot better if I went also." His voice rumbled as he said the statement, but his solid undertone left no room for doubt that he meant the words.

Relief filled her. Good. Jonah hadn't made it weird, which was what she'd been afraid might happen.

"Perfect." Rachel offered a brief nod.

Maybe she could sleep a little better knowing that.

THE NEXT MORNING, Cassidy took a bite of her eggs—fried over easy by Ty.

He really did spoil her.

It was still early, and Faith was sleeping. Cassidy and Ty were able to grab a few minutes of alone time before their day started.

Alone time was something Cassidy had learned to treasure. She adored time when she, Ty, and Faith were all together. But talking uninterrupted to Ty also helped her keep a cool head.

"What's on your mind?" Ty studied her from across the table.

"I just have a lot to think about."

"Does this have something to do with the dead man pulled out of the ocean this week?"

She put her fork down on the table and frowned,

ignoring the tantalizing scent of bacon and coffee that surrounded her. "Maybe. Really . . . it's everything. I'm trying to put it all together. But there's more to it than I know right now."

"What do you mean?" He took a sip of his coffee as he waited for her response.

"There's something about that new lab that bothers me."

"The lab? Or Rachel?"

Cassidy frowned. "Not Rachel. She seems nice enough. And she's new here. If there's something going on with the lab, I doubt she knows about it yet."

"I agree." Ty nodded slowly.

"The fact that Essence chose this island bugs me," Cassidy continued. "It's such an unlikely place for a business of this size."

"I think everyone on Lantern Beach would agree with that." Ty took another sip of coffee. "What about Rachel's friend, Jonah? What do you think of him?"

"I think he's hiding something also. There's more to him than he's letting on."

"You think he's involved with some of the things going on here on the island?"

Cassidy let out a long breath. "I'm not sure. I want to say no. But he has no online presence at all. That seems suspicious."

Ty raised a triangle of toast toward his mouth.

"He said he works for an organization called the Shadow Agency. I did my own search for it, just out of curiosity. I can't find out anything about it either."

Cassidy frowned. "Jonah is like a ghost. His agency is a ghost. It's all unnerving."

"I can see why you'd feel this way."

"I can't let this go. I need some answers."

"If there's anything I can do for you, let me know." Ty pushed his food aside and leaned toward her, his rich eyes full of loyalty and love.

She smiled. "I will. Thank you."

She loved that about Ty. He would do anything for her, and he always made time when she needed him.

But that same foreboding sense that a storm was brewing here on the island came rushing back to Cassidy, leaving her feeling on edge.

It was her job to protect the residents and visitors here.

She took her responsibilities seriously.

Her fists tightened. Cassidy needed to figure out what was going on before someone else got hurt.

CHAPTER
TWENTY-SIX

LAST NIGHT'S WINNING
SCRABBLE WORD: PROGRESS

RACHEL BRIEFLY CONSIDERED MAKING a big breakfast and sharing it with Jonah the next morning. But that felt too friendly—and she needed to keep her distance.

Instead, she made some oatmeal with nuts and fruit. She wasn't sure if her dad had left the groceries or if Jonah had bought them, but she made a mental note to pay Jonah back if that was the case.

Breakfast in hand, she sat at a window seat with her coffee and watched the ocean as she ate. It was much calmer today than it had been when she arrived. The waves were peaceful and rolling, and the sky was sunny.

The truth of the matter was that her thoughts had gone to a different place of worry this morning.

Do not worry about tomorrow, for tomorrow will worry about itself.

The Bible verse had always been one of her favorites—probably because she tended to worry. But it was true. This anxiety wasn't adding anything to her life—it was only robbing her of today's joy.

Even though she'd gotten that text message from her dad, something about the way it was worded just didn't ring true to her.

She'd tried to call him again this morning. He still hadn't answered.

Last night, she'd tried contacting a few of his colleagues. Each said they hadn't heard from him either.

Rachel had been trying to deny the truth, but she couldn't any longer.

Something had happened to her dad.

What if someone had grabbed him? Did this have to do with what happened in Colorado? Had one of Carl's guys taken her dad in order to teach Rachel a lesson?

What if Jonah really was one of the bad guys? If he worked for Carl?

A tremble of fear captured her muscles.

Rachel was so deep in her thoughts that when Jonah stepped into the kitchen, she jumped. Coffee sloshed onto her pajama bottoms, and she sprang to her feet, feeling clumsy.

"I didn't mean to scare you." Jonah was already dressed for the day in jeans and a gray sweater. His hair was wet as if he'd just showered—and the clean scent of soap drifted from him. His eyes looked bright. "I apologize."

Rachel grabbed a napkin and dabbed at her pajamas. "No, it's okay. I'm a deep thinker, and when I get lost in my thoughts . . ."

He poured himself a cup of coffee and then pulled up a chair, placing it close to the window seat. "Everything okay?"

Rachel nibbled on her bottom lip a moment as she contemplated how much to say.

Jonah seemed trustworthy. But trusting people—especially men—was something she found difficult. However, everything about Jonah seemed to indicate that she could rely on him.

Did she trust him enough to tell him what happened in Colorado? What if he was working for Carl Nevada? That question kept echoing in her mind.

Yet he'd saved her life. He'd helped her.

Though she didn't believe Jonah was telling her everything, another part of her felt certain she could trust him.

Rachel let out a sigh and set her half empty coffee mug down on the table beside her. She was taking a calculated risk here.

But she wanted to watch Jonah's reaction to what she told him.

She licked her lips. "The truth is there's more to me being here than I told you."

His eyes widened. "Is there?"

Jonah didn't press her for more information, which actually inclined her to share more.

Rachel cleared her throat. "I . . . I actually witnessed a murder back in Colorado."

"What?" His voice dipped with surprise.

She nodded as the memories pummeled her. "As I was leaving work one night, I had to drop off something at another building in downtown Denver. It was late, and I didn't think anyone would be in the office of this land developer. But when I got there, I noticed people were inside."

She sucked in a deep breath as she tried to compose herself.

A moment later, she continued. "I stepped inside the office, sure they'd heard me come in. They didn't. I rounded the corner, and that's when I realized they were arguing. Like, really arguing. The next moment, I heard gunfire."

Jonah reached for her and squeezed her arm. "I'm so sorry."

"I ran," Rachel continued, knowing if she stopped, she might not start again. "But I saw the man's face—

the one who pulled the trigger. Carl Nevada was hard to miss since he's a well-known businessman in the area. But people also suspect him of being behind some nefarious deals. In fact, the rumor is he's dangerous."

"What happened?"

"I made it to the police station and reported what I'd seen." Rachel watched his expression but saw no signs of deceit—only surprise.

Maybe he really wasn't working for Carl.

"Was this guy arrested?" Jonah asked.

She swallowed hard. "He was. But he sent his men to intimidate me, knowing I'd be the sole witness at his upcoming trial. All the other evidence disappeared—security footage, the murder weapon. Everything."

"How long ago was that?"

"About a month or so."

Surprise washed through Jonah's gaze before quickly disappearing. Then his gaze darkened. "What did these guys do to intimidate you?"

"His guys followed me. Left messages. Talked to my friends. Tried to make them turn against me, probably so I wouldn't have a support system in place."

"That's terrible."

She rubbed her throat as she felt it tighten, worry lodging there. "It wasn't fun. But I just heard Carl

Nevada was released on a technicality. He's out on the streets."

Jonah's eyes widened. "The police didn't call and offer to put you in witness protection?"

She shook her head. "I haven't heard from them. I have, however, heard that Carl is one of the biggest donators to the police's fraternity.

"Do you think he'll come after you here?"

Rachel frowned. "I'm afraid he already has."

———

Jonah hadn't expected to hear what Rachel told him.

From everything he'd researched, she had been a respectable scientist and an esteemed member of the community. He hadn't expected trouble to be following her.

If Carl Nevada had murdered a man a month ago . . . that would explain why Rachel had dropped off the radar for a week. She'd probably gone off grid after seeing that man die—both to stay safe and to come to terms with what had happened.

She hadn't been in Baltimore, had she?

She'd given up a lot to come here to Lantern Beach. She'd been afraid enough to uproot her entire life and move far away to this remote island. He'd seen that haunted look in her eyes and wondered if there was more to her story.

Now he knew.

But was what had happened in Colorado connected with her dad's disappearance?

His doubts continued to disappear as pieces fell into place.

Rachel had nothing to do with Ganon's death. He now felt more certain than ever. Her jitters were because she was being threatened.

Against Jonah's better instincts, he reached forward and squeezed her hand. "I'm sorry, Rachel. I can't imagine what you're going through."

"Thank you." Her voice cracked as she said the words, and she glanced down at her hands as tears filled her eyes. "I didn't tell you this earlier but . . . that man you pulled out of the ocean?"

"What about him?"

"He had a dolphin necklace in his hand." She reached beneath her shirt. "One just like this one."

His eyes widened when he saw the matching pendant. "Wow."

"My dad gave it to me. And there were numbers written on that man's hand . . . numbers that match Dr. Hensley's phone number."

His thoughts raced. "Did you tell Cassidy?"

Rachel nodded. "I did. But . . . I don't know what to do. Especially now that my father is missing. What if someone is targeting him because of me?"

His jaw tightened at her words. "I think you should talk to Cassidy about your dad."

She looked up at him as if surprised by his words. "But what can she do?"

"She'll at least be able to keep her eyes open for any trouble. Maybe she has some contacts she can tap into to see if she can help find your dad."

"I'm wondering if I should just leave the island and go look for him myself." Heaviness drew out her words.

"Where would you go? Would you drive up to his home in DC? You know he's not there, right?" Jonah had to talk some sense into her before Rachel did something unwise.

Rachel's frown deepened. "But maybe there's a clue in the house. Maybe someone left a ransom note."

"If there was a ransom note, the culprits would be sure you got it."

"You're right. I guess that makes sense. But . . . if I could talk to people face-to-face, maybe I could get some answers."

Jonah waited for her to think things through, not wanting to push her. But he wasn't sure that plan would work—especially if she didn't know who she could trust.

Finally, she sighed. "Maybe I *will* start by talking to Cassidy."

A sense of relief filled him. Jonah couldn't help but think Rachel would be safer on Lantern Beach, where he could look out for her.

Because that's what he wanted to do—to help her.

Rachel was no longer his enemy. Larchmont wouldn't change Jonah's mind about that.

"Would you like me to go with you?" he asked.

Rachel stared at him a moment as if contemplating her choices.

Then she nodded. "If you wouldn't mind, that would be great." She frowned. "But first, there's something I need to show you."

He stiffened, sensing there was more bad news coming. "Okay."

She pulled out her phone and showed him a text she'd received. A text saying she couldn't trust him.

Alarm flashed through him.

Who would have sent this? Who knew who he really was? He didn't recognize the number.

Jonah glanced at Rachel and realized she was waiting for his response.

He licked his lips, contemplating how much to say. Finally, he settled on, "I have no idea why someone would send you that."

"You think someone is just trying to confuse me?"

Guilt pounded him. He wanted to tell her everything. He really did.

But he couldn't.

"I do," he said instead.

"But why . . . ?"

"Because someone clearly wants to mess with your head." Jonah swallowed his regrets.

Those words were true.

He would never hurt Rachel—even when she'd been a suspect.

But now a seed of distrust had been planted in her mind.

Someone was playing a deadly game.

And he and Rachel were both pawns.

AT THE POLICE STATION, Rachel finished telling Cassidy about her dad.

She hadn't been sure if she should share that information about the text concerning Jonah. The man *had* risked his life for her.

He wouldn't do that if he wasn't trustworthy . . . right?

She bit down and decided to remain quiet.

"Thank you for sharing." Cassidy leaned forward on her desk and glanced at Rachel and Jonah. "I'm sure that wasn't easy."

"It wasn't. I didn't mean to hide this from you." Rachel frowned and reconsidered her words. "Well . . . maybe I did. But I didn't expect there to be trouble either. I just wanted to leave that mess with Carl Nevada behind me. I'll do whatever I need to find my father. But now I'm beginning to think that coming to Lantern Beach was a mistake."

Cassidy's jaw tightened as if she wasn't pleased with the update—and the danger that came with it.

But her voice didn't sound harsh or judgmental as she said, "I'll do some digging and see what I can find out. As soon as I learn anything, I'll let you know, okay?"

Rachel nodded. "Thank you."

As they finished, Jonah placed his hand on her back and led her from the station. When they stepped outside, an unseasonably warm breeze greeted them.

"How would you feel about a walk on the beach?" Jonah nodded toward a wooden walkover crossing the dunes in the distance. "It's beautiful out here, and it might help you clear your head."

"That would be nice."

They crossed the street, one that would be flooded with cars in the summer when tourists arrived. Right now, hardly anyone was here. That was why some people liked this shoulder season the most.

Neither said much as they headed to the walkover and crossed the dunes to the shoreline. But as they began to stroll beside each other along the shore, Rachel pointed to a horseshoe crab that had washed up. The shell was old and cracked, and the animal inside long since dead.

"Do you even realize how fascinating horseshoe crabs are?" Rachel started.

"Horseshoe crabs?"

"They're amazing creatures. They have a protein in their blood called limulus amebocyte lysate. It's used by pharmaceutical and medical device manufacturers to test products for the presence of endotoxins and bacterial substances that can cause fevers—or even be fatal to humans."

"You said a lot that I don't truly understand, but it sounds interesting."

Rachel let out a laugh. "Sorry. I don't mean to speak in scientific jargon. But horseshoe crabs have been an integral part of medicine in this country for a long time. In fact, horseshoe crabs themselves are believed to have been around back when the dinosaurs roamed the earth."

"Interesting. When their blood is used for this testing you mentioned, are the animals killed?"

"Not at all. The blood can be extracted in certain safe quantities, and then the crabs returned to their habitat."

"That is fascinating. Just like you."

She flashed a grin and felt her cheeks flushing. "I know I'm talking nerd."

"You just sound smart—because you are. Beauty and brains? I'd say you're the total package."

Her cheeks flushed again.

They strolled a few minutes in silence before Jonah asked, "Not to change the subject, but do you think that man who died on the beach is somehow connected with the lab? Or to Carl?"

Any of the giddiness Rachel had felt at Jonah's compliment disappeared.

She shrugged. "I don't know. It's hard to say. I mean, I'm not sure about the connection. Why would someone affiliated with the lab be murdered? What sense does it make? I assume Carl was behind it."

"Or maybe it has something to do with you," Jonah offered.

Rachel paused as her breath caught. "What do you mean?"

"I mean, this all started when you came here. Maybe someone doesn't want you working at this lab."

She let out a nervous laugh. "Why would you say that? I'm not exactly a threat."

"I'm just trying to put the pieces together."

Unease churned inside her. "I can understand why someone might target me after Colorado—but why would this guy put everything at risk to follow me here, especially if the DA dropped the charges? Even if he did, I have no idea what the lab would have to do with any of this."

Jonah stared at her a moment, something swirling in his gaze. Finally, he shrugged. "I don't either."

But Rachel didn't believe him.

She couldn't pinpoint why exactly. But there was just something about the way he said the words that left her with doubt.

What wasn't Jonah telling her?

———

Jonah sensed Rachel's apprehension, and he couldn't blame her for feeling anxious.

Things felt as if they'd reached a boiling point, yet he suspected Rachel's troubles were far from being over.

He hoped maybe some fresh air and a walk on the beach might help her feel better.

The scent of the ocean—salty yet fresh—swept around them. The wind brought a smattering of sand that pricked any exposed skin. Seagulls squawked overhead, circling as if keeping an eye on them.

What Jonah really wanted to do was to tell Rachel the truth about why he was here. She'd opened up to him, and he wished he could do the same.

But if she knew Jonah was there to investigate his friend's death, that might put her in more danger, and he didn't want that. Besides, he'd signed a confidentiality agreement promising to keep the details of his career and assignments under wraps.

If he broke that agreement, he could be fired or even sued.

"I'm truly beginning to wonder if coming here was a bad idea," Rachel murmured as she shoved her hands into the front pockets of her jeans.

"It sounds like you really wanted to come back to Lantern Beach."

"I did. I wanted a simpler life." She let out a hesitant laugh. "That doesn't appear to be what I've gotten, though."

"Everything that has happened is puzzling. Do you really think Carl's guys could have found you here?"

She shrugged. "It's my best guess. If not that then I don't know what else to think. But between that situation and my father missing, I almost feel beside myself."

Jonah didn't bother to tell her that his presence here could also have something to do with the danger surrounding them. Although he and his colleagues had kept their operations under wraps, there was still a certain risk that followed him wherever he went.

He'd made a lot of enemies in his line of work.

Too many to count.

Could one of them have sent Rachel that text, warning her about him?

"Cassidy seems capable," Jonah said instead. "I'm

sure she'll do everything within her power to figure this out."

"I'm one of those people who's never sat back and waited for life to lead me where it wants. I'm a go-getter, as my father often says. So it's killing me that I can't do anything to find him. That I'm just taking a lazy walk on the beach while my father could be suffering somewhere."

"I'm still praying it's all a misunderstanding and that he'll turn up with a simple explanation about where he's been and why he wasn't answering his phone."

Rachel glanced at him. "To be honest, I'm still a little confused about why he hired you. The whole situation feels off. I didn't want to say anything before, but that's how I've felt all along."

The woman was astute. Jonah had known that from the moment they met.

He needed to be careful around her in order not to blow his cover.

"I can understand your concerns," he finally said. "Basically, what I do is I look for breaches in companies' security systems, and then when I hack into their systems, they hire me to strengthen their security."

"Isn't that illegal to hack into their systems? Even though you don't mean the company any harm, don't some of them take legal action against you?"

Jonah shook his head. "No, because I market my services to the companies first. They sign an agreement with me, giving me the right to hack into their systems at random. It's kind of like a lottery. For example, I like to keep permission from about seventy-five to a hundred companies at any given time. They don't know if I will target them or not. The companies actually want me to choose them to try and get past their security."

"Why would they want it all to be random?"

"To save them money. This way, I only get paid if I can hack into their systems. They don't have to pay me to look for their weak spots. That can save them thousands. Also, it keeps their IT departments vigilant, knowing they could be targeted by my company at any time."

Rachel continued to study him. "And out of all those businesses, you just so happened to pick my father's company to hack into?"

Jonah's neck muscles tightened. Her question was valid. Her instincts were probably telling her that something smelled fishy.

"It's not completely random on my end," he explained. "I usually target the larger corporations more because they just make more sense. They have greater resources, and they are more of a target for hackers."

"But my dad runs a company that employs the

newest technology—and his new company is basi-cally a startup. How is it possible that he doesn't have the best security out there already?"

"It's because things are always changing. What may have been the best even a year ago may not be today. As far as his company being a startup . . ." He shrugged. "What can I say? I was fascinated by your father's work."

Rachel stole a glance up at him. "How did you learn to stay so up-to-date with all the latest technology?"

Again, another good question. "Because it's what I do. I study things to learn what the hackers are doing now and then I come up with ways to prevent it."

"I see." Rachel slowed her steps as if she had another question she might want to ask.

Jonah braced himself for whatever that might be.

"So you hacked into my father's business, identi-fied the vulnerabilities, and then he hired you to fix them?"

"That's right. I offered to meet with him to discuss details. He told me he was on Lantern Beach, and I told him that wasn't a problem. I could meet him here."

"And then?"

"I arrived here two days before you and discussed everything with him," Jonah said. "He liked what I showed him and the ideas I had, so he hired me. Since everything is digital, I'm able to work wherever I want. When he heard I was looking for a rental place here, he told me I should just stay with him, that there wasn't any use in paying all that extra money. At first, I refused, but he insisted."

Rachel continued to study him. "It sounds like the two of you get along well then."

"We do. We talked a lot about fishing and golf. Some people you just click with, and your dad is one of those people."

Rachel strolled down the shoreline but didn't say anything.

Jonah wished he could reach out to her and offer her some kind of comfort. But it wasn't that easy. The more he got to know her, the more guilt he felt over his deception.

He wanted more than anything to come clean.

Maybe he should stop overthinking this and just tell her the truth. It would feel good to get things out in the open. To stop pretending around Rachel.

But being honest with her didn't come without risks.

Though he didn't think she would sell him out, there was a chance Rachel wouldn't understand his reasoning. Or that she'd try to get involved. Or that she'd feel loyalty toward Ocean Essence and tell someone in leadership what was going on.

Jonah licked his lips as he contemplated his options.

But before he could say anything, a new sound sliced through the air.

A bullet, he realized.

The next instant, he threw Rachel onto the sand.

CHAPTER
TWENTY-EIGHT

RACHEL WASN'T sure what was happening.

She heard the pop. The next thing she knew, she was on the ground, Jonah covering her body with his own.

Then more noises split the air.

She glanced up at the water.

She saw a boat floating in the distance.

A man onboard with a hat pulled low over his head faced them, something in his hands.

A gun.

Her heart pounded harder.

Out here, there was nothing to block the bullets—only the waves.

And Jonah.

Her lungs tightened at the thought.

"What are we going to do?" Rachel's voice cracked.

"Just stay low."

More bullets split the air, one landing in the sand only inches from her.

She bit back a cry.

What if Jonah had been hit? All while protecting her?

Please, God. I know I haven't been talking to You much lately. But protect Jonah. Protect us. Please.

I can't handle losing anyone else.

She froze, hardly able to breathe as she waited for whatever would happen next.

A shout sounded.

Then the boat zoomed away.

Jonah rolled into the sand and glanced at the water as if making sure the gunman was gone.

He was.

But that had been close.

Jonah turned back toward her. "Are you okay?"

Rachel quickly scanned her sand-covered clothing to make sure. Adrenaline could conceal a lot of things —including pain sometimes.

"I'm fine." Her voice quivered. "You?"

He nodded and stood. "I'm good."

He quickly wiped the sand from his hands before reaching to help her to her feet.

Just as he did, Cassidy and another cop appeared in the distance.

They must have heard the gunfire—the police station wasn't far away. The gunman must have seen them coming and that's why he'd zoomed away.

It looked as if she and Jonah were going to need to give their statements . . . again.

———

Jonah didn't like what was going on here in Lantern Beach.

He was so glad that Rachel had asked him to go to this party with her tonight.

If he could, he wouldn't let her out of his sight at all. But that would be weird considering that they didn't know each other that well—though it felt as if they did.

He took one last glance at himself in the mirror. Thankfully, he'd brought a suit with him when he came.

Even if he wasn't investigating Ocean Essence, he would go to this party with Rachel. He was honored she'd asked him, and the thought of getting to know her more secretly thrilled him.

But he had to admit he was excited about the possibility of learning more about this company and the people who worked there.

Ganon deserved some answers, and Jonah was determined to bring justice to his friend.

He adjusted the collar of his white dress shirt then stepped out of his room and wandered into the living room. Rachel waited for him there, nervously running her hands over her hips.

His eyes widened when he saw her olive-green dress—one that hugged her in all the right areas. But the gown was still modest, covering her neck and arms.

She looked up and flashed a self-conscious smile at him. "Don't you look nice."

He let out a low whistle. His voice dropped low as he said, "You look gorgeous."

Rachel's cheeks flushed. "Thank you."

"No, I mean it. You really do look gorgeous."

Her hair flowed down past her shoulders in waves like it normally did. But it didn't look quite so untamed right now. She'd put on more makeup than usual, and her eyes looked even bigger and brighter.

Jonah swallowed hard.

Being attracted to Rachel was one thing he hadn't counted on when he'd come here.

But he had to wonder if God had brought her into his life for a purpose.

"You sure you're ready for this?" Jonah swallowed hard as he tried to push down his growing feelings.

Rachel nodded, but the motion almost seemed hesitant.

She was nervous about this party, and rightfully so. Anyone in their right mind would be.

Cassidy had taken their statements at the beach. She'd called the Coast Guard so they could be on the lookout for that boat.

But so far, Jonah and Rachel hadn't heard anything.

Jonah had known this situation could escalate. But everything had happened even faster than he'd thought. Things had gone from break-ins and theft to shooting at them.

Was someone at the lab targeting Rachel? Did they perceive her as a threat?

Or was the person behind these attacks associated with Carl Nevada?

Rachel nodded toward the door, a touch of hesitation in her gaze. "Are you ready to go?"

Jonah put those thoughts aside and nodded. "Of course. Let's go wow your new colleagues."

CHAPTER
TWENTY-NINE

RACHEL HAD ONLY BEEN at Dr. Hensley's party for an hour, and she was already anxious to leave.

But she couldn't do that. It would be rude.

She reminded herself of that as Lloyd cornered her and talked her ear off about world affairs.

She'd already answered many of the same questions several times. That was to be expected. She was thankful no one here seemed to know about the fact she was shot at today. Or if they did, no one brought it up.

That was the last kind of attention she wanted to receive.

The good news was that she had a good opportunity to talk a little more with Noelle Purdy, the dermatologist under Rachel.

Noelle was petite with light-brown hair that was pulled back into a high ponytail. She had bright eyes and a curiosity in her voice—a curiosity that any good scientist should have.

Also, Dr. Hensley's wife, Margaret, was here. The woman loved to talk fashion and fancy restaurants. Rachel wasn't sure why the woman seemed to have taken an interest in her, but every time Rachel turned around, Margaret seemed to be there.

She was probably lonely, Rachel mused.

"Can I steal you away for a minute?" Jonah murmured beside her.

Rachel looked up at him, surprised by his statement.

He gave her a look that almost seemed to show that he understood how overwhelmed she was right now.

Rachel nodded and excused herself from Lloyd.

She'd stopped listening ten minutes ago.

Instead, she and Jonah wandered toward a built-in bookcase on the other side of the room.

"You looked like you needed to get away," Jonah murmured once they were out of earshot.

"I did. Thank you."

Rachel's gaze went to the pictures on the shelves. Even though Dr. Hensley was only here long enough to get the new development lab up and running, he'd obviously made himself at home at this short-term rental.

The man had numerous photos of himself with people Rachel didn't recognize. Of course, why would she recognize anyone? She didn't know his family.

She picked up a framed picture of Dr. Hensley. A Middle Eastern type of background stretched behind him in the image. She supposed it could be the southwestern United States, but she didn't think so, especially because the men around Hensley wore clothing that didn't fit what she typically saw here in the US.

"Checking out pictures, I see?"

Rachel turned when she heard Dr. Hensley's voice behind her.

She set the picture back down. "I hope you don't think I'm being nosy."

"Not at all. I put these pictures out so I could enjoy them. I don't mind if others do as well."

"Is this in the Middle East?" Jonah asked as he studied the photo.

"Very good. Not many people would be able to pinpoint that." A touch of admiration filled Hensley's voice.

"I served in the Middle East for several years so I'm familiar with the area."

"I guess you are. And, yes, that's one of my friends who lives in Dubai. I like to go over and visit about once a year if I can. He's also one of the investors in Ocean Essence."

"Good to know," Rachel murmured. "I'm learning new things about Ocean Essence every day."

Dr. Hensley flashed a tight smile. "There's a lot to learn."

"I appreciate you hosting this tonight," Rachel continued, her gaze scanning the crowd behind him. "It's nice to be able to get to know everyone here a little better."

"I was hoping it might be." Dr. Hensley glanced at his phone, and his expression darkened. "Would you excuse me a moment?"

"Of course," she told him.

Her boss slipped away.

What was that about? Rachel wondered.

Whatever it was, Dr. Hensley didn't look happy.

Was he hiding something as well?

Was everyone on this island, for that matter?

———

"Would you like to get some fresh air?" Jonah nodded toward the balcony.

"I'd love that." Rachel flashed a grateful smile.

He led her through the double doors and outside.

But Jonah wanted to come out here for more than fresh air.

Whatever text Dr. Hensley had gotten, it seemed to have upset him. Jonah had seen the man go downstairs. Then he'd heard a door open and slam shut soon after.

Jonah suspected the man had stepped outside.

No one else was on the balcony—it was a little too chilly for most people. But they could use some privacy right now, so he wasn't complaining.

Jonah took his coat off and put it around Rachel's shoulders as the wind swept around them.

She shivered and pulled the jacket closer. "Thank you."

"Of course."

"I don't suppose you have work functions like this in your line of work," she murmured.

"It's only me, two colleagues, and our boss, so not really. We do get together outside of work, but we're all friends so we enjoy the downtime together." He shrugged as he remembered Vincent and Tex. He meant the words.

He trusted those men with his life.

"That sounds wonderful." Rachel studied him for a moment. "I feel like there's still so much I don't know about you."

"There is," Jonah answered honestly. An internal nudging pleaded with him to share more.

But he didn't. He couldn't.

Or could he?

He didn't often doubt himself. But that was exactly what he was doing now.

And he didn't like it.

Before he and Rachel could talk more, voices drifted up from downstairs.

It was hard to make out the words, but Rachel also seemed to sense they were important. She grew quiet.

Jonah walked in silence to the other side of the balcony.

When he peered over it, he spotted Dr. Hensley meeting with another man. Whoever it was, the guy wore all black, and Jonah couldn't make out the guy's features. He stood in the shadows beneath a small tree.

Jonah stepped into the shadows himself and listened. Rachel moved beside him, her eyes wide as she eavesdropped.

"Are you sure the money is gone?" the unknown man asked.

"I'm positive. This is unacceptable."

"I'm doing what I can."

"Do more!" Dr. Hensley growled.

The man didn't say anything for a moment until finally conceding. "I'll keep working on it."

Working on what?

What exactly was that conversation about?

Jonah wanted to hear more, but the man in the shadows stepped away, and Dr. Hensley headed back toward the house.

Which left Jonah with the question: did their clandestine meeting have anything to do with Ganon?

CHAPTER
THIRTY

WHAT WAS THAT CONVERSATION ABOUT?

Rachel replayed it in her head.

What Hensley and the shadowed man had talked about didn't make sense. It must be a personal matter, she mused. Hensley couldn't be talking about something regarding the company.

Right?

Jonah grasped her elbow and whispered, "We should get back inside."

Rachel nodded, though part of her wanted to stay out here. Still, she didn't want Dr. Hensley to catch her out here and realize they'd been snooping.

Before she could take a step, a hiccup escaped.

Her cheeks reddened.

She usually hiccupped when she lied. Apparently, the act of telling an untruth caused her to hold her breath, which then caused her to hiccup.

What if Hensley had heard her?

Another pang of worry shot through her.

She shouldn't have come here to Lantern Beach. This job change was a mistake. It could get her killed.

But it was too late to run back to Colorado now—even if she wanted to.

It seemed as if she couldn't escape her problems. That was usually the way they worked.

She and Jonah stepped back inside, and warmth hit her.

Maybe Hensley hadn't heard her hiccup. Maybe he hadn't realized they'd overheard his conversation.

She handed the coat back to Jonah, but immediately missed the scent of his piney cologne. It had brought her a surprising comfort.

How was it possible that she had feelings for this man already? She barely knew Jonah, and she'd sworn off men for the immediate future.

She frowned.

She didn't know what to think.

"Listen, if you could excuse me for a minute, I'm going to run to the bathroom," Jonah murmured as he leaned closer.

"Of course."

Rachel watched him disappear.

Immediately, she missed his presence.

Why did she somehow feel that without him by her side she was surrounded by sharks?

Maybe because she was.

———

Jonah glanced behind him to check that no one was watching.

They weren't.

He hated to leave Rachel alone, but there was something he needed to do—and it wasn't running to the bathroom.

Being here at Dr. Hensley's house offered him the perfect opportunity to enact the next part of his plan.

He bypassed the bathroom and slipped into the next room down the hallway instead.

Dr. Hensley had given them a tour earlier, and Jonah knew exactly where his office was located.

That was just the area where Jonah wanted to be.

He slipped inside and pulled something from his pocket. A bug.

He worked quickly as he planted it in the lamp in the room.

If Dr. Hensley had any secret conversations, Jonah could listen.

He stared at the computer sitting on the desk, wondering if he should download what was on it. He had no doubt that the man had firewalls in place. But if Jonah was able to load his program directly on the device, he'd be able to see what Hensley might be up to.

He considered his options a moment, knowing if he was gone too long it would raise suspicions.

But he couldn't pass this up either.

He hurried toward it and clicked on the keys. The screen lit.

Quickly, he inserted his jump drive into the computer.

The program on the drive broke through the password screen.

Perfect.

Jonah held his breath as he waited for the device to do its work.

It would only take a few minutes until all the contents of the computer were loaded onto the jump drive.

As he waited, footsteps sounded outside the door.

Jonah tensed.

What was his excuse going to be if someone came in here?

If he made one wrong move, his cover would be blown.

That would make things much more difficult for him and make Rachel look bad.

He didn't want to pull her into this mess any more than she already was.

He glanced at the door again, his throat tightening.

He had to think quickly if he was going to get out of this without somehow hurting her as well.

RACHEL GLANCED AT HER WATCH.

What was taking Jonah so long? Was he okay?

She considered going to knock on the bathroom door, but that seemed awkward.

They didn't know each other *that* well yet.

But the longer she stood here, the more unease she felt.

"So how are you enjoying your time here in Lantern Beach?" Mark Williams paused in front of her, a glass full of an amber-colored liquid in his hand. The normally uptight numbers guy had dressed down tonight, wearing jeans and a sweater instead of his normal business casual suit.

"It's a beautiful island." Her answer felt rehearsed. It wasn't. She'd simply been asked the question many times already.

This was the kind of small talk she'd been making all night—the kind she hated. It didn't matter that her coworkers seemed kind. This just wasn't her thing.

"I know it can be a bit overwhelming. Dr. Hensley can be intense sometimes. I suppose that's what's gotten him this far in the beauty industry. But I assure you that we're all very excited to have you on board at the new lab."

"I appreciate that." Rachel's gaze wandered toward the hallway again as she waited for Jonah to reappear.

Mark shifted. "Not to bring up work stuff here at the party, but I can't stop thinking about the break-in at the lab. I just can't understand why someone would ransack your desk. That doesn't make any sense."

Now *this* was a subject Rachel could dig into.

"That was supposed to be Ganon's office, you know. Did you ever meet Ganon Jones?"

At the mention of Ganon's name, Rachel frowned. "I did."

"Then you know he recently died."

"His death was such a shame."

Mark's voice turned somber. "He was a brilliant man. We were sorry to lose him."

"I can imagine," Rachel said. "He was a really good guy. I have big shoes to fill."

"I'm sure you're going to do a great job." Mark patted her arm reassuringly.

Of all the leadership Rachel had met at the new Ocean Essence lab since she'd arrived, Mark seemed the most down-to-earth and approachable.

Unlike Dr. Hensley and Lloyd, who both had a certain arrogance about them.

Rachel glanced at the hallway again, trying to fight the concern that rose in her.

Certainly, Jonah was fine.

But, given everything that had happened lately, maybe she shouldn't feel so certain.

———

As the door opened, Jonah clicked the computer screen off and slipped under the massive desk inside Hensley's office.

Rather than coming up with an excuse as to why he was in here, he would hide.

He prayed his decision paid off.

Because if he was caught underneath the desk, then there was no way he'd be able to talk himself out of this situation. It would be clear to whoever came in here that he was snooping.

The door opened wider, and his breath caught.

This was it, the moment he'd figure out if his whole operation was blown or not.

As he waited, his heart thumped in his ears with anticipation.

"I prefer not to talk about that here," Dr. Hensley said.

Not talk about what here?

What exactly was the man talking about?

Jonah listened, hoping to maybe hear something significant.

"Yes, Ganon was a good man. I don't want to see the same thing happen to Rachel."

Jonah's muscles tightened.

It *was* somebody at the company targeting Rachel, wasn't it? Maybe this didn't have to do with Carl Nevada at all.

Jonah waited to hear what else Hensley had to say to whoever he was speaking with.

But before the conversation could continue, the door closed.

Had they left?

Why had they opened the door in the first place without coming inside? Had someone seen him step into this room and come to check things out?

The questions raced through Jonah's head.

He waited a few moments to see if they would come back.

They didn't.

He climbed out from beneath the desk and turned the computer screen back on.

The hard drive was now loaded onto his jump drive.

Perfect.

He pulled the device from the computer and jammed it back into his pocket.

All he had to do now was to slip from this room without being seen.

He stepped toward the door, hoping he wouldn't be caught.

RELIEF WASHED over Rachel when she saw Jonah striding toward her.

When he was close enough, she leaned toward him and lowered her voice. "Are you okay?"

He waved a hand in the air as if it wasn't a big deal. "I'm fine. I just needed a breather."

A breather? Had he needed a breather from her?

Jonah seemed to sense her confusion and admitted, "I have moments of being an introvert too, believe it or not."

"Or not," Rachel quipped.

They shared a smile.

A second later, she nodded toward the door. "What do you say we get out of here?"

"And play Scrabble?"

She tilted her head in surprise. "I didn't realize you liked Scrabble as much as I did."

Jonah shrugged. "I didn't realize it either. Not until I came here. But the game is growing on me. I kind of like our little nighttime routine."

Rachel flushed at the warm tone of his words. She understood exactly what he was saying.

Because she felt the same way.

"I'm glad to hear that," she murmured. "Because I do too."

They shared a lingering glance.

Did Jonah feel the same way that she did?

It was hard to say for sure.

But if Rachel had to make a scientific guess . . . she would say a definite yes.

That possibility thrilled her.

———

Jonah felt sweat spreading across his forehead.

So far, he had gotten through this evening without blowing his cover.

But at every turn, he felt like the possibility of that happening grew stronger and stronger.

And he wasn't just talking about the investigative part of being here.

It was being with Rachel.

There was a chance she might even be the next victim.

That she might meet the same fate as Ganon.

Jonah couldn't let that happen.

Though it was too soon to have developed deep feelings for anyone, Jonah knew that he was beginning to care about Rachel. Much more than he expected. In fact, it surprised him in amazing ways.

How could he find answers and protect her?

He wasn't sure.

But he could get her out of this party and to somewhere safe.

Because he had a feeling that someone here was a killer.

They made their rounds and told everyone goodbye before slipping outside to the car. They both let out an audible sigh of relief as they climbed inside and shut the doors.

"Thanks for going along with me tonight." Rachel rested her head against the headrest and barely turned toward him. "I know that wasn't exactly fun."

"You work with some interesting people," Jonah said. "What do you think about all of them?"

Maybe he was fishing for information here, but it seemed like a good opportunity to ask.

"Dr. Hensley is brilliant as a scientist and businessman. He built this company from the ground up forty years ago, and that's something to truly admire."

"I'm surprised he's here overseeing this lab."

"He's very hands-on, and he wants to make sure that we get a good start here. But I don't believe he wants to stay here very long. It's only temporary, which is why he's renting this place instead of buying."

"His wife seems like a handful."

Rachel smiled. "Yes, she does. Margaret won't last long on an island like this. Her tastes are too expensive."

"And Lloyd?"

"He'll be managing this lab. He's brilliant in his own right, but he doesn't have the people skills that Dr. Hensley has. He doesn't try to hide his arrogance."

"I can see that. And the other guy? What's his name? Mark?"

"He's the most down-to-earth one I've met in the administration. I'm a little surprised he's here, but they decided to base his operations out of this office. I heard through the grapevine that Mark was looking for a new place to live and had always wanted to come to the beach. So here he is."

"And everyone else there? My impression is they were either scientists or assistants."

"That's right." Rachel nodded enthusiastically. "Noelle is a dermatologist I'll work with."

Jonah started the car and pulled down the road. "I'm glad you're excited about the job. That's important."

He noticed Rachel spoke about her career with so much passion.

But he feared she'd ultimately be crushed. If these people were as corrupt as he thought they were, then it really would be difficult for Rachel to work with them.

Apprehension pressed on him again.

A few minutes later, they pulled up to the house. He scanned the outside as the headlights illuminated the place.

He didn't see any signs that anything was wrong or that anyone had been there.

But still, until Jonah knew what was going on, he wouldn't let down his guard.

He rushed to the other side of the car and opened the door for Rachel.

"Thank you," she murmured as he helped her out.

Then he placed his hand on the small of her back and led her up the front steps.

He'd definitely check this place out before Rachel went inside.

RACHEL WASN'T sure why she felt so nervous.

It wasn't necessarily because of the danger surrounding her.

It was probably more because of her time with Jonah.

A thrill of excitement rushed through her at the thought of having a casual evening with him again. It surprised her how much she was looking forward to their time together. Even though they'd only played Scrabble a few times, it still felt like a nice routine.

Jonah had checked the house out and cleared it.

No one was here, and no strange messages had been left.

That brought her a definite measure of comfort.

As she went to change into something more comfortable, Jonah started some tea. By the time she got back downstairs, the Scrabble board was set up and two steaming mugs of tea were on the table in front of a warm fireplace.

She settled on her side of the table but then decided to scoot toward the center and lean against the couch.

If she angled her letters in the right direction, Jonah wouldn't be able to see them.

He did the same, and they ended up beside each other.

"Why did you want to work for this lab?" Jonah asked as she grabbed some tiles from the bag.

"What do you mean?"

"I mean, you're clearly brilliant. You could have worked anywhere, really. But you chose the beauty industry."

She felt her cheeks warm at his compliment "That's a fair question. The truth is that I have personal reasons for wanting to work in this industry."

Jonah waited for her to continue, and she considered how much to say.

Finally, Rachel pulled up the sleeve of her sweatshirt and showed him her skin there. "I have something called vitiligo."

"Vitiligo?"

She pointed to several white patches on her skin. "It's loss of pigmentation. It's not life-threatening, but it can make people feel self-conscious. Especially teenage girls who just lost their mothers."

"I bet." His voice dipped with compassion.

"I was so self-conscious about it when I was younger. I wouldn't go out of the house without long sleeves and a turtleneck. Part of that is because you can't have sun exposure. It makes it worse. But I was also embarrassed. You know how tough kids can be."

"I do. I was in foster care, so I had my fair share of unkind comments."

"I imagine that you did. But when I decided to get my degree, I wanted to do something to help kids who were in similar situations. There's really no known cure for vitiligo. But when I was hired here at the lab, they gave me permission to work on some formulas that might help with it. It's not 100 percent their mission to do projects like this. A lot of times it's the pharmaceutical companies. But I would rather find a natural cure for this. That's why I'm so excited about helping here."

Jonah's gaze caught with hers, and he nodded. "It's starting to make sense now."

"You've been trying to figure me out?" Rachel's voice held a teasing tone.

He shrugged. "Maybe."

"I've been trying to figure you out also."

He turned toward her. "Like what?"

"I don't know where to start." She tapped her lips

and remembered him calling out "Anna" in his sleep. She was still curious about that, but asking him outright seemed awkward. Instead, she asked, "Have you ever been married before?"

"I have not."

"Ever been in a serious relationship?"

He glanced down a moment. "I thought I was once. I dated someone, and I thought I could see myself with her for . . . well, for a long time. Maybe the rest of our lives."

A lump formed in her throat.

"What happened?" Rachel asked.

"She told me I wasn't the man she thought I was. She walked away, acting like the last six months didn't mean anything to her."

Was he talking about Anna? That was Rachel's best guess. "Ouch. I'm sorry. But she didn't tell you why?"

"I guess the more she found out about me, the less she liked."

Rachel tilted her head. "I can't imagine that being true."

Jonah shrugged. "It is."

She licked her lips as she tried to think of what to say. She finally settled on, "My fiancé cheated on me multiple times, and I had no idea until the end. Everyone else did, apparently."

Jonah's gaze met hers. "That had to be tough."

"I guess it was better I found out before we were married rather than after."

"That's a good way to look at it. He was a fool to walk away from you, you know."

"And I think your girlfriend made a big mistake also. But her loss—" Rachel swallowed hard. She'd almost said, "My gain."

But she wasn't the type to be that forward. What had she been thinking?

Jonah stared at her, waiting for her to finish.

"Her loss just means someone else better is waiting out there for you."

A smile stretched across Jonah's face. "I hope you're right."

As their gazes caught again, Rachel couldn't help but wonder what he was thinking.

———

All Jonah could think about was how much he wanted to kiss Rachel.

Knowing a little bit more about her struggles only made her more attractive and real to him. He admired her determination to find a cure for her skin issue so she could help others who struggled with it.

It had felt good to tell her about Anna—although, he hadn't told her all the details. In truth, what he'd said had happened. But as Anna had left that conversation, some men had grabbed her.

Men Jonah had made angry.

They'd abducted her, and her dead body had washed ashore two days later.

It was all Jonah's fault.

He didn't deserve to ever love again.

He knew that.

But as Rachel stared at him with the firelight flickering across her face, she'd never looked so beautiful.

Jonah knew without a doubt that he'd been wrong about her earlier.

She wasn't involved in Ganon's death.

In fact, Jonah wanted to get her as far away from this company as he could.

But after hearing her reasons for being here, he realized that probably wouldn't happen.

She believed in the mission of this company and embraced the freedom they'd given her to do what she was passionate about.

"Rachel . . ." Jonah licked his lips as he stared at her.

He should tell her the truth. Tell her why he was really here. Because of his past in foster care and then his job with the military, he'd become a master at compartmentalizing.

But, for once, he didn't want to do that.

He wanted to bring all the different parts of his life together.

All he could think about was kissing her.

But he couldn't. Not without telling her the truth first.

The words seemed to catch in his throat and refused to leave his lips.

"Yes?" Rachel stared up at him with those big brown eyes of hers.

He could see himself with this woman.

He hadn't thought that since Anna. But he and Anna had never really been a great match anyway. Sure, there were sparks between them, but that was because they both lived on adrenaline.

Rachel was different. She was the kind of woman men wanted to marry and start a family with. She had the nurturing, sweet qualities any man would want in a wife or mother. But she also had a fiery side, and she was so smart.

Jonah had it bad. He hadn't realized it until right now. But he did.

"Were you going to say something?" Rachel's soft voice cut through his thoughts.

Say it . . . an internal voice urged him.

Or just kiss her.

Both sides of himself warred with each other.

"Rachel, the truth is that . . ." Jonah's gaze stopped on her lips.

She looked up at him, raising her face.

She wanted to kiss him too, didn't she?

"The truth is that . . ." He swallowed hard, trying to gather the nerve to say what he needed to say.

Before he could, a phone buzzed.

The moment disappeared faster than a spy vanishing into the night.

Jonah should have moved more quickly.

But it was too late now.

"IT'S MY DAD AGAIN," Rachel muttered as she stared at her phone. "He just texted me."

Jonah scooted closer. "What did he say?"

She showed him the screen. The message was simple.

> Sorry to make you worry. I'll be back
> soon. No time to talk right now.

"What do you think of that?" Jonah turned toward her.

"It doesn't even sound like him." Rachel quickly dialed his number. "I'm going to see if he'll answer."

If her dad had his phone on him long enough to send that message, then he should still be close to it. Maybe Rachel could catch him and set some of her worries at ease.

But when she dialed his number, the phone rang and rang and rang.

Her dad didn't answer.

She ended the call and frowned. "This just doesn't make any sense."

Jonah wrapped his arm around her shoulders and pulled her close. "I know it doesn't. I'm sorry for what you're going through."

She didn't stiffen at his touch. Instead, she leaned into him, finding comfort in his partial embrace. "I'm going to have to go try to find him soon. I can't just keep sticking my head in the sand."

"Do you really think you'd be able to find him?"

She thought about his question a moment before shrugging and shaking her head. "I really don't know. But I can't just do nothing."

"Look, I have a few connections within the security industry. Why don't you let me look into it? Would you mind that?"

Her heart pounded harder at his offer. "You would do that for me?"

"Of course I would. I would be more than happy to help in any way I can. I probably should have offered earlier."

The next moment, she threw her arms around him. His arms wrapped around her waist also, and he pulled her closer.

Rachel loved the feel of Jonah against her. The

strength of his muscles. The calming scent of his piney cologne.

She was getting carried away with this, wasn't she?

Yet she didn't seem to know how to put the brakes on her emotions.

She pulled away, and her gaze locked with his for a moment.

She wanted more than anything to kiss him.

But instead of giving in to that, she scooted to the other side of the table. Anxiety thrummed inside her as she remembered Digby. As she remembered how badly it had hurt when Digby had betrayed her.

She couldn't put herself in that position again.

Besides, she hardly knew Jonah. And given everything that was going on . . .

Acting on her impulse was just a bad, bad idea.

She rubbed her throat, and her voice sounded strained as she said, "Maybe we should finish this game."

Jonah glanced at her, a flash of surprise—and maybe hurt—in his gaze.

"Yeah, of course," he finally said.

Letting her emotions lead her right now could be a fatal mistake.

Rachel needed to keep that at the forefront of her mind.

———

As soon as Jonah went to his room that evening, he pulled out his computer and stared at it a moment.

What had happened downstairs?

He'd almost kissed Rachel.

But he knew that would have been a mistake.

If she hadn't pulled away, he would have.

But he couldn't deny that, more than anything, kissing Rachel was exactly what he wanted to do.

He swallowed hard and pushed those thoughts aside.

That wasn't why he was here in Lantern Beach. He had other things to focus on. He wanted to check out the contents of Hensley's hard drive.

But he'd told Rachel he'd look into her dad, and that was what he planned on doing first.

He'd tried to avoid breaking into Roman's computer and finding anything too personal. That wasn't the nature of this mission after all.

But what if he discovered something that was going on with Roman by doing so?

Jonah contemplated what to do. He hadn't wanted to suggest doing this very thing in front of Rachel. Partly because he feared what he might find out.

What if he saw that something unscrupulous was

going on with her father? How would he tell her that? It would only make things worse.

In his line of work, he'd dealt with truth and lies all too often.

Sometimes in order to find the truth, he had to perpetrate a lie. It was something he struggled with at times.

Did the end justify the means?

He wasn't sure.

But when it came to people he cared about, lying was the worst possible thing he could do. Yet it had come so naturally to him in so many areas of his life.

He pressed his eyes closed. *Lord, how should I even proceed with this?*

Jonah didn't know the answer to that question. Everything felt complicated, and he hated the fact that the lines were blurred.

It shouldn't be this way. But reconciling his old life with his new life definitely had its challenges. Every day he strode toward making the best choices that he could.

God's going to do great things through you.

Those words echoed in his mind.

One of his youth sponsors at the church he'd begun going to his senior year of high school had told him that once.

Jonah had never believed him.

How could God use someone as broken as he was?

Jonah had adopted so many personas that sometimes he wasn't sure exactly who he was. He'd done terrible things under the guise of following orders. And his heart was so cracked and broken it didn't seem as if it would ever be whole.

Something about being around Rachel made him feel like that might be possible.

He opened his eyes again and looked at the computer.

He needed to see what he could find out about Roman, and he would start by examining the files on the man's computer.

But Jonah prayed that whatever he found wouldn't devastate Rachel.

As he glanced over at the dresser beside him, he saw one of the drawers was slightly open.

His eyes narrowed.

He hadn't left it like that.

He was certain of it.

Had someone been in his room? Snooping through his things?

Who might it have been? And what exactly were they hoping to discover?

THE NEXT MORNING, Rachel and Jonah decided to go to church, where they met Ty and Cassidy.

The service was small, but the worship seemed authentic, and the sermon by Pastor Jack Wilson was powerful.

Being here reminded Rachel so much of her time growing up.

How had she let herself drift away from this?

That had been a mistake on her part.

The good news was it was never too late to turn things around. That's exactly what she planned on doing.

As long as she was in Lantern Beach—and even after she left, if she decided to do that one day—she would make church a priority. As well as reading her

Bible and prayer. Maybe she could even get involved with a small group.

Suddenly, the possibilities of how she could get back to her faith seemed bright and evident.

Just what she needed right now.

Being here with Jonah made everything feel even better.

After church, the two of them grabbed a bite to eat at a new seafood restaurant that had opened on the island a few weeks ago—The Fisherman's Wife. They kept their conversation casual, which was a nice change from the intense conversations they'd been having about everything going on.

There had been no incidents so far today. She hadn't felt any unseen eyes watching her.

Even though she knew danger could still linger close, the day so far was a much-needed break.

After they finished eating, Jonah turned to her. "What now?"

"What are you up for? You want to do some sightseeing?"

"Sightseeing? That sounds fantastic."

"I've been wanting to check out the lighthouse. What do you say?"

"That sounds perfect."

Before they reached his truck, a familiar face caught her eye.

It was Margaret—Dr. Hensley's wife.

The woman waved them down as she hurried toward them.

"Fancy seeing the two of you out here." Margaret was dressed to the nines in her linen pants, sky-blue sweater, and expensive-looking flowered scarf. Her hair was coifed and her makeup perfectly applied.

"Just out enjoying the day," Rachel said.

"Listen, I'd love to get together sometime," Margaret continued. "I need to get to know some women here on the island. I thought the two of us might get along."

"Sure, I'd love to schedule something sometime."

Margaret didn't even acknowledge her words. "Plus, you understand all the stress that Hensley brings home."

"He brings home stress?" Rachel tried to keep her voice casual.

"Oh, does he." Margaret rolled her eyes. "I can hardly stand it. I'm ready for him to retire. But the only thing that makes him feel important is money. There can never be enough."

Rachel's thoughts raced.

Could Hensley be behind Ganon's death? Was money truly his bottom line?

Rachel suddenly felt chilled at the thought.

———

Jonah paused as he stood in front of the lighthouse with Rachel.

The structure really was a sight to behold as it stood on the end of the island with the waves crashing around it.

The lighthouse keeper's quarters beneath it had been restored, and he wished he could see the inside.

He had always been fascinated with lighthouses. He'd learned from one of his foster parents that lighthouses had their own flashing patterns to communicate with mariners and send various messages.

Back before technology had grown to the point it was today, human innovation had still found ways to communicate.

Without all the bells and whistles of the modern world.

Sometimes, he wanted to go back to a different time. A time when life was simpler. When communication wasn't so complicated.

Then again, maybe it didn't have to be.

He glanced at Rachel as she stared up at the structure.

He didn't want to ruin Rachel's day by sharing the truth about his presence here.

But he couldn't put it off much longer.

"This has been a really nice start to the day." Rachel smiled up at him.

Jonah felt warmth flood his heart—followed by an immediate flash of guilt.

He needed to come clean with her. If he really cared about her, he should tell her what was going on.

Yet the words wouldn't leave his lips.

Maybe this wasn't the time and place to do it. Maybe it would be better back at the house, where she felt safe and secure. Where they could sit down. Get some of that tea that she loved to drink.

That's what he would do, he decided.

He would wait, but he would tell her.

Because she deserved to know the truth about what was going on . . . especially considering the danger that she was probably facing.

CASSIDY PUT her phone away and turned to Ty as they sat in the living room.

Ty held Faith, bouncing her on his knee and blowing on her belly until she giggled.

But one glance at Cassidy and he clearly knew something was wrong.

"Bad phone call?" he asked.

Cassidy's thoughts continued to race. "I guess you could say that. I was curious about Jonah Gray, so I decided to make a few calls and use some of my contacts to figure out who this guy really is."

"I take it it's bad news?" Ty stopped blowing on Faith's belly for a moment as he turned to Cassidy. But Faith continued to reach for him, trying to turn his head toward her to get his attention.

Any other time, Cassidy would think that the

interaction was adorable. She thought that now also. But she was distracted by what she'd just learned.

"There's more to Jonah Gray than he's letting on," Cassidy started. "And there's a good reason why I couldn't find any trace of him in the system. Maybe even a good reason that his last name is Gray—a last name that he picked himself."

"What?" A knot formed between Ty's eyes.

"He grew up in the foster care system, and as soon as he was out, he officially changed his name and joined the military. But it turns out a special project snagged him while he was in the military, and he worked some clandestine operations for them."

Ty's eyebrows shot up. "Is that right?"

"It gets even better. It turns out one of his friends, another guy who was in the foster care system with him, died about a month ago. And guess what?"

"What?" Ty stared at her as he waited for the answer.

"Ganon worked for Ocean Essence."

Realization washed over Ty's features. "Do you think Jonah is targeting Rachel? Do you think he killed Ganon?"

Cassidy took another sip of coffee before saying, "I'm not sure what's going on. But I definitely need to bring him in for questioning."

Ty shook his head. "That's too bad. I actually kind of liked the guy."

CHAPTER
THIRTY-SEVEN

RACHEL STILL FELT REFRESHED as she stepped inside her father's house. She took off her coat and hung it by the front door before depositing her purse near the table.

Then she headed toward the living room and turned to Jonah. He really had surprised her. She had enjoyed spending today with him much more than she had anticipated.

Could there really be something brewing between them?

But when she looked at him, she saw something new in his gaze.

There was something he wanted to say, wasn't there?

"Everything okay?" Rachel studied his face as she waited for his answer.

"There's something I need to tell you."

Alarm raced through her at the implication of his words. "Is it about my dad?"

His frown deepened, and he didn't confirm or deny her words.

"Maybe we can fix some tea and sit down to talk?" he asked instead.

Rachel nodded, even though the apprehension building inside her already felt overwhelming.

"I'll fix the tea," she said.

"And I'll start a fire to warm this place up a bit."

She slipped into the kitchen and reminded herself not to get ahead of herself. Whatever he had to say, maybe it wasn't as big of a deal as she was making it out to be.

Still, it seemed to take forever for the teakettle to whistle. Finally, it did, and she poured the boiling water into two coffee mugs.

Her hands trembled so badly as she carried the mugs back into the living room that she feared she might spill something.

She didn't.

She set the mugs on the coffee table and noted the warm fire that Jonah had started.

Just seeing that brought her a moment of comfort.

Then she sat on the couch and curled her legs beneath her as she turned to Jonah. "So what's on your mind?"

"There's something I need to tell you," Jonah repeated, hesitation marring his voice. "I should have probably told you from the start, but I didn't know if I could trust you."

She was certain this had to do with her dad. What did Jonah know?

Was her dad okay?

"You're killing me here," she admitted. "What's this about?"

Jonah wasn't the type of guy who ever looked insecure—at least not since Rachel had met him. The fact he looked so nervous right now really threw her for a loop.

"It's just that . . . I came here to Lantern beach for a reason." Jonah pressed his lips together, his gaze strained.

"To help my father, right?"

He shifted his head in a half nod. "Kind of. But there's more to it than that."

"What are you talking about, Jonah?" Did he have something to do with her father's disappearance?

The silent question startled her.

No, Jonah would never have anything to do with that.

So why did Rachel's heart race as if it were a possibility?

Jonah licked his lips as their gazes met. "Rachel, there's a lot more going on here than meets the eye."

But before he could say anything else, a knock sounded at the door.

Rachel let out a frustrated sigh. He was just about to explain.

Now who was here?

She rose to her feet. "I should get that. Hold that thought."

As she walked toward the door, she noticed that Jonah was close behind her.

He was probably still worried that trouble might have shown up.

But what if Jonah was the very trouble she'd been trying to hide from all this time?

———

As soon as Jonah saw Chief Chambers standing there, he knew something was wrong.

She charged inside the house and paused in front of him. "You and I need to talk. Down at the station."

"What?" Rachel strode up beside them and let out a gasp. "What's going on? Are you arresting him?"

Cassidy's gaze remained on Jonah, the look in her eyes accusatory.

"I'm afraid that Jonah Gray isn't exactly who he is pretending to be."

Rachel looked at him, her eyes widening as she let out an airy, "What?"

"Do you want to tell her or do you want me to?" Cassidy stared at him.

Regret sloshed inside Jonah as he shifted his gaze toward Rachel. This wasn't the way he wanted this to go down. Not at all.

"I was about to tell you." He knew how lame his words sounded, even if they were true. "I'm sorry."

Rachel crossed her arms as she stared at him, a new standoffishness about her. "What's going on here, Jonah? Who are you?"

He licked his lips. "My foster brother that I told you died?"

"I remember you mentioning him."

"He was . . . Ganon."

"You knew Ganon?" Her lips parted with surprise. "You didn't come to the island to help my dad, did you?"

Jonah knew he couldn't lie any more—not if he wanted to salvage the fragile remains of their relationship. "I didn't. I'm pretty sure someone from Ocean Essence killed Ganon. I'm here to investigate his death."

Rachel gasped and shook her head. "What are you talking about?"

Maybe this was his chance to plead his case, to help Rachel understand. "Someone at Ocean Essence is dirty. They killed my friend. Now I'm afraid they're going to kill you too."

"But Ganon had a heart attack."

"Ganon thought someone at Ocean Essence was selling top-secret formulas to someone for a big payout. I was with Ganon when he died. He handed me a paper with your name on it and muttered the word 'killed.'"

"Killed?" Rachel shook her head as if flabbergasted. "Why was my name on the paper? I don't understand."

"I don't either. At first, I thought he meant that you'd killed him. You weren't in Colorado when his death occurred."

Her skin went white. "I took a week off after seeing that murder, and I stayed home."

"I know that now. Besides, after I got to know you, I realized my theory wasn't true. I've been pushing for a tox screen or autopsy. I believe Ganon was poisoned, though I'm not sure with what."

Rachel gasped. "Box jellyfish venom . . ."

"What?"

Rachel opened her mouth and then shut it again. "Nothing."

"Rachel . . ."

She stared at him another moment, her gaze heavy with questions and confusion.

Before they could say anything else, Cassidy took Jonah's arm and pulled him toward the door. "We have a lot to talk about, especially since I have a warrant for your arrest."

"A warrant?" Rachel's voice sounded shrill with surprise.

"For what?" Jonah's mind raced.

"A breaking and entering that happened five years ago." Cassidy pulled out handcuffs and tugged his arms behind him before snapping them on his wrists.

That breaking and entering was supposed to be wiped from his record. Larchmont had told him it was taken care of. Apparently, his boss had been wrong.

As Cassidy led him outside, Rachel followed behind, a storm of emotion playing out in her gaze.

"So the fact that you're at my house . . . it's not a coincidence, is it? You wanted to get to know me so you could find answers, didn't you?" Betrayal stained her voice.

"I can explain more," Jonah said as Cassidy led him away.

"Don't bother."

Failure pressed down on Jonah. Rachel was one of the best people he'd ever met.

Now, he'd ruined it.

Based on the look in her eyes, Jonah knew Rachel would never forgive him.

Part of him couldn't blame her.

But if Jonah was behind bars, he'd never find justice for his friend.

Nor could he protect Rachel.

At once, he felt as if everything was falling apart.

RACHEL STOOD in the doorway and watched as Jonah was escorted to Cassidy's police vehicle.

Her mind still reeled over everything that had happened.

Just when she'd begun to think she might really have feelings for Jonah, she'd discovered all of this was an act.

He'd just been playing nice so he could get information from her. That was probably what he'd been about to tell her—that he needed help figuring out what had happened to his friend.

He hadn't been about to confess his feelings or anything that Rachel might have been dreaming about.

She was so pathetic.

Rachel squeezed her eyes shut and shook her head.

No, she wasn't pathetic. She'd just let her feelings grow too quickly. She should have known better. Past wisdom had tried to warn her to keep her distance, but she hadn't listened.

Her dad had always taught her if something seemed too good to be true then it probably was.

Jonah was a case in point for that.

As Cassidy's SUV pulled away, Rachel closed her door and locked it. Then she leaned against the wall and pressed her eyes shut again.

Okay, enough feeling sorry for yourself. Sure, he betrayed you and he hurt you. You should have known better than to let him do that. You should have kept your distance. But you didn't. So now what?

Her thoughts drifted back to her rushed conversation with Jonah as he'd been arrested.

He'd mentioned Ganon.

That man on the beach had possibly died from the jellyfish venom. Ganon had obtained some of that very venom for his project.

What if he was murdered? The venom could mimic a heart attack . . .

Her throat tightened at the thought.

Could someone at Ocean Essence really be involved in his death? Ganon had ordered some of the venom for this project, so the lab would have small quantities. And if the wrong person got their hands on it . . .

Since she'd come here, Rachel *had* heard some strange conversations between people working at the company.

Conversations that made her wonder about the intentions of those who'd hired her.

Was she easily replaceable?

Or had someone wanted her here for a specific reason?

What if Rachel had been brought here under false pretenses? What if the board of Ocean Essence really didn't believe in her plan to find a natural cure for vitiligo, and instead they wanted something else from her?

She shook her head. No, what sense would that make?

Then again, what sense did all the incidents that had occurred here recently make? How were they connected?

Her head began to pound.

She didn't know the answers to any of those questions.

But finding answers and solutions was what she did.

Rachel pushed herself from the wall and opened her eyes.

Then she went into the kitchen and pulled out a

pen and some paper.

She would jot down some hypotheses.

Then she'd try to make sense of this mess that had become her life.

———

"You need to start talking." Chief Chambers stood on the other side of the interrogation table and stared at Jonah. "Because right now you're my best suspect as to who killed Travis Metcalf."

"It's not what you think." Jonah shifted in the uncomfortable metal chair.

Cassidy raised her eyebrows, no longer looking like the friendly woman he'd had dinner with only two nights ago.

"I did come here with ulterior motives," he admitted, adrenaline thrumming through him. "But I haven't hurt anybody."

"Go on."

Jonah resisted a sigh.

How had Cassidy even discovered this information?

This wasn't the time to ask.

"I believe someone at Ocean Essence killed my friend," he admitted. "I'm here to figure out who."

"You're using Rachel?"

Guilt pounded at him at her statement. But he couldn't deny her words.

"Not totally," he said. "Sure, Rachel was a great connection with the lab so I thought she might be able to provide some answers. But I didn't mean her any harm."

"It may be too late for that."

He heard the underlying truth in Cassidy's statement.

He may not have hurt Rachel physically, but the betrayal she no doubt felt right now would cut deep.

He regretted that immensely.

"I told you that I used to be military." Jonah decided not to hold back.

Cassidy crossed her arms. "You did."

"I was recruited for a secret project. Everything was off book. Essentially, my team and I didn't exist. If we were caught, the government would deny any connection to us."

"Keep going."

"I suppose, through that, I perfected the art of subterfuge. So I came here to find some answers. Yes, I did need an inside connection at the lab. For a while, I suspected Rachel may have been involved with Ganon's death."

"What changed your mind?" Cassidy continued to study him.

"Once I got to know Rachel, I realized there was

no way she was a killer. She's a good person. I was about to tell her the truth about why I'm here when you came by."

Cassidy gave him a skeptical look, but Jonah couldn't blame her. It seemed an unlikely story.

"Tell me what you think is going on at this lab." Cassidy lowered herself into the seat across from him and waited.

"I'm not sure. But before my friend died, he gave me a piece of paper with Rachel's name on it. He'd started to tell me that something happening at the lab was bothering him."

"You think someone there is trying to cover something up?"

Jonah shrugged. "I really can't say. But if I had to guess, someone received a large payout for selling information and didn't want to be caught. That's when someone decided to kill Ganon and cover up the crime."

Cassidy nodded slowly, but Jonah couldn't read her body language. He wasn't sure if she believed him or not.

"Do you really think I killed that man on the beach?" Jonah finally asked. "I'm not sure what the timeline of his death was, but I was with Roman in the morning, and then I was talking to Rachel when we heard him in the ocean. Why would I have risked my life to rescue him if I had actually intended to kill him?"

"You wouldn't have." Cassidy frowned. "I wasn't sure about your whole involvement in that, I only knew I needed to bring you into the station so I could find out some answers."

He leaned closer. "Look, I know you don't owe me anything. You don't even know me. But I need to keep my true identity under wraps. If people know who I am . . . that will only bring more trouble here on the island. I promise you, my intentions aren't nefarious. Even when I figure out who killed Ganon, I don't plan to make trouble."

Cassidy stared at him, her expression still unreadable.

But Jonah hoped he hadn't just ruined his entire investigation.

THIRTY-NINE

AN HOUR LATER, Rachel sat at the kitchen table still and stared at the list she'd jotted of potential suspects, mulling over their possible motives, means, and opportunities.

Now her head pounded.

She leaned back in her chair and sighed.

She had lots of ideas, but she was no closer to finding any answers than she'd been before.

What was happening with Cassidy and Jonah at the police station? Part of her wanted to go down there and find out for herself. She wanted answers.

However, she knew she didn't have any right to do that or to even be there. So, instead, she decided to wait. Maybe Cassidy would give her an update.

However, as time continued to slowly tick

forward, Rachel realized she just couldn't sit here at the house with her thoughts any longer.

She grabbed her keys and headed to the Ocean Essence office instead. She wasn't sure what she hoped to discover there, but at least she'd be doing *something*.

Her car was the only one in the lot when she arrived, but she knew she could access the lab whenever she wanted.

A thrum of nerves swept through her as she walked toward the door. She pulled her jacket closer, though she knew the coat wouldn't do any good. Her chill came from deep inside her.

Using her badge to access the building, she crept inside, feeling like a stranger in this place.

She paused just inside the doorway to the office area.

What if what Jonah said was true? What if someone at the lab was up to no good?

Could someone here have murdered Ganon?

She shuddered at the thought of it.

How had she walked away from one nightmare only to amble into another?

Rachel glanced around as if seeing this place in a new light. All the latest technology had once seemed so alluring. But what if all this was a cover-up? The change of locations? The remote island?

The bad feeling continued to grow in her stomach.

She paced the perimeter of the first floor, taking her time as she soaked things in.

Finally, she paused by the "Authorized Personnel Only" door.

What was behind those doors? Answers about Ganon's death?

Or would that be too simple?

Nothing made sense.

Her heart began to pound.

Rachel glanced behind her again as if to double-check she was the only one here—even though she knew she was.

Then she glanced in the corner.

A security camera stared at her from above.

Of course.

No one had told her about them, but she'd noticed they were there on her first day in the office.

If she tried to get into this room, someone would see her.

Then she might *really* be a target.

Tension pulled across her shoulders.

The idea had been foolish anyway.

Jonah was probably just blowing off steam. Trying to deflect from the real issue.

Maybe there was no meat to his theory that someone at Essence had killed Ganon.

But even as much as she didn't like Jonah right now, she thought she'd heard some truth in his words.

She glanced at the "Authorized Personnel Only" door again.

How could she find out if what he'd said about Ganon was true?

That was the question swirling in her mind.

Before she could figure out an answer, a footstep sounded behind her.

Rachel froze as Ganon's face flashed in her mind.

What if his killer was here?

———

"You're letting me go?" Jonah stared at Cassidy from across the interrogation table, unsure if he'd heard correctly.

"We don't have enough to hold you here."

Her words weren't especially friendly or encouraging—more matter of fact. She stood and walked toward him.

"I called about that arrest warrant, and it turns out those charges should have been dropped several months ago." She uncuffed him.

Jonah rose. "Okay then."

"I suggest you find somewhere else to stay rather than at Rachel's place. In fact, I can pick up your things at Rachel's. I'm not sure it's a good idea if you go over there again."

Jonah's heart pounded harder.

She was right.

It probably *wasn't* a good idea.

But he desperately wanted to explain himself. He wanted to somehow take the hurt from her eyes.

Was that even possible?

He wasn't sure.

Regret panged inside him.

Instead, Cassidy escorted him out to her police SUV.

They silently drove down the road until she stopped in front of an inn. The building was plantation-style with white shingles and a double balcony. However, the place looked rundown—shingles were missing, the paint was peeling, and the septic tank was partly exposed.

Just as he was about to get out, Cassidy called his name, and Jonah paused, looking back at her.

"Just for the record, I know what it's like to be in your shoes." Her gaze locked with his. "I'm not totally discounting what you said. But I have to be cautious."

What did she mean by that? Jonah was more curious than ever about her story.

"I appreciate you giving me the benefit of the doubt," he finally said.

Cassidy's gaze remained standoffish, but she nodded. "Of course."

"What about my truck? It's still at the other house."

"Give me your keys. I'll have an officer drive it over."

Jonah fished his keys from his pocket and handed them to her.

Then he climbed out and looked at the inn in front of him.

It wouldn't be nearly as fun to stay here as it had been to stay with Rachel.

But his accommodations were the least of his concerns.

He needed to figure out how to make things right with Rachel somehow.

Currently, he had no good ideas.

CHAPTER
FORTY

RACHEL SWIRLED AROUND and saw a man standing behind her.

"Dr. Hensley?" Her hand rushed over her heart. "I didn't even hear you come in."

"I guess I'm quieter than I thought." His eyes narrowed as he studied her. "Is everything okay?"

Her hand rested on her chest as her pulse raced out of control. "I felt restless, so I decided to come in to straighten up my office."

He glanced at the door behind her but didn't ask the question in his eyes. Clearly, he was curious why she'd stopped in front of the room full of classified information.

"I was just walking around the office, making sure it's clear." She shrugged, praying a hiccup didn't escape. "In case you didn't know, I was shot at yesterday. It's put me on edge. I must have stopped here right when you walked in."

"I see. I can imagine all of that has you shaken."

"It does. The island usually seems so safe. But it feels anything but since I've arrived."

"Hopefully, it's just a phase that will pass."

"Hopefully." She flashed a tight smile.

Hensley nodded toward his office. "I came in to do a little extra work. So, if you'll excuse me . . ."

Rachel watched him walk away. Only once he was in his office did she release her breath.

That had been close.

Was he suspicious of her?

Dr. Hensley had made her list of suspects. After all, this was *his* company. He had the most to lose if something illegal was uncovered going on here.

But the man seemed so uptight and business-minded.

Still, what if Ganon had been poisoned? That was usually the murder method of women.

Could one of the females who worked in the lab be behind this?

Rachel shook her head. Everyone here had an interest in science. Poison seemed the most logical choice as a murder weapon for *anyone* here.

She didn't like the thought of it.

She glanced at the doorway behind her one more time.

She wouldn't be getting in that room today. Maybe not ever.

For now, she needed to straighten her office, just like she'd told Hensley she'd be doing.

But Rachel would remain on edge . . . from now until the person behind these crimes was caught.

———

Jonah paced his room at the inn.

His things had been delivered a few minutes ago, but he didn't like the fact he was here and away from Rachel. Yet he understood the reasoning behind the move. He'd known that something like this might happen, and it had.

Now he needed to figure out what to do about this latest turn of events.

He glanced outside his window. It had been a long day, and the darkness had already fallen.

Was Rachel okay? Had she checked the doors and windows at the house to make sure they were secure?

Because it appeared that she was the intended target here. Jonah had felt better when he was close and could keep an eye on things.

How would he ever win back her trust?

An image of her father entered his mind again.

Jonah needed to find Roman. To figure out exactly

what had happened to him.

If he could do that, maybe Rachel would trust him again.

He thought about the prototype of some glasses he'd seen in Roman's bedroom.

On a whim, he remotely logged onto Roman's personal computer. A few minutes later, he tracked down the software linked with those glasses.

Roman had been wearing glasses when he'd left Lantern Beach. Could they have been his prototype?

Jonah found a live video feed from them.

His heart rate quickened.

After only a moment of hesitation, he hit Play.

He watched as, through Roman's eyes, he strode up to a generic-looking office building. Knocked on the door.

Then a man pulled a gun on him.

Grabbed him, despite Roman's protests.

Then his glasses must have fallen off and been smashed.

The feed died.

The investor Roman had met with wasn't really an investor at all, Jonah realized with clarity.

Jonah didn't recognize the man who'd grabbed Roman, but at least they had evidence now that something had happened.

He needed to tell Rachel.

Now.

RACHEL ARRIVED BACK at the house, making a mental note of how empty and cold it felt being here alone.

The thought was crazy because she had lived by herself back in Colorado. She was used to being on her own.

But she and Jonah had fallen into a nice little routine.

Despite her logic, she knew she'd miss it.

At the memory of Jonah, another sting of betrayal hit her.

How could he have kept those secrets from her? Rachel had felt as if they'd bonded. As if she had grown closer to him and opened up.

But it was all just an act on his part.

Her gut twisted at the thought of it.

That was okay. She raised her chin.

She'd do just fine on her own. She would make herself some tea tonight and start a fire and then she would play Scrabble on her iPad against the computer.

She'd done it plenty of times before, and there was nothing wrong with doing those things alone again.

That was what she told herself, at least.

Just as she sat down ready to begin to unwind with her tea and iPad, her phone rang.

She frowned when she saw Jonah's number there.

He had a lot of nerve to call her after everything that had happened.

She started to ignore it but then paused.

She wasn't going to be a shrinking wallflower. She needed to let him know exactly how she was feeling.

She put the phone to her ear. "What do you want?"

"Rachel, I discovered something," he rushed.

Her jaw hardened. "Sure you did."

"No, I really did. It's about your father."

Her breath caught, but she reminded herself to remain cautious.

Could she really believe anything he told her? Probably not.

"Are you just saying that to get back into my

good graces?" She tucked her legs beneath her. "How do I know that you're not behind all of this in the first place?"

Jonah paused a second. "I'm so sorry about everything that happened, Rachel. If I could go back and do it over—"

"But we can't do that, can we? We make choices, and then we have to live with those consequences." Her voice hardened with bitterness.

She'd been taken advantage of one too many times.

When would she ever learn that life was safer when she kept people at a distance? When she didn't let others get close?

"Rachel, I know you're mad." Urgency stretched through Jonah's voice. "But please, listen to me."

Before she could respond, a shadow lunged from the darkness.

At a dizzying speed, a hand covered her mouth. An arm locked her arms in position against her.

She let out a muffled scream as she dropped the phone.

The last thing she heard was Jonah yelling her name.

———

Jonah wasted no time.

He ran outside and jumped into his truck. Then he headed down the road to Rachel's place.

He only hoped he didn't get there too late.

As he drove, he dialed Cassidy's number and told her what was going on.

She promised to be on her way also.

Worst-case scenarios continued to play out in his head. Scenarios where Rachel was hurt.

Or worse.

Where she was killed.

Looking back, Jonah would have handled this in an entirely different way. But it was too late to go back and change any of that now.

He gripped the steering wheel as he continued down the road.

Finally, he pulled up to Rachel's house—at just the same time as Cassidy and one of her officers.

The police chief gave Jonah a warning glance before muttering, "Stay behind me."

He wouldn't argue. He was just happy she hadn't sent him away.

She directed her officer to check the outside of the place.

Then, at the front door, Cassidy turned to him. "Do you still have the key?"

He fished it from his pocket and handed it to her. Cassidy unlocked the door and stepped into the relatively dark house.

As she rounded the corner, Jonah saw the fireplace had been lit.

His heart panged with another moment of regret.

Had Rachel been sitting there drinking tea when he had called her?

He scanned the place, looking for signs of what might have happened to her.

He saw the tea that had spilled on the floor. A lamp that had been turned over.

Then he saw the blood on the carpet.

His breath caught.

What had happened to Rachel? Where was she now?

"I'll check upstairs, and you check the rest of the downstairs, okay?" Cassidy said.

Jonah nodded.

At least, the police chief hadn't completely written him off.

He continued down the hallway.

As he did, he prayed that he would find Rachel and that she was okay.

CHAPTER
FORTY-TWO

RACHEL'S HEART slammed against her ribcage over and over again.

The masked man still held a hand over her mouth, pressing it so hard that her teeth hurt.

He'd begun to question her when the cars had pulled up outside.

Then he'd forced her into a closet in the master bedroom. He held her close and threatened that she shouldn't make any sound, or she would die.

She believed him.

This guy was big and strong.

She tried to think of someone at the lab who might fit his description and strength, but she couldn't think of anyone.

What if she'd been off base this whole time? What

if the person behind everything that had happened wasn't affiliated with the lab?

Would the same killer poison someone and use this kind of physical force?

The two didn't fit in her mind.

Rachel would figure that out later. First, she needed to survive long enough to do so.

Downstairs, someone called her name.

Was that Cassidy?

Her heart beat faster.

Maybe Jonah had called the police when he had heard the altercation over the phone.

Maybe there was hope that she would survive this.

The words the man had whispered to her when he'd taken her by surprise flooded back to her mind.

Where is it?

Rachel had told him she didn't know what he was talking about.

Don't play dumb with me. You have something I want.

Rachel had asked exactly what that was.

The man had gotten rough with her afterward. For a moment, she'd thought he might kill her.

But not until he tortured her into spilling everything.

The problem was, she had no idea what he was asking about.

Silence stretched throughout the house.

What was Cassidy—Rachel assumed that's who it was—doing?

That was when she heard the footsteps above her.

The police chief was checking out the second floor, wasn't she?

Her abductor seemed to draw that same conclusion.

"We need to move," he growled. "Not a sound from you."

Another shot of ice-cold fear rushed through Rachel.

If she left this place with this man, she wasn't sure she'd ever be seen alive again.

Yet this guy easily overpowered her. How would she ever get away?

Just as they stepped from the closet, another shadow appeared.

This one lunged at the man.

Then, there in the darkness, chaos ensued.

———

Jonah saw the closet door open.

He waited until two people emerged.

A man wearing all black.

And Rachel.

He knew he didn't have much time to act, especially if he wanted to take this guy by surprise.

He lunged at the man and tackled him to the floor. The man let out a gasp, followed by a string of expletives.

"Rachel, run!" he yelled.

Instead, she stood there staring as if in shock.

As the man came after Jonah again, Jonah tried one more time. "Rachel, go! Now!"

Finally, she left.

Good. Now he could concentrate on figuring out who this guy was.

The guy rose to his feet, towering above Jonah's six-foot-one stature.

The guy was big. He grunted and puffed as he stood in front of Jonah, reminding him of a bull about to charge.

Just as Jonah thought that, the man came at him.

Jonah ducked, trying to throw the thug over his shoulder.

But this guy was large and heavy—just like the man who'd broken in earlier.

Instead, the man rammed Jonah into the wall.

As he did, Jonah's head hit something hard.

Then everything blurred around him.

CHAPTER
FORTY-THREE

RACHEL HEARD the crash and paused.

She gasped as she considered what might be happening in the other room.

Was Jonah okay? Should she go back and check on him?

Then again, what could she do to help? There was no way she could overpower that man.

Panic raced through her as indecision gripped her.

"Rachel." She looked up and saw Cassidy running toward her. "Are you okay?"

Rachel nodded and then pointed toward the door. "But Jonah . . ."

Cassidy took one more look at her before darting into the room.

As the door flung open, Rachel peered inside.

Jonah slumped on the floor.

Rachel's heart pounded harder.

Was he dead?

A cry caught in her throat.

No, he couldn't be dead . . .

Cassidy quickly checked his pulse then nodded at Rachel. Then she rose and searched the room.

Rachel saw that the patio door was open.

Her attacker must have run outside.

Cassidy stepped outside also and radioed her officer.

As she did, Rachel rushed toward Jonah and knelt beside him. "Are you okay? Jonah. Wake up!"

But he remained unmoving.

Jonah jerked his eyes open. The events that had just happened rushed back to him.

"Are you okay?" Rachel asked again.

He pressed his eyes shut and started to nod. But the motion only made pain pulse through his head even more.

He pressed his eyes closed again as he fought a groan.

Then he said, "I think so. Are *you* okay?"

"I'm fine." She gripped his arm as if she wanted to lift him herself and take him to safety.

It was a sweet thought, but that would never be happening.

Then Cassidy appeared on the other side of him. "It looks like you hit your head pretty hard. An ambulance is on the way."

"I'll be fine," he insisted.

"Maybe, but you need to have that checked out anyway to be sure."

"Did you catch that man?" He avoided what she said.

"He got away. But I called in some more officers for backup. They're going to search the beach for him."

That was a nice thought, but Jonah doubted they would find this guy.

Whoever he was, he knew what he was doing.

"Did he hurt you?" Jonah couldn't hide the concern in his voice.

She shook her head. "We struggled, and I hit my head on the table. But I'm okay. It's a good thing you guys got here when you did, though."

"What did the man say to you?" Cassidy turned toward Rachel. "What did he want?"

Rachel swallowed hard and rubbed her throat, a pinched look in her gaze. "He asked me to give him something."

"To give him what?" Cassidy squinted as she waited for Rachel to respond.

Rachel shrugged and shook her head. "I have no idea what he was talking about."

Jonah frowned. He didn't like the sound of any of this.

WHEN RACHEL REALIZED that Cassidy would be here for a while, she fixed something warm for everyone to drink.

The paramedics had come to check out Jonah, but he'd refused to go to the island's clinic. Instead, he'd been warned to keep an eye out for any symptoms of a concussion.

Butterfly bandages had been placed on Rachel's forehead as well. But every time she looked at the blood on the floor, she shivered.

That had been too close. If Cassidy and Jonah hadn't come when they had . . . she might be dead right now.

The person behind these crimes was growing more desperate.

That thought terrified her.

Cassidy sat down beside her. "I want to assure you that we're doing everything we can to find out answers here. I plan on questioning some people at the lab."

Another shot of panic rushed up Rachel's spine. This could make things uncomfortable in her workplace. Yet whoever was behind this couldn't get away with it either.

"I know you are doing everything you can." Rachel rubbed her arms, hating the chill she felt. "I appreciate it."

"If there's anything else you can think of that could help us find these guys, please let us know," Cassidy said. "In the meantime, I'll continue to have an officer patrol past the house. I'm sorry this guy somehow got inside. It looks like he snuck around back and jimmied one of the sliding glass doors. Do you want to come stay at my place tonight? We have some extra rooms."

Although the thought was tempting, Rachel waved her off. "I'll be okay. But thank you."

But *would* she really be okay? She wasn't sure.

She glanced at Jonah, who sat close by listening to every part of their conversation.

What exactly was he thinking? Could she trust him?

Rachel desperately wanted to say yes.

But desperation might get her killed.

Jonah stared at Rachel as she sat across the room.

For once in his life, he felt at a loss for words.

There was so much he wanted to say, but he knew the words would fall on deaf ears.

What he'd done had caused irreparable damage between the two of them.

Now Rachel's life was on the line, and there was little he could do to help her because of their broken trust.

"I'm glad you're okay," he finally said.

She nodded and pulled the blanket up around her.

"Rachel, I never meant—"

She raised a hand. "I'm so tired of hearing excuses. That's all I heard with Digby. He always had excuses as to why he acted the way he did. In his mind, he was justified. But that's just not how you treat people you care about."

"Rachel, I've grown to care about you. But at first, I didn't know if I could trust you."

"Well, now you've proven that I can't trust *you*."

Jonah felt as if he had been slapped.

But he understood where she was coming from.

"I hate to think about you being here by yourself tonight."

"I doubt the man will return." But her words lacked conviction.

"Can I at least tell you what I discovered about your dad? Please? It's not for my sake but for yours."

Her gaze fluttered up to meet his and finally she nodded. "Sure."

But that hardness still remained in her voice.

"I found the software your dad developed for those glasses he was working on," Jonah started.

A spark of interest ignited in her eyes. "And?"

"And I found some video of him wearing them right before he disappeared."

"What was on it? I want to see it."

Jonah shook his head. "You don't want to see it."

She went still. "Why not?"

"That supposed investor he met with . . . he wasn't an investor. He abducted your dad. The glasses must have flown off when he did."

Rachel gasped, and her face went pale. "What?"

"I'm sorry, Rachel. I wanted to tell you earlier . . . but I wish it was better news. I've been working on a few other angles, but I don't have anything yet."

"What should I do, Jonah?" Rachel stared at him as if she hoped he had all the answers.

"We should call Cassidy. She can call the FBI."

Rachel finally nodded. "Okay. Let's do that."

EXCITEMENT THRUMMED through Cassidy the next morning.

She finally had a lead on Travis Metcalf.

One of her officers had found his car.

The vehicle had been left in a parking lot at the general store, and the owner had finally reported the car had been abandoned there for a few days.

Officer Dillinger had checked it out already and found multiple guns inside.

Yes, guns.

Now Cassidy was on her way to check out the car herself.

As she made her way down the road, her thoughts wandered to everything that had happened.

Rachel had called last night with the update on her dad. Then Jonah had sent the video footage.

It was chilling.

Cassidy had called one of her FBI contacts, who promised to put a team onto it.

She prayed they found Roman Atwood before something happened to the man.

Her earlier prediction that trouble was brewing on the island seemed to be accurate.

All the island's most recent suspicious activities seemed to center around this new lab and its newest employee.

Cassidy only hoped Rachel wasn't hurt in the middle of all this chaos. She liked the woman.

She wanted to like Jonah also.

She'd put in some calls to verify that what he'd told her was accurate.

His story appeared to be true.

Cassidy wanted to be upset with him, yet considering the circumstances of her own arrival on the island, how could she be? Still, she'd remain cautious around him until she knew more.

She pulled up to the store and parked. A beat-up gold sedan sat empty in the corner of the lot. Dillinger waited there with it. He'd already used a Slim Jim to unlock the car so they could search inside. The trunk was also open.

Cassidy strode toward the back of the vehicle and peered inside. She let out a whistle when she saw the stash of guns there.

"This guy meant business," Cassidy muttered.

"You can say that again."

She glanced at Officer Dillinger. "Anything else of note?"

"His cell phone was in the glove compartment. The screen is locked, and I couldn't get into it."

"Maybe I can find someone who can." Cassidy pulled on some gloves before sitting in the driver's seat and looking around.

Just who was this Travis Metcalf guy? Why did he have that dolphin necklace? Those numbers on his hand? That poison in his system?

He was connected with the lab also. She felt certain of it.

She searched through his vehicle but didn't find anything beneath the seat or in the glove compartment.

Then she spotted something poking out from beneath the floor mat.

With her gloved hand, she grabbed it.

Her breath caught when she saw what it was.

A picture of Rachel.

This photo, combined with the guns in the back of the man's vehicle, led her to only one conclusion.

This guy had come here to harm Rachel.

But the question of why remained.

CHAPTER
FORTY-SIX

LAST NIGHT'S WINNING
SCRABBLE WORD: UNEASY

RACHEL STILL FELT on edge the next morning as she went into work.

Nothing else had happened at the house last night. But she'd hardly gotten any sleep as she'd waited to hear another footstep or see another movement in the darkness.

There had been none.

Part of her had wanted to ask Jonah to stay the night at her father's place, just so she could know someone else was near.

But that might send the wrong message.

Besides, Rachel was still upset with him, and her trust had been broken. She couldn't easily invite him back into her life as if nothing had happened.

Sure, he'd gone out of his way to protect her last

night. He could have even been killed. That meant something to her.

But she still needed to keep her boundaries in place. Her heart had been ripped in two after Digby had cheated on her. She couldn't let herself go through something like that again. So it was best if she kept her distance.

Several people at the office this morning had asked her about the bandages on her forehead. Rachel had simply told them she'd fallen, and that explanation seemed to satisfy their curiosity.

At any moment, she expected Cassidy to arrive to question people here. Though Rachel knew it needed to be done, the thought still set her on edge as she wondered what that would mean for her afterward.

She didn't want her coworkers to think she'd thrown them under the bus. That wouldn't make for a good workplace experience. Yet the person behind this just couldn't simply get away with what they were doing either.

Her head pounded at the thought.

"You sure you're doing okay this morning, Rachel?"

She looked up as she refilled her coffee cup in the break room and saw Mark standing there.

"I'm trying to adjust to being here, I suppose." She shrugged.

"That's understandable." He glanced at the cut on her forehead and frowned but said nothing.

Out of everyone here at the office, Mark seemed the most approachable and unpretentious. If Rachel was going to find out information, maybe he was the one to ask. Besides, he worked in finance. He probably didn't know much about proprietary formulas.

She raised her cup of coffee to her lips and took a sip before asking, "You mentioned Ganon Jones at the party?"

"I did."

She stepped closer. "I know this sounds strange, but what if his death had something to do with our work here?"

Mark quickly drew his eyebrows together in surprise. "Why would you think that?"

Rachel scrambled to gather her thoughts. "I received an anonymous text. Whoever sent it indicated that there was more to Ganon's death than police suspect. That it wasn't a heart attack that killed him and that his murder is somehow connected with this lab. Needless to say, it's left me shaken."

"I would say so." He shook his head, a wrinkle of concern forming on his brow. "I don't know why anyone would say that. Ganon worked on anti-aging serums and retinol products. They're not exactly something that would make people hate him."

"Have we had many complaints here? Have

people been having bad side effects from any of the serums?"

"No. You know if that happened, we'd have to report it. Otherwise, we'd be facing a huge lawsuit. That's not something we could sweep under the rug. It's best if we have full disclosure when things like that happen. But the worst effects of the products he was working on would maybe be a rash or something. That's not anything to kill somebody over."

She wasn't so sure about that. The wrong kind of chemicals could cause serious illnesses, including cancer. But she didn't want to get into that argument now.

Mark stepped closer. "It sounds to me as if someone is simply trying to stir the pot. I wouldn't worry about it too much."

Rachel nodded. His words made sense.

Yet, on the other hand, none of this made sense.

Rachel wouldn't be able to breathe easy until she had some more answers.

She thanked Mark and then took a step toward the door.

Today, she would learn the ins and outs of the lab upstairs.

Noelle Purdy would be giving her the official tour.

The timing was convenient. Rachel wanted to get to know some of the people upstairs anyway.

Had any of them worked with Ganon?

This could be her opportunity to find out some answers.

———

The next morning, Jonah grabbed some coffee and then sat with his computer in his room at the inn.

He wanted to find out if the bug he'd planted at Hensley's place and the tracker he'd placed on the man's computer would lead anywhere.

As of last night, they hadn't.

But he wanted to dig more deeply into this.

He put on some headphones and then played the audio from Hensley's bedroom.

He fast-forwarded through hours, but there was nothing—only Hensley snoring.

With that lead going nowhere, he tried the man's computer to see if there was anything new there.

It held a lot of information to dig through, so it would take a while. He was especially interested in Hensley's emails.

Jonah scanned those messages again, going back more than six weeks, but frowned.

Nothing popped out at him.

Had that whole song and dance he'd gone through at the party been for nothing?

Maybe it was time to take more aggressive measures.

He could break into the man's home. Look for any evidence he might find that way.

But that move would be risky—especially since he didn't know Margaret's schedule. He'd need to run surveillance on her first.

Jonah sighed and leaned back in his chair.

He had to find answers. But he kept reaching dead ends.

It was time to change that.

FORTY-SEVEN

"SO THIS IS OUR LAB," Noelle said as she presented the space with a flourish. "I think you're really going to like it here."

Rachel hadn't met Noelle before coming to Lantern Beach, but she already liked the woman. She was friendly and smart and matter-of-fact. Rachel had enjoyed talking to her at the party at Hensley's place.

"I'm looking forward to it. How long have you been here?" Rachel took another sip of her coffee. She was on her fourth cup this morning, and jitters were beginning to kick in.

"Two years. I started at the Baltimore lab. At first, I wasn't thrilled about moving down here. I like the conveniences of big box stores and shopping centers.

But I decided to see this as a new adventure. Since I'm single, I figured, why not?"

"Makes sense to me."

"But I still haven't gotten used to the fact that this place takes a lot longer to get Amazon packages, doesn't have Uber Eats, and this lab doesn't always get cell phone service."

Rachel glanced at her phone. "It doesn't?"

She didn't check her phone very often at work, but she had made a couple of phone calls—including those to her dad.

"It's spotty at best. What do you expect on an island, right?" Noelle smiled and leaned against her desk.

Rachel studied her a moment. "I'm surprised I didn't meet you at the company's yearly conference in Texas."

"I never made it there myself, but I heard it was a lot of fun."

"It was." Rachel shifted as she tried to casually bring up the next subject. "Say, did you happen to know a man named Ganon Jones?"

Noelle's smile slipped. "Yes, I knew Ganon. He was a wonderful man. Unfortunately, he passed away about a month ago. I'm sure you've probably heard. I think a company-wide memo went out about his passing."

Rachel frowned at the memory. "I heard. What a huge loss."

"It came as a shock to all of us."

"I can imagine." Rachel paused and shifted her line of questioning. "Listen, I'm supposed to be picking up where he left off, but I can't find any of his project notes."

Noelle shrugged. "I'm not sure where they would be. I'm assuming one of the higher-ups have it."

Did something in those notes get Ganon killed?

The answers seemed to be getting further away instead of closer.

Rachel wanted something more definitive. But she knew if she asked too many questions that she'd only raise people's suspicions.

So her next task was to try and figure out where Ganon's notes or research materials may have gone.

Maybe the answers waited there.

Sometimes, she wished life was more like a game of Scrabble. She wished she was simply given some letters that she needed to make sense of.

On second thought, maybe life *was* like that.

Because she suddenly felt as if she'd drawn the worst letters possible—the ones incapable of forming any words.

———

Jonah leaned against Rachel's car in the parking lot of Ocean Essence as he waited for her to leave on her lunch break.

He was taking a risk by being here, and he knew that. Rachel might not even leave for lunch. She was a practical type of gal who could have packed her own food.

But she hadn't been answering his phone calls or texts, and he needed to talk to her.

He wanted to share a surprise discovery he'd made.

Finally, after he'd stood outside for forty minutes, the front door opened.

He held his breath as he waited to see who would emerge.

A moment later, Rachel stepped out, her hair blowing behind her in the breeze and her heels clicking against the sidewalk.

Relief filled him.

Until she looked up and spotted him.

Her expression instantly became stormy, and she slowed her steps.

At least, she didn't turn around and run back inside.

Instead, she paused in front of him and crossed her arms. "What are you doing here?"

"I need to talk to you."

She narrowed her eyes. "I guess you didn't

understand when I wasn't responding to you that I might not be in the mood to talk . . ."

She was mad—and rightfully so. But Jonah had to figure out a way to reach her. "No, I understood that. But this couldn't wait."

"What couldn't wait?"

Jonah glanced around to see if anyone was nearby listening.

The two of them were alone.

But this wasn't a conversation Jonah wanted to have here.

"Can we at least sit in my truck for some privacy?"

Rachel let out a sigh to let him know she was annoyed. Finally, she nodded. "Fine."

They climbed into his truck. The day was temperate enough that Jonah didn't need to roll down the windows or turn on the heat.

"What's going on?" Rachel stared at him.

There was so much he wanted to say. But he'd stick to the facts right now instead of diving into his personal life or begging for forgiveness.

"Walter sent me a document before he died," he started. "But I didn't realize he'd sent it at first. He used a different email, and the message went to my spam folder."

Her eyes brightened. "How did you find it then?"

"I was looking for an email I hadn't received yet

from someone else. Then I spotted this email advertising a new skincare line. I got curious and clicked on it. Sure enough, I found a hidden link in the text of the message. I realized Walter had sent it to me, so I clicked on the link and downloaded some documents. He obviously wanted to conceal the information—probably because he feared for his life."

"And rightfully so." Rachel shifted, unable to hide her curiosity. "What was in these documents?"

"It was an unfinished formula." Jonah shrugged. "It doesn't make sense to me, but maybe it will to you."

"Can I see?"

"I thought you'd never ask." Jonah reached into his pocket and pulled out the paper he'd printed. He handed it to Rachel and watched her expression, anxious to hear her thoughts.

Her eyes widened as she scanned the text there. "This is the project Ganon and I were working on."

"You worked on a project together?" Surprise washed through him.

"Only during off hours," she murmured.

"You didn't mention that . . ."

Rachel cast him a look. "And there's a lot you didn't mention to me."

Jonah pressed his lips together, knowing he couldn't argue. "That's a fair statement. Can you tell me about this project?"

"It's a formula Ganon and I were working on to cure acne. He was so excited about it."

"I know he had bad acne as a teen, and he hated it."

"He told me that. The only reason we worked together on the acne serum was because I shared an idea with Ganon at the conference. It was about a study I'd read up on about the use of benzoyl peroxide for clearing up acne. Ganon had been wanting to try a similar formula, but this one used colloidal silver. We realized if we put our ideas together, we might be able to come up with a true solution."

"Fascinating."

"Then he told me he wanted to try the jellyfish venom as part of the formula as well—that it had amazing healing properties after it was neutralized. I told him he was crazy. But he'd done some research and thought it might be the missing ingredient we needed."

"Keep going."

"Our experiments weren't in the budget, so we ventured out on our own with plans of sharing our ideas once we had something solid." She frowned. "That day never came. While some aspects of our formula worked, I felt like we were missing something that would counteract the venom for some people who might be sensitive to it. We needed more tests."

Rachel continued studying the paper and sucked in a breath.

Jonah's curiosity skyrocketed. "Rachel?"

"You'll never believe this . . ."

"Believe what?"

"It sounds like he figured something out. He doesn't say what, however. He ran some trials on the new formula, and it worked. It appears like Ganon wanted to move forward and tell people at the company about the project."

"Could this be the formula someone was trying to sell?"

"There's big money in the acne business. There's a good chance that's accurate."

"That's why someone is trying to get to you, Rachel." Jonah stared at her as realization clicked in his mind. "They want you to finish the formula. They don't know what that other ingredient is."

"If that's true, then that's a problem . . ." She frowned. "Because I have some of our notes but . . . I don't know how to finish it."

CHAPTER
FORTY-EIGHT

RACHEL'S MIND raced as she stepped back inside the office after her break.

Jonah hadn't wanted her to return to work. He'd wanted her to go somewhere safe.

But he didn't have any authority over her life, especially not after his deceit. She had, however, promised him that she'd call him before she left tonight.

It just seemed smart.

Maybe some time they would talk about his deception.

But not now.

Not after what Jonah had shared with her.

She smiled at Kari as she stepped through the reception area.

If someone had killed Ganon, Rachel might be

one of the few people who could figure out what happened. Her best chance of finding those answers were inside this lab.

Poison was the weapon women most often used. That was what Rachel had always heard, at least.

Could Noelle be behind this? Rachel had her doubts about that.

But what about Margaret? The woman certainly seemed to love money. She'd been especially friendly toward Rachel. Maybe that was on purpose. Maybe Margaret suspected Rachel might have the answers she needed.

How would Rachel find out any of these answers, though?

She wasn't sure, especially since all of Ganon's possessions seem to have disappeared.

She sat at her desk to ruminate on everything.

"Everything okay?" Lloyd paused by her office door.

Rachel pulled herself together and smiled. "Of course. Yes."

"Listen, I was going through a few things from the move. I found a folder that Ganon Jones gave me a while back. I hadn't had a chance to go through the contents yet. I thought I would hand it over to you to see if you can make sense of his notes. He was always full of good ideas."

Her heart raced. Was this the information she was looking for? "That sounds great."

She swallowed hard as she considered her options.

She could be treading into dangerous territory here.

But she didn't have much time. The person behind these crimes was escalating, and she was in the crosshairs.

Rachel leaned back in her chair, trying to remain composed and not raise any suspicions. "Has anyone else seen this folder?"

He pushed his glasses up higher. "Not to my knowledge."

"I look forward to seeing what he was working on."

"I'll bring it by sometime before I leave for the day."

"Perfect. Thank you."

Excitement thrummed through her.

Maybe she could finally find some answers.

———

Jonah hadn't wanted to leave Rachel at the lab.

But he couldn't convince her to leave.

However, before he could pull from the parking lot, he saw Noelle step outside.

The woman glanced around before briskly walking toward her mint-green Volvo.

As she climbed inside and pulled away, Jonah decided to follow her.

He'd have to be careful. On an island this size with little other traffic, tailing someone could be obvious.

He didn't want to be caught.

But he was curious about the woman.

As he followed behind Noelle, his phone rang. It was Cassidy.

Jonah's breath caught.

Would she throw out more accusations?

"Are you with Rachel?" she rushed instead.

"No, I just left the lab." He gripped the steering wheel. "What's going on?"

"I believe the man found on the beach was a hitman and that Rachel was his target."

His heart pounded faster. "What?"

"That's our working theory. Any idea why someone would want to kill her?"

He shared his theory about the stolen proprietary formula that could have been worth millions. He'd kept that information from her until now. But he honestly thought he could trust this woman.

"Interesting," Cassidy muttered.

Jonah's thoughts raced. "Do you think Rachel is safe at the lab?"

"She's not answering her phone."

"She said service is spotty inside the building."

Cassidy paused a moment before saying, "I think she'll be okay there, at least during business hours."

Jonah's chest tightened. "I hope you're right."

"I'm going to head out there now to talk to Hensley."

He stared at the woman's car on the road in front of him. "Sounds like a good idea."

"If you hear anything else, let me know."

"Will do." But as he said the words, Noelle pulled up to a small cottage. No other cars were in the driveway.

She hadn't led him anywhere suspicious.

So now he'd head back to the lab.

One thing felt certain: the noose was tightening.

FORTY-NINE

RACHEL FELT her nerves thrumming as she sat at her desk.

If what Jonah had told her was correct, then the trouble developing at Ocean Essence was even worse than she thought.

She stood, suddenly needing to stretch her legs.

She stepped from her office and fisted her hands, trying not to show her anxiety to anyone who might be watching.

She glanced around.

There was a good chance that *someone* here was truly watching her.

Rachel didn't want to believe any of the theories circling in her mind might be true. They sounded too outlandish. But she couldn't deny the facts in front of her either. Couldn't deny the encounters she'd had and the danger she'd faced.

She headed toward the breakroom. She wanted to grab some water from the fridge.

As she walked, she tried to figure out a way to find out more information about what Ganon was working on.

The two of them had talked about their idea when they had met at a conference, but Ganon wasn't ready to present it to the company yet. So they had begun to play with some formulas, mostly via phone conversations.

They had been getting closer and closer to finding a solution, but they weren't there yet. However, if they were able to develop the formula that they wanted—and what they had so far was showing promise—then it would be an amazing advancement for skin care.

And something that someone would be willing to pay a lot of money for.

Rachel stepped into the breakroom and grabbed a bottle of water.

As she did, Rachel heard a voice in the hallway and peered through the door.

Cassidy was here, walking toward Lloyd's office.

Rachel's back muscles tightened.

The police chief was following up, just as she should.

But whoever was behind these crimes certainly wouldn't be very forthcoming.

This whole time Rachel had been leaning toward Noelle or Margaret as a possible suspect. Of course, if that was the case, the guilty party would have had to hire someone else to do their dirty work. It had clearly been a man who'd attacked both Jonah and Rachel.

But now Rachel was beginning to question the assumption that a woman was behind the murder.

She worked in the scientific field, so death by poisoning might be more of a natural fit for any scientist working here.

Could it be Hensley? Lloyd?

They were both scientists by trade.

She disappeared inside her office and sat. As she leaned back in her chair, she realized her concentration was shot.

When her phone buzzed, she glanced at the screen.

It was another text from her dad.

Only, it wasn't what she had expected.

Instead, it was a video.

On the screen, her father was bound and gagged. The background was dark.

Nausea gurgled inside her at the sight of him.

But the voiceover made the situation clear.

"Do exactly what we say, or your father will die."

A cry caught in her throat as her worst fears came to fruition.

———

Jonah arrived back at Ocean Essence in time to see Cassidy disappear inside.

Then, as he'd waited, he'd seen her leave.

She even stopped by to talk to him for a moment. She didn't have any updates yet, however.

It wasn't until Jonah saw Dr. Hensley leaving that Jonah put his car into Drive. Following Noelle hadn't led him anywhere, but maybe Dr. Hensley would be different.

Besides, there was a good chance that whoever was guilty was now feeling spooked. Since Dr. Hensley was his number one suspect right now, he wanted to see what he would do after Cassidy's visit.

Would he meet with the person he'd hired? Would he try to destroy any evidence?

That's what Jonah wanted to know.

He maintained a good distance behind the man as he traveled north on the island.

Part of him wanted to stay with Rachel and to wait until she left. But he knew she probably wouldn't appreciate that. Plus, she'd promised to text him before she left.

As he drove, Jonah couldn't help but wonder if the CEO of the company would sell his own exclusive information. Was what Margaret said correct? Did Dr. Hensley feel as if he could never have enough money? Would he do whatever it took to get more?

Jonah wasn't sure. The whole situation didn't make sense to him. He'd grown up with nothing, and material possessions had never been important to him.

A few turns later, Dr. Hensley pulled up in front of his rental house.

Jonah slowed his car as he went past so he could see what the man was doing.

But Dr. Hensley didn't even glance around when he got out of the car.

Instead, he climbed the steps to the front door and opened it. Margaret appeared in the entryway, and Dr. Hensley gave her a kiss on the cheek.

Jonah frowned.

Had his theory about Hensley being guilty totally been off base? Had following this man been a complete waste of time?

Possibly.

Jonah was grasping at straws here, wasn't he?

He continued down the road. He'd make a U-turn in a moment and then head back to the lab so he could be ready when Rachel left.

But as he passed some smaller rental houses, his foot hit the brake.

Someone matching the description of the man who'd attacked him wove between the buildings.

Jonah hadn't seen the man's face.

But he'd seen that the man was at least a good six inches taller than Jonah was, and unusually broad and muscular.

It was hard to miss someone who was that big.

Big just like the guy who'd broken into Roman Atwood's house and fought Jonah.

Jonah couldn't let this guy get away now.

FROM HER DESK, Rachel glanced out the doorway of her office.

Cassidy appeared to already be gone.

She couldn't report the video of her father to the police chief.

Instead, she grabbed her phone and dialed Jonah's number.

But the call didn't go through.

Rachel gritted her teeth.

Why now of all times was cell phone service down?

She wanted to talk to Jonah. To tell him about that video of her dad. To tell him she was ready to leave and go home for the evening.

She'd been counting down the moments until her workday was over.

It was 4:55.

Close enough.

Since her cell wasn't working, she picked up her landline. But there was no dial tone.

What? Was this phone service out also?

She repressed a sigh.

Rachel gripped her cell phone as she contemplated what to do. She'd promised Jonah she'd call him before leaving. But what could she do since her reception was so bad out here?

She would simply leave, she decided.

Rachel stood, her chair rolling behind her and hitting the bookshelf.

She jumped at the sound.

Ever since she'd gotten that video of her dad, she'd been a mess.

She had replied to the sender, asking what this person wanted her to do.

They'd said that instructions would follow.

Rachel practically felt beside herself as she waited for further instructions to come through.

Just as she grabbed her purse, a shadow blocked the doorway.

Rachel gasped and drew back.

Lloyd stood there.

"Didn't mean to scare you. But I'm about to head out. Here's that information I told you about." He held up a folder. "Maybe you can make sense of it."

She practically held her breath as Lloyd handed her the folder.

Was this it? The information she'd been looking for?

As soon as Lloyd walked away, she glanced at the folder.

Though Rachel knew she should wait until she got in the car to open it, she didn't think she could do that.

Instead, she opened the manilla folder and stared at the handwritten notes inside.

She narrowed her eyes as she scanned Ganon's notes. They didn't make any sense—not at first glance, at least. But he'd definitely been brainstorming some new ideas.

She needed to study this more, but she wanted to do it in the privacy of her home.

Here at the lab she felt . . . almost exposed.

Just as she tucked the folder into her oversized purse and stepped out, she spotted Mark walking toward her office.

His expression looked pinched, however.

He paused in front of her and leaned close. "Can we talk?"

"Is everything okay?" Something about the sound of Mark's voice sent alarm through her. It was almost as if he knew something was wrong.

"It's about Ganon." He glanced around. "There's

something I want to show you."

"Where would you like to talk? My office?"

"No, I have a better idea." He nodded toward the atrium area. "Follow me."

———

Jonah pulled his truck onto the side of the road and threw it into Park.

He jumped out and began to chase the man on foot.

Jonah knew there was no way he could catch this guy in his truck—not with the way the guy wove between the houses.

But this might be Jonah's chance to talk to this guy and get some answers once and for all.

The guy must have seen Jonah before he even stopped.

Because now the man sprinted away, hardly looking back.

As he cut between some other buildings, Jonah lost sight of him.

But when Jonah finally emerged from between all the houses, he paused.

The guy appeared to be gone.

But he couldn't have disappeared. Not again.

This guy was somewhere close, and Jonah needed to find him.

Jonah glanced around, looking for any signs of movement.

Where did this guy go?

His gaze finally stopped on an old yellow building in the distance.

A sign on the roof read ARCADE, even though it was missing a couple of letters and the remaining ones were crooked and faded.

The screen door fluttered open with the wind.

Was that where this guy had gone?

It was Jonah's best guess.

His shoulders tightened as he started that way.

He was about to find out what was going on.

MARK POINTED toward a door in the distance. "It's in here."

It was the "Authorized Personnel Only" room.

Her excitement turned into a moment of fear.

She knew this place was not only locked up as tight as Fort Knox, but it was also soundproof inside —that's what Dr. Hensley had told her while on the tour.

Soundproof could be good, she mused.

No one could overhear their conversation.

But a small niggle of worry also formed inside her.

Soundproofing could also be a disadvantage. If she were to cry out for help . . . no one would hear.

She glanced at Mark again, and her throat tightened.

But Mark wasn't a threat. He hadn't even made her list of suspects.

He was a finance guy. He no doubt wouldn't even know what any of these formulas were about.

He'd simply found some information he wanted to share with her. Probably because Rachel had been asking about Ganon earlier.

She pushed aside her nerves and watched as he used the biometric scan to unlock the door.

A moment later, Mark pushed it open and motioned for her to follow.

Rachel cast one more glance behind her to see if anyone was watching.

They weren't.

Most of the people from the office were gone for the day. Those who hadn't left for home yet were gathering their things so they could leave.

Rachel's phone was tucked in the pocket of her navy-blue blazer.

Would Jonah try to call her? Would his call even go through if he did? Or were the phone lines still down?

Though Rachel was still upset with him, another part of her felt safer when he was nearby.

She stepped into the room, listening as the door clicked closed behind her.

Then she glanced around.

When she had caught a brief glimpse inside the

room earlier, she'd only seen filing cabinets. But on the opposite wall there was a case of various products, chemicals, and ingredients, mostly kept behind locked glass.

The room was just as big as Rachel had imagined. There were also some smaller pieces of lab equipment, almost as if someone had set that up just in case an employee wanted to do some top-secret work in here.

She glanced up at Mark, anxious to hear what he had to show her.

"You said you found out something about Ganon?" she started.

Mark nodded, his expression still pensive. "Apparently, he was working on a top-secret project in his free time. I guess that made some people like Hensley mad. Lloyd also."

Rachel swallowed hard wondering if Mark knew about the project she'd been working on with Ganon.

She knew that under contract anything developed while she was employed here was officially property of Ocean Essence, at least for a year after employment was terminated. She'd signed a noncompete clause when she'd come to work here. Everyone did.

She and Ganon hadn't planned on doing anything illegal. But they weren't ready to come forward with the project until they had more solid evidence that the serum was valid.

"I don't know what kind of project Ganon was working on, but I guess he stirred a hornet's nest. I just found out that there was a lot of fighting behind the scenes."

Rachel stepped closer, more curious than ever now. "Fighting between Ganon and Dr. Hensley? Or Lloyd?"

"Both of them. I've suspected for a while that the two of them may be up to something."

Her thoughts raced. "Why are you telling me this now?"

"Because you said that man on the beach died from the same poison Ganon did."

Rachel froze.

How did Mark know that? Rachel hadn't told him, and Cassidy had kept the fact under wraps.

The only way he would know would be . . . if he'd been the one who poisoned the men.

Rachel's blood went cold at the thought.

———

Jonah drew his gun and stepped inside the old, abandoned arcade.

It took a moment for his eyes to adjust to the darkness. He glanced around, looking for any signs of where the man may have gone.

The musty building looked bigger on the inside

than it did on the outside. Lots of freestanding video games, an old claw machine, and even a small rock-climbing wall cluttered the space.

Keeping his back to the wall, Jonah began to edge around the room.

Just as he was about to walk by two freestanding arcade games—Pacman and Donkey Kong—a shadow lunged from between them.

Jonah's gun fell to the floor with the impact.

A fist hit his jaw, and pain radiated through him.

It was the same man as before.

He'd recognize those punches anywhere.

Jonah quickly came to his senses.

He sprang to life and threw a punch also.

Then the two faced off.

"Who are you?" Jonah demanded, his muscles bristled and tense.

As a sliver of light hit the man, his craggy face came into view. Jonah didn't recognize the guy. He hadn't expected to.

This guy was obviously hired help.

"Wouldn't you like to know?" the man growled.

They began to pace in a circle, both daring the other to make the first move.

"What do you want with Rachel?" Jonah asked.

"You don't know yet?" The man's hands fisted in front of him.

"Why don't you tell me so I don't have to keep guessing?"

The man let out a throaty chuckle. "She has something my client wants."

"And who's your client?"

"I can't tell you that."

Jonah poised his arms to throw another punch. "You need to leave her alone."

"You're not having much luck stopping me."

"Well, my luck is about to change." Anger rippled through him.

"I doubt that . . . especially considering this was all a distraction to get you out of the way while the real fun begins."

The real fun begins? It wasn't an accident that Jonah was in this arcade right now, was it?

This guy's client was moving in on Rachel.

More anger rushed like lava through his blood.

Then Jonah charged at the guy.

FIFTY-TWO

RACHEL STARED at Mark as they stood in the locked room, her nerves thrumming through her. "I didn't tell you that."

"What? Of course you did." He released a nervous laugh.

"But I didn't." She took a step back, suddenly realizing what a mistake it was to come in here with him.

Mark didn't want to tell her anything.

He wanted to trap her.

Because he was behind Ganon's death and the subsequent attacks on her.

She glanced at the door behind her.

Could she make a run for it?

Mark could certainly reach her before she got there. But could she take him down?

She might be a scientist, but she was fairly spry and strong.

"Don't do it." His voice hardened as he stepped toward her, his shoulders rolling back as if he were transforming into someone else.

Rachel glanced at his hand.

He held a gun.

Where had that come from?

Her trembles deepened.

"Do what?" Her voice quivered as she asked the question.

Mark nodded at the door. "Don't even bother trying to escape. You have to have the right badge to get in and out."

Rachel glanced beside the door and saw his words were true. A scanner had been installed on the wall near the lock.

"We thought of everything," Mark explained with a smirk. "We had a security breach once, and we didn't want that to happen again. Safeguarding our property is the name of the game."

The trembles started inside her again.

She stared at Mark as her thoughts raced. "You're the one who did this, aren't you? The one who killed Ganon? Or, should I say, the one who had him killed?"

"He started asking too many questions. Kind of like you." Mark's voice didn't hold any emotion, almost as if he were talking about his morning routine.

"So why kill him?"

"I knew he was working on something. When I asked him about it, he finally told me the truth. As soon as I heard the idea he was developing, I knew how much I could get for it from the competition. So I stole the information I needed, and I sold it to the highest bidder." He frowned. "The problem was, the formula was incomplete."

That made sense. Because Mark would have no idea how to read all the scientific jargon on the papers. He'd only assumed the formula was done.

"So then you killed Ganon?" Rachel couldn't believe she was saying those words out loud.

"Ganon began to get suspicious, and I knew I had to do something. We met the morning he died to talk about the project—but no one knew about our little meeting. That's when I added some of that jellyfish venom he'd been telling me about into his coffee. I wasn't sure how long it would take to have effect. Longer than I'd assumed."

"But later you realized the formula wasn't complete, and you'd killed Ganon prematurely. You began to panic."

Mark's gaze darkened. "I got word back from my buyers about it, and they weren't very happy. They began threatening me, and I knew I had to do something. Then I saw your name on some paperwork I stole from Ganon's place."

"That's why you hired me here for this new lab." Rachel's heart lodged into her throat.

Her promotion hadn't been on merit, had it? She'd simply been a means to an end.

"I had to get that information, and you were the best way to do it." Mark raised his gun higher. "Now I need you to tell me what the rest of this miracle formula is."

"But I don't know the rest," Rachel said. "Ganon and I hadn't gotten that far. We thought we did, but the tests were inconsistent. But Ganon thought he'd figured out what the missing ingredient was. We were supposed to talk the day after he died so he could tell me. We never had the chance to have that conversation."

"So you're useless to me?" Mark stared at her, disgust dripping from his words.

Rachel's lungs tightened even more. "Do you have my dad?"

"I knew I was going to need some leverage. But if what you're telling me is true, then I could just kill both you and your father."

———

"I have been wanting to kill you since the first time I laid eyes on you," the man muttered to Jonah before lunging at him again.

This time, the guy's shoulder caught Jonah in the abdomen.

Jonah flew backward and hit a wall.

Pain pulsed through him, and his head spun.

But he didn't have time to dwell on that.

As the man charged again with his fist raised, Jonah ducked.

The guy's hand rammed into the wall, and he muttered curses beneath his breath as he flexed his wounded fingers.

Jonah had known this guy would be strong, but he was even stronger than Jonah had anticipated.

Not missing a beat, Jonah swung his leg.

His foot caught the guy in the side of his face, and the guy stumbled backward, buying Jonah a few minutes.

Jonah's gun was on the floor somewhere. If he could only grab it . . .

The man suddenly growled as if he hadn't liked being taken by surprise. He sprang to life and charged at Jonah again.

This time, Jonah ducked low. He caught the guy at his waist and flipped him over his shoulder and onto the floor.

As he did, Jonah quickly grabbed him. Turned

him facedown. Pulled his arms behind him and subdued the man before he could do more damage.

"Who do you work for?" Jonah demanded.

"Not that it makes a difference, but I'm with an organization called Dagger."

Jonah had heard of the agency before. Those guys were no good—mostly people who'd gotten out of the military for less than honorable reasons and who continued to do their dirty work, just now for more money.

In fact, one of Jonah's colleagues had been offered a job with the company, but he'd refused.

"Who hired Dagger to hurt Rachel?" Jonah pressed his knee into the man's back.

"I don't know." His voice sounded strained. "I never saw his face. He tells me what to do and pays me."

Just then, the door behind him flew open.

Cassidy and two officers flooded inside, guns drawn. "Police!"

Relief washed over her features when she saw that Jonah had apprehended the guy already.

Her officers surrounded him and grabbed the man's arms, handcuffing him as they read him his rights.

Jonah stood and wiped off his pants. He ignored the trickle of blood coming from his lips and the pounding in his head.

"I saw your truck and figured something was wrong," Cassidy explained. "My guys and I started looking for you."

"I'm glad you did." He turned to Cassidy. "Rachel is in trouble. We've got to find her. Now."

RACHEL TREMBLED.

The look in Mark's eyes made it clear he wasn't afraid to kill her.

Gone was the meek man she thought she knew. In his place was a cold-hearted killer.

A killer who knew numbers. Who knew a good payout when he saw it.

Mark was willing to kill to get what he wanted. He'd already killed Ganon, and he wasn't afraid of killing Rachel and her dad also.

She had to figure out a way to get out of this.

But as she glanced around again, she didn't see anything that would help her—especially when considering his gun was aimed at her. She was trapped in this room with Mark, and no one knew she was here.

Even if they did, they wouldn't be able to get inside.

Mark reached into his pocket and pulled something out.

A syringe.

Rachel's throat tightened.

"What's inside that?" She knew the answer, but she asked anyway.

"One guess."

"Poisonous venom from the box jellyfish." Her voice cracked as she said the words.

"Very good. Everyone says you're astute. Looks like you are."

She ignored the sarcasm in his words. "Ganon thought you were on his side, didn't he?"

Mark grinned and pushed the air from the needle. "Of course."

"You're very unassuming. I can see why he thought he could trust you. What I don't see is how you can live with yourself in light of the decisions you've been making."

Mark shrugged. "Once I get the rest of this payout, I can leave this job. Buy my own island in the Caribbean. All this will be behind me."

"How are you going to explain my death?"

He shrugged again. "I'll figure out a way. An experiment gone wrong or something."

Rachel's pulse quickened. "So you're the guy who hired that man to try to kill me?"

"He was supposed to be looking through your notes for the formula—not hurting you. He wasn't very good at what he did."

"Why did he have a necklace that matched mine?"

Mark shrugged as if annoyed. "I don't know. Because he was an idiot who liked to get into 'the mind of his victims.' Stupid man. Hiring him was a mistake."

"He also had Hensley's phone number written on his hand."

"I wondered how much Hensley knew, so he was supposed to check him out also. But, like I said, hiring that guy was a mistake. That's why I had to correct my error."

"So you killed Travis Metcalf?"

His gaze darkened. "I couldn't allow for any sloppy work."

A timeline began to form in her mind. "I see. Then you stole my notebook, hoping I'd written down something inside it—the missing pieces of the formula."

"I saw you jotting ideas there. I figured it was a good bet." Mark scowled. "It wasn't."

"How are you going to get the rest of this formula if you kill me?" Rachel stared at that syringe again, imagining how it would feel if the needle was to pierce her skin.

It wouldn't be a fun way to die. She knew that for sure.

"I'll find someone," Mark spit the words out. "Noelle might be a good candidate. I know she still has a ton of debt from her student loans from college so maybe I can offer her some incentive to pay that off."

"You think Noelle is a better bet than I am?" The last thing Rachel wanted to do was to help Mark. But she had to figure a way out of this situation. She needed to prey on his logic.

Mark stepped closer, a new gleam in his eyes. "Are you offering to help?"

Rachel swallowed hard.

Was that what she was offering?

She wasn't sure.

Right now, she was just trying to stay alive.

But she prayed that, whatever happened, she didn't hiccup right now and ruin any scheme she might develop to keep her alive.

————

Jonah practically threw his phone on the floor of his truck.

He'd just tried to call Rachel again, but there was still no answer.

He needed to warn her but couldn't.

Instead, he sped down the road toward the lab.

Cassidy drove in front of him followed by her officers.

When they pulled into the lot, only two cars were there. One of them was Rachel's.

He and Cassidy met in the parking lot.

"Do you know who the other car belongs to?" Cassidy nodded toward the Mercedes.

Jonah shook his head. "No, but I have a few ideas."

"We'll talk about this in a moment." She pointed toward the door. "Let's go."

When they reached the door, it was locked.

Of course.

The company had used all the latest technology to make the glass unbreakable.

"Can you pick the lock?" he asked.

Cassidy examined it before frowning.

"I could, but it would take a while. We don't have a while." She grabbed her phone. "I'm going to call Dr. Hensley if I can get a signal."

She paced from the front door, walking farther into the parking lot as she called the man.

As she did that, Jonah ran around the lab and tried to peer in the windows.

Rachel wasn't anywhere within eyesight.

He felt certain she was in grave danger.

The person who'd killed Gannon now had her. If Jonah didn't find her soon enough, she would also be dead.

His heart leapt into his throat at the thought.

He hadn't realized how much he cared about her until he'd lost her. Of course, he never really had her either.

But he wanted to change that.

If Rachel would forgive him.

Right now, his first priority was keeping her alive.

Cassidy jogged back toward him. "Hensley is on his way. It will take him about five minutes."

Jonah's muscles tightened.

Did they have five minutes?

He wasn't sure.

While they waited, he filled Cassidy in on everything the Dagger agent had said and what he'd learned.

Cassidy shook her head. "I don't like the way any of this sounds."

"Me either. We've got to get to Rachel."

A couple of minutes later, Hensley's vehicle sped into the lot.

Hensley quickly climbed from his Audi and met them at the door. "Rachel's in trouble?"

His hands were practically shaking as he pulled out his badge.

"She's in a lot of danger right now," Cassidy said. "We've got to get inside."

Sweat trickled down the man's forehead. "Of course."

He scanned his badge, and the door clicked.

"You should wait out here," Cassidy told him. "I'm not sure what exactly is happening inside."

"You might need me. There are other doors in there that are locked."

"We'll find you if we need you," Cassidy said.

Then she and Jonah and the other officers rushed inside.

"DO you know what's missing from the formula?" Mark glared at Rachel as he pointed the gun at her.

"I haven't even had a chance to look at the new research again." Rachel took a step back but hit the wall. She had nowhere else to go. "In fact, I didn't know he was finished with it. I thought he was still working on it."

Mark stared at her, clearly still skeptical about her words.

He waited, almost as if expecting her to hiccup.

She didn't.

"Is that what's in the folder?" He nodded toward her bag.

Rachel glanced at her purse where she'd stuffed the folder. "I think so. Lloyd just found it and gave it to me. I don't even know where he got it."

"Look at it. Tell me what you think."

Her hands trembled as she pulled out the folder. In fact, they shook and quivered so much that she couldn't even read anything there.

"I need to set this down," she told Mark. "I can't read it right now. My hands are shaking too badly."

He grunted and pointed with his gun toward the table against a wall on the other side of the room. "Go over there. Don't try anything stupid."

But Rachel already had an idea of how she might get out of this.

She just needed to wait for the right timing.

Mark remained close, his gun still drawn.

It was just the two of them.

If Rachel was going to get out of this, she needed to figure out a solution for herself.

She not only had to figure this out for herself but for her dad also.

She placed the folder on the table and opened it, pretending to stare at the words written there.

"What do you think?" Mark demanded.

"I don't know." Her voice quivered. "I can't think clearly with that gun aimed at me."

"I'm sorry I'm making you uncomfortable." He paused and sneered. "Not really."

Out of the corner of her eye, Rachel saw his badge still on his coat. To get into this room required a retinal scan.

But to leave, one just needed the approved badge.

If Rachel could grab it . . .

Her thoughts raced.

"Just give me a minute." She turned back to the folder. "I need to breathe a second."

"Don't be too long. I'd hate for anyone to come here looking for you."

She pretended to study the words. Instead, she looked at a bottle of acid sitting about three feet from her.

If she could just get her hands on that . . .

"Well?" Mark practically breathed down her neck as he waited.

"Like I said, I just need a minute to sort through all this. Gannon scribbled notes everywhere, and I don't know exactly what everything means."

"You're really testing my patience. This venom is sounding more and more tempting all the time."

How could this man be so vile? So greedy?

Ganon's life had been worth more than whatever this formula was worth. When Rachel thought about the cures Ganon could have developed . . . she swallowed hard as disgust rose in her.

It was time to end this.

Rachel grabbed the acid and flung it at Mark.

He howled with pain as the liquid hit his face. "You little . . . what have you done?"

A pungent fume filled the air, followed by the sound of sizzling.

Sizzling flesh.

Rachel quickly grabbed Mark's badge and sprinted toward the door.

The lock clicked open.

She threw the door open and ran out only to collide with someone else.

Her breath caught.

Was his hired henchman here?

She glanced up, trying not to let fear overtake her.

Instead, she whispered, "Jonah . . ."

He grasped her arms. "Are you okay?"

She nodded and then looked through the doorway. "It was Mark. I just threw acid on him and . . ."

Cassidy rushed past.

As she did, Jonah pulled Rachel close.

Rachel melted into his arms, grateful to feel a moment of safety.

Two hours later, Jonah and Rachel sat on a bench outside the lab.

The nighttime sky was dark now. The only light around them came from a few lights on the Ocean Essence building and the blue and red flashing lights of first responder vehicles.

Blankets had been placed over both of their shoulders.

Mark had been taken away—handcuffed—in an ambulance.

Dr. Hensley was being questioned.

Cassidy had called someone to rescue Rachel's father. The man who'd been hired to intimidate Rachel had apparently known Roman Atwood's location.

Jonah slipped his arm around Rachel.

Rachel hadn't pushed him away. He was grateful for that.

"Thank you for coming for me," she murmured.

"Of course. I'm . . . well, I'm really sorry I wasn't truthful with you, Rachel."

She pulled away from him and looked into his eyes. "Did you really think I could have murdered Ganon?"

"He gave me your name before he died and then muttered, 'killed.' What was I supposed to think?"

"He probably said that because he wanted you to talk to me to get some answers or he thought I was in danger."

Jonah nodded. "It makes more sense now. But at the time . . ."

Rachel was quiet a moment before shaking her head. "I just don't know what to think about all of this."

"It's a lot. But Ganon will finally get the justice he deserves."

"We can be thankful for that. I know Mark hired that man who broke into the house. He was clearly looking through my things, trying to find information. But what about the guy who shot at us on the beach? I keep trying to figure out how he fits. Because Mark didn't want me dead."

Jonah's spine tightened. He'd thought of that also.

He didn't like the conclusions he'd drawn.

"Jonah?" Rachel stared at him, waiting for his response.

He let out a breath, tired of lying to her. "I'm not sure. But the shooter could have been . . . he could have been after me."

Her eyes widened with surprise. "Why would people be after you?"

"Do you have a few hours?"

She tilted her head. "I might."

"I'll give you the short version. I was recruited from the military for an experimental project. I didn't realize it involved scientists and injections and covert missions."

Her eyes narrowed. "Like the Jason Bourne novels?"

"Not exactly. But these people tested some drugs on us. Some of the effects . . . well, they weren't good." He rolled up his sleeve and showed her some of his scars.

She sucked in a breath and gently ran her finger across one of them. "I wondered about these. I thought it was a knife wound."

His gaze darkened. "It was. But that's a story for another day. Anyway, I eventually left. The thing is, the leaders didn't expect anyone to leave the program on their own time. As a result, I made some people mad. Really mad."

"Mad enough to kill you?"

"I'm not sure. But maybe. If not them, then it could be any one of the enemies I made while doing operations for them."

Rachel stared up at him, more questions in her gaze. "What about Anna? Was what you told me about her true?"

He nodded. "I met her while on an assignment. When I told her the truth about what I did, she couldn't handle it. Her rejection . . . well, it broke me."

"I'm sorry to hear that."

"But there was more to the story." His voice caught. "When she left that conversation, three men I'd been spying on grabbed her. They thought she had information and they . . . they killed her."

"Oh, Jonah. That's terrible."

"I haven't been able to forgive myself."

"You couldn't have known . . ."

"Her death turned my world upside down."

"I can imagine." Rachel squeezed his arm.

"I'm okay now. It's just that I've never been one to easily trust. Now it's even worse."

Rachel shifted to fully face him, a new determination in her gaze. "How about if you and I start from scratch?"

A smile tugged at his lips. "I like that idea."

She extended her hand. "I'm Rachel Atwood."

"Jonah Gray."

She grinned. "It's nice to meet you, Jonah. That's a great name you know. Biblical."

"I've been told that before. In fact, I picked my name myself as soon as I turned eighteen."

Rachel raised her eyebrows. "Did you? I can't wait to hear that story."

Jonah slipped his arm around her, grateful for a second chance.

But for now, they still had more questions to answer and a long night ahead of them.

CHAPTER
FIFTY-FIVE

THE NEXT MORNING, Rachel heard a vehicle rumble into her driveway and threw open the front door.

She stepped outside into the sunshine-filled day, and a smile spread across her face when she saw someone step out of an SUV.

Her dad.

She flew from the house and threw her arms around his thin frame. She held on for a long time. Maybe too long.

She didn't care.

Once she finally pulled away, she studied him for any signs of injury. There were none she could see.

"Are you okay?" she murmured.

He rested his palm on the side of her face. "I'm fine now that I see you."

"I was so worried about you." Her voice cracked.

"I heard how brave you were. I'm so proud of you." The skin around his eyes crinkled as he gazed at her affectionately.

"I'm so sorry that I pulled you into this mess. I had no idea."

"Of course, you didn't. I'm just glad we're all okay." His gaze traveled beyond her to Jonah, who'd followed her outside.

Rachel stepped back to let the two interact.

Her dad observed him a moment, an aloofness in his gaze. "I heard you . . ."

She held her breath as she wondered where he was going with this conversation.

". . . helped save my daughter," her dad finally finished.

Jonah cast her a quick smile. "I think Rachel did just fine on her own. But I'm glad I could be there to offer her support."

Her dad held out his arm and smiled. "So am I. She means everything in the world to me."

The two shook hands in a friendly truce.

Rachel and Jonah exchanged a glance.

Last night, she and Jonah had played Scrabble and drank tea in front of the fireplace.

It would take time to rebuild her trust with him. But a new beginning felt like a distinct possibility.

However, she wasn't even sure Jonah would stay on the island now that Ganon's murder had been closed. Why would he? Jonah worked jobs all over the country. Staying on an isolated island like this would only hinder him.

But Rachel didn't want to think about that at the moment.

For now, she was simply grateful her father was okay. That a killer was now behind bars. That the air had been cleared between her and Jonah.

She'd found out that the conversation she'd heard between Hensley and Lloyd had been about business. Neither of them was guilty in this crime. Hensley had, however, been suspicious that something was going on inside the company. He'd noticed some money disappearing from Ocean Essence's account—thanks to Mark.

That was why he'd hired an independent investigator to check the company's books. That was the conversation she and Jonah had overheard at Hensley's party.

Carl Nevada was apparently in Colorado still. The threats against her hadn't been made by him.

Rachel wrapped her arm around her father's shoulder. "Why don't we get you inside? I'll fix something to eat, and you can relax a little and tell me about everything that's been going on. I want to hear about all of these new inventions you're working on."

"I'd love to tell you. Let's get inside and do just that. It sounds like the perfect evening."

Rachel grinned. "Yes, it really does."

She wasn't sure what the future held. As of right now, she still planned on staying with Ocean Essence. Mark wouldn't be bothering her, and she truly believed in the mission of what she was doing at the company.

But it would be a while before she felt comfortable in that office.

Hensley had reached out to her and offered his apologies. He'd even given her a week off.

Rachel wasn't sure if she would take it or not. That remained to be seen.

But for tonight, she would enjoy being with her father.

And Jonah.

———

After they finished eating dinner, Jonah's phone rang.

He glanced at the screen and saw it was Larchmont.

Excusing himself, he stepped upstairs to his bedroom to take the call.

He'd tried to contact his boss last night to give him an update, but Larchmont hadn't answered, which was unlike him.

"Hey, what's going on?" Jonah pushed the phone against his ear as he closed his bedroom door behind him.

"I hear there's been progress."

Jonah's muscles stiffened at his words.

How did Larchmont know there was an update? Jonah hadn't even told Vincent or Tex yet.

"How did you hear that?" Jonah's back muscles bristled as he stared outside.

"I have eyes and ears everywhere. I'm glad you finally found some answers for your friend. Now, are you ready for a new assignment?"

As Larchmont asked that question, the sound of Rachel's laughter drifted upstairs to him.

Jonah smiled.

He loved that sound.

More than anything, he wanted to get to know Rachel better. She was everything he could ever want, and when Jonah imagined his future . . . he couldn't stop dreaming about what it would be like with her.

He desperately wanted the family he'd never had growing up. He wanted stability. Normalcy.

That would be hard to do if he left this area for a new assignment.

Because Jonah knew what would follow after that.

There would be a new assignment.

Then another new assignment.

Was this really the life Jonah wanted to live? He'd thought it was. He'd thought he didn't have anything to live for. No one to hold him down.

But now that he'd met Rachel, a new hope sprang to life inside him.

God is going to do great things through you.

Jonah remembered the words of his high school mentor.

Was God's plan for his life for him to continue with the Shadow Agency?

Or was it for him to find a new purpose here in Lantern Beach with Rachel?

Jonah might even be able to talk to Ty and see if he could work for Blackout. Jonah wasn't sure.

For now, Larchmont's question lingered in the air.

Are you ready for a new assignment?

He frowned.

The memory of being shot at on the beach also filled his thoughts. The memory of that text that had been sent to Rachel, warning her not to trust him.

That hadn't been Mark. At least, Mark hadn't admitted to it.

Jonah had a feeling one of his enemies had sent it.

Danger still could be following him. If that was the case, did he want to stay here and put Rachel in the line of fire again?

Jonah had some major thinking to do before he made that decision.

Rachel's smile flashed into his mind.

He'd be a fool to walk away from her.

He planned on letting her know just how much she meant to him.

"Jonah?" Larchmont's voice cut into his thoughts.

Jonah swallowed hard. "I'm going to need some time . . ."

"How much time?"

"I'm not sure."

"I don't know . . ." Larchmont's voice made it clear he wasn't happy.

"Give me a few weeks to figure some things out. Then we'll talk again. Okay?" Jonah held his breath, hoping his boss understood.

Finally, Larchmont sighed. "Fine. A few weeks. But not a moment longer."

A smile stretched across Jonah's face.

He couldn't remember the last time he felt so much hope inside him.

He ended the call and went back downstairs to meet Rachel and Roman . . . and maybe to play a game of Scrabble.

~~~

Thank you for reading *Fractured Lies*. If you enjoyed this book, please consider leaving a review.

Stay tuned for *Shattered Whispers,* coming next!

~~~

ALSO BY CHRISTY BARRITT:

OTHER BOOKS IN THE LANTERN BEACH SERIES:

LANTERN BEACH MYSTERIES

Hidden Currents

You can take the detective out of the investigation, but you can't take the investigator out of the detective. A notorious gang puts a bounty on Detective Lady Matthews's head after she takes down their leader, leaving her no choice but to hide until she can testify at trial. But her temporary home across the country on a remote North Carolina island isn't as peaceful as she initially thinks. Living under the new identity of Cassidy Livingston, she struggles to keep her investigative skills tucked away, especially after a body washes ashore. When local police bungle the murder investigation, she can't resist stepping in. But Cassidy is supposed to be keeping a low profile. One wrong move could lead to both her discovery and her demise. Can she bring justice to the island . . . or will the hidden currents surrounding her pull her under for good?

Flood Watch

The tide is high, and so is the danger on Lantern Beach. Still in hiding after infiltrating a dangerous gang, Cassidy Livingston just has to make it a few more months before she can testify at trial and resume her old life. But trouble keeps finding her, and Cassidy is pulled into a local investigation after a man mysteriously disappears from the island she now calls home. A recurring nightmare from her time undercover only muddies things, as does a visit from the parents of her handsome ex-Navy SEAL neighbor. When a friend's life is threatened, Cassidy must make choices that put her on the verge of blowing her cover. With a flood watch on her emotions and her life in a tangle, will Cassidy find the truth? Or will her past finally drown her?

Storm Surge

A storm is brewing hundreds of miles away, but its effects are devastating even from afar. Laid-back, loose, and light: that's Cassidy Livingston's new motto. But when a makeshift boat with a bloody cloth inside washes ashore near her oceanfront home, her detective instincts shift into gear . . . again. Seeking clues isn't the only thing on her mind—romance is heating up with next-door neighbor and former Navy SEAL Ty Chambers as well. Her heart wants the love and stability she's longed for her entire life. But her hidden identity only leads to a tidal wave of turbulence. As more answers emerge about the boat, the danger around her rises, creating a treacherous swell that threatens to reveal her past. Can Cassidy mind her own business, or will the storm surge of violence and corruption that has washed ashore on Lantern Beach leave her life in wreckage?

Dangerous Waters

Danger lurks on the horizon, leaving only two choices: find shelter or flee. Cassidy Livingston's new identity has begun to feel as comfortable as her favorite sweater. She's been tucked away on Lantern Beach for weeks, waiting to testify against a deadly gang, and is settling in to a new life she wants to last forever. When she thinks she spots someone malevolent from her past, panic swells inside her. If an enemy has found her, Cassidy won't be the only one who's a target. Everyone she's come to love will also be at risk. Dangerous waters threaten to pull her into an overpowering chasm she may never escape. Can Cassidy survive what lies ahead? Or has the tide fatally turned against her?

Perilous Riptide

Just when the current seems safer, an unseen danger emerges and threatens to destroy everything. When Cassidy Livingston finds a journal hidden deep in the recesses of her ice cream truck, her curiosity kicks into high gear. Islanders suspect that Elsa, the journal's owner, didn't die accidentally. Her final entry indicates their suspicions might be correct and that what Elsa observed on her final night may have led to her demise. Against the advice of Ty Chambers, her former Navy SEAL boyfriend, Cassidy taps into her detective skills and hunts for answers. But her search only leads to a skeletal body and trouble for both of them. As helplessness threatens to drown her, Cassidy is desperate to turn back time. Can Cassidy find what she needs to navigate the perilous situation? Or will the riptide surrounding her threaten everyone and everything Cassidy loves?

Deadly Undertow

The current's fatal pull is powerful, but so is one detective's will to live. When someone from Cassidy Livingston's past shows up on Lantern Beach and warns her of impending peril, opposing currents collide, threatening to drag her under. Running would be easy. But leaving would break her heart. Cassidy must decipher between the truth and lies, between reality and deception. Even more importantly, she must decide whom to trust and whom to fear. Her life depends on it. As danger rises and answers surface, everything Cassidy thought she knew is tested. In order to survive, Cassidy must take drastic measures and end the battle against the ruthless gang DH-7 once and for all. But if her final mission fails, the consequences will be as deadly as the raging undertow.

LANTERN BEACH ROMANTIC SUSPENSE

Tides of Deception

Change has come to Lantern Beach: a new police chief, a new season, and . . . a new romance? Austin Brooks has loved Skye Lavinia from the moment they met, but the walls she keeps around her seem impenetrable. Skye knows Austin is the best thing to ever happen to her. Yet she also knows that if he learns the truth about her past, he'd be a fool not to run. A chance encounter brings secrets bubbling to the surface, and danger soon follows. Are the life-threatening events plaguing them really accidents . . . or is someone trying to send a deadly message? With the tides on Lantern Beach come deception and lies. One question remains—who will be swept away as the water shifts? And will it bring the end for Austin and Skye, or merely the beginning?

Shadow of Intrigue

For her entire life, Lisa Garth has felt like a supporting character in the drama of life. The designation never bothered her—until now. Lantern Beach, where she's settled and runs a popular restaurant, has boarded up for the season. The slower pace leaves her with too much time alone. Braden Dillinger came to Lantern Beach to try to heal. The former Special Forces officer returned from battle with invisible scars and diminished hope. But his recovery is hampered by the fact that an unknown enemy is trying to kill him. From the moment Lisa and Braden meet, danger ignites around them, and both are drawn into a web of intrigue that turns their lives upside down. As shadows creep in, will Lisa and Braden be able to shine a light on the peril around them? Or will the encroaching darkness turn their worst nightmares into reality?

Storm of Doubt

A pastor who's lost faith in God. A romance writer who's lost faith in love. A faceless man with a deadly obsession. Nothing has felt right in Pastor Jack Wilson's world since his wife died two years ago. He hoped coming to Lantern Beach might help soothe the ragged edges of his soul. Instead, he feels more alone than ever. Novelist Juliette Grace came to the island to hide away. Though her professional life has never been better, her personal life has imploded. Her husband left her and a stalker's threats have grown more and more dangerous. When Jack saves Juliette from an attack, he sees the terror in her gaze and knows he must protect her. But when danger strikes again, will Jack be able to keep her safe? Or will the approaching storm prove too strong to withstand?

Winds of Danger

Wes O'Neill is perfectly content to hang with his friends and enjoy island life on Lantern Beach. Something begins to change inside him when Paige Henderson sweeps into his life. But the beautiful newcomer is hiding painful secrets beneath her cheerful facade. Police dispatcher Paige Henderson came to Lantern Beach riddled with guilt and uncertainties after the fallout of a bad relationship. When she meets Wes, she begins to open up to the possibility of love again. But there's something Wes isn't telling her—something that could change everything. As the winds shift, doubts seep into Paige's mind. Can Paige and Wes trust each other, even as the currents work against them? Or is trouble from the past too much to overcome?

Rains of Remorse

A stranger invades her home, leaving Rebecca

Jarvis terrified. Above all, she must protect the baby growing inside her. Since her estranged husband died suspiciously six months earlier, Rebecca has been determined to depend on no one but herself. Her chivalrous new neighbor appears to be an answer to prayer. But who is Levi Stoneman really? Rebecca wants to believe he can help her, but she can't ignore her instincts. As danger closes in, both Rebecca and Levi must figure out whom they can trust. With Rebecca's baby coming soon, there's no time to waste. Can the truth prevail . . . or will remorse overpower the best of intentions?

Torrents of Fear

The woman lingering in the crowd can't be Allison . . . can she? Because Allison was pronounced dead six years ago. Musician Carter Denver knows only one person who's capable of helping him find answers: Sadie Thompson, his estranged best friend and someone who also knew Allison. He needs to know if he's losing his mind or if Allison could have survived her car accident. Could Allison really be alive? If so, why is she trying to harm Carter and Sadie? As the two try to find answers, can Sadie keep her feelings for Carter hidden? Could he ever care for her, or is the man of her dreams still in love with the woman now causing his nightmares?

<h1 style="text-align:center">LANTERN BEACH PD</h1>

On the Lookout

A runaway woman. A dead body. A mysterious compound. When Cassidy Chambers accepted the job as police chief on Lantern Beach, she knew the island had its secrets. But a suspicious death with potentially far-reaching implications will test all her skills—and threaten to reveal her true identity. Cassidy enlists the help of her husband, former Navy SEAL Ty Chambers. As they dig for answers, both uncover parts of their pasts that are best left buried. Not everything is as it seems, and they must figure out if their John Doe is connected to the secretive group that has moved onto the island. As facts materialize, danger on the island grows. Can Cassidy and Ty discover the truth about the shadowy crimes in their cozy community? Or has darkness permanently invaded their beloved Lantern Beach?

Attempt to Locate

A fun girls' night out turns into a nightmare when armed robbers barge into the store where Cassidy and her friends are shopping. As the situation escalates and the men escape, a massive manhunt launches on Lantern Beach to apprehend the dangerous trio. In the midst of the chaos, a potential foe asks for Cassidy's help. He needs to find his sister who fled from the secretive Gilead's Cove community on the island. But the more Cassidy learns about the seemingly untouchable group, the more her unease grows. The pressure to solve both cases continues to mount. But as the gravity of the situation rises, so does the danger. Cassidy is determined to protect the island and break up the cult . . . but doing so might cost her everything.

First Degree Murder

Police Chief Cassidy Chambers longs for a break from the recent crimes plaguing Lantern Beach. She simply wants to enjoy her friends' upcoming wedding, to prepare for the busy tourist season about to slam the island, and to gather all the dirt she can on the suspicious community that's invaded the town. But trouble explodes on the island, sending residents—including Cassidy—into a squall of uneasiness. Cassidy may have more than one enemy plotting her demise, and the collateral damage seems unthinkable. As the temperature rises, so does the pressure to find answers. Someone is determined that Lantern Beach would be better off without their new police chief. And for Cassidy, one wrong move could mean certain death.

Dead on Arrival

With a highly charged local election consuming

the community, Police Chief Cassidy Chambers braces herself for a challenging day of breaking up petty conflicts and tamping down high emotions. But when widespread food poisoning spreads among potential voters across the island, Cassidy smells something rotten in the air. As Cassidy examines every possibility to uncover what's going on, local enigma Anthony Gilead again comes on her radar. The man is running for mayor and his cult-like following is growing at an alarming rate. Cassidy feels certain he has a spy embedded in her inner circle. The problem is that her pool of suspects gets deeper every day. Can Cassidy get to the bottom of what's eating away at her peaceful island home? Will voters turn out despite the outbreak of illness plaguing their tranquil town? And the even bigger question: Has darkness come to stay on Lantern Beach?

Plan of Action

A missing Navy SEAL. Danger at the boiling point. The ultimate showdown. When Police Chief Cassidy Chambers' husband, Ty, disappears, her world is turned upside down. His truck is discovered with blood inside, crashed in a ditch on Lantern Beach, but he's nowhere to be found. As they launch a manhunt to find him, Cassidy discovers that someone on the island has a deadly obsession with

Ty. Meanwhile, Gilead's Cove seems to be imploding. As danger heightens, federal law enforcement officials are called in. The cult's growing threat could lead to the pinnacle standoff of good versus evil. A clear plan of action is needed or the results will be devastating. Will Cassidy find Ty in time, or will she face a gut-wrenching loss? Will Anthony Gilead finally be unmasked for who he really is and be brought to justice? Hundreds of innocent lives are at stake . . . and not everyone will come out alive.

LANTERN BEACH ESCAPE

Afterglow

What if you married someone, only to discover that she was suspected of killing her former fiancé? While on their honeymoon, Grayson and Rachel Stewart are confronted with dark details of Rachel's past. As more facts begin emerging, their new marriage is thrown into a tailspin. The newlyweds must figure out how to move forward . . . and Grayson must figure out if he married a killer.

LANTERN BEACH BLACKOUT

Dark Water

Colton Locke can't forget the black op that went terribly wrong. Desperate for a new start, he moves to Lantern Beach, North Carolina, and forms Blackout, a private security firm. Despite his hero status, he can't erase the mistakes he's made. For the past year, Elise Oliver hasn't been able to shake the feeling that there's more to her husband's death than she was told. When she finds a hidden box of his personal possessions, more questions—and suspicions—arise. The only person she trusts to help her is her husband's best friend, Colton Locke. Someone wants Elise dead. Is it because she knows too much? Or is it to keep her from finding the truth? The Blackout team must uncover dark secrets hiding beneath seemingly still waters. But those very secrets might just tear the team apart.

Safe Harbor

Guilt over past mistakes haunts former Navy SEAL Dez Rodriguez. When he's asked to guard a pop star during a music festival on Lantern Beach, he's all set for what he hopes is a breezy assignment. Bree hasn't found fame to be nearly as fulfilling as she dreamed. Instead, she's more like a carefully crafted character living out a pre-scripted story. When a stalker's threats become deadly, her life—and career—are turned upside down. From the start, Bree sees her temporary bodyguard as a player, and Dez sees Bree as a spoiled rich girl. But when they're thrown together in a fight for survival, both must learn to trust. Can Dez protect Bree—and his carefully guarded heart? Or will their safe harbor ultimately become their death trap?

Ripple Effect

Griff McIntyre never expected his ex-wife and three-year-old daughter to come to Lantern Beach. After an abduction attempt, they're desperate for safety. Now Griff's not letting either of them out of his sight. Bethany knows Griff is the only one who can protect them, despite the fact that he broke her heart. But she'll do anything to keep her daughter safe—even if it means playing nicely with a man she can't stand. As peril ripples through their lives, Griff and Bethany must work together to protect their daughter. But an unseen enemy wants something from them . . . and will stop at nothing to get it. When disaster strikes, can Griff keep his family safe? Or will past mistakes bring the ultimate failure?

Rising Tide

Benjamin James knows there's a traitor within his former command. The rest of his team might even think it's him. As danger closes in, he must clear himself and stop a deadly plot by a dangerous terrorist group. All CJ Compton wanted was a new start after her career ended under suspicion. Working as the house manager for private security group

Blackout seems perfect. But there's more trouble here than what she left behind. As the tide rushes in, the stakes continue to rise. If the Blackout team fails, it's not just Lantern Beach at stake—it's the whole country. Can Benjamin and CJ overcome their differences and work together to find the truth?

LANTERN BEACH GUARDIANS

Hide and Seek

During a turbulent storm, a child is found on the beach, washed up from the ocean. Making matters worse— the girl can't speak. Lantern Beach Police Chief Cassidy Chambers can feel the danger lurking around them. As more mysterious incidents happen on the island, Cassidy fears each crime is somehow connected to this child—a child no one has reported missing. Cassidy knows the girl's life depends on finding answers. With the help of her husband, Ty, a former Navy SEAL, she scrambles to discover what exactly is going on. Someone appears to be playing a deadly version of hide-and-seek—and using the girl as a pawn. But what will happen when the game finally ends? *Hide and Seek is the first book in a three book series. Though the main storyline of each book will be wrapped up at the end, some plot lines will not be resolved until the end of book three.*

Shock and Awe

They thought the worst was over—but they were wrong.When Police Chief Cassidy Chambers arrives at a grisly crime scene, she's shocked at where the evidence leads. Then the threats start coming. Threats against her. Threats that could upend her life.As more clues are uncovered, a sinister plot is revealed, and Cassidy fears the little girl in her care may be tangled in a deadly scheme. Cassidy and her husband, Ty, will do anything to protect the child, each other, and the island. But what happens when they might not be able to save all three?

Safe and Sound

A call for help draws Police Chief Cassidy Chambers deep into a wooded, isolated area on Lantern Beach. What she finds shakes her to the core—a friend is bleeding out, and his last words before dying are: They know. Figuring out who killed her friend and what his final words meant becomes Cassidy's mission. Have members of the notorious gang that placed a bounty on her head discovered her new life? Or is someone else trying to teach her a twisted lesson? Elements from past investigations surface and threaten more than one person's safety. Cassidy and her husband, Ty, must make sense of the deadly secrets that unfold at every turn. If not, the life they've built together might come to a permanent end.

LANTERN BEACH BLACKOUT: THE NEW RECRUITS

Rocco

Former Navy SEAL and new Blackout recruit Rocco Foster is on a simple in and out mission. But the operation turns complicated when an unsuspecting woman wanders into the line of fire. Peyton Ellison's life mission is to sprinkle happiness on those around her. When a cupcake delivery turns into a fight for survival, she must trust her rescuer—a handsome stranger—to keep her safe. Rocco is determined to figure out why someone is targeting Peyton. First, he must keep the intriguing woman safe and earn her trust. But threats continue to pummel them as incriminating evidence emerges and pits them against each other. With time running out, the two must set aside both their growing attraction and their doubts about each other in order to work together. But the perilous facts they discover leave them wondering what exactly the truth is . . . and if the truth can be trusted.

Axel

Women are missing. Private security firm Blackout

must find them before another victim disappears. Axel Hendrix likes to live on the edge. That's why being a Navy SEAL suited him so well. But after his last mission, he cut his losses and joined Blackout instead. His team's latest case involves an undercover investigation on Lantern Beach. Olivia Rollins came to the island to escape her problems—and danger. When trouble from her past shows up in town, she impulsively blurts she's engaged to Axel, the womanizing man she's seen while waitressing. Now, she may not be the only one in danger. So could Axel. Axel knows Olivia might be his chance to find answers and that acting like her fiancé is the perfect cover for his latest assignment. But he doesn't like throwing Olivia into the middle of such a dangerous situation. Nor is he comfortable with the feelings she stirs inside him. With Olivia's life—as well as both their hearts—on the line, Axel must uncover the truth and stop an evil plan before more lives are destroyed.

Beckett

When the daughter of a federal judge is abducted, private security firm Blackout must find her. Psychologist Samantha Reynolds doesn't know why someone is targeting her. Even after a risky mission to save her, danger still lingers. She's determined to use her insights into the human mind to help decode the deadly clues being left in the wake of her rescue. Former Navy SEAL Beckett Jones needs to figure out who's responsible for the crimes hounding Sami. He's not sure why he's so protective of the woman he rescued, but he'll do anything to keep her safe—even if it means risking his heart. As the body count rises, there's no room for error. Beckett and Sami must both tear down the careful walls they've built around themselves in order to survive. If they don't figure out who's responsible, the madman will continue his death spree . . . and one of them might be next.

Gabe

When former Navy SEAL and current Blackout operative Gabe Michaels is almost killed in a hit-and-run, the aftermath completely upends his life. He's no longer safe—and he's not the only one. Dr. Autumn Spenser came to Lantern Beach to start fresh. But while treating Gabe after his accident, she senses there's more to what happened to him than meets the eye. When she digs deeper into his past, she never expects to be drawn into a deadly dilemma. Gabe has been infatuated with the pretty doctor since the day they met. Now, can he keep her from harm? Could someone out of his league ever return his feelings or will her past hurts keep them apart? As danger continues to pummel them, Gabe and Autumn are thrown together in a quest to find answers. More important than their growing attraction, they must stay alive long enough to stop the person desperate to destroy them.

LANTERN BEACH MAYDAY

Run Aground

A dead captain on a luxury yacht leads to a tumultuous seafaring journey . . . Med student Kenzie Anderson, tired of letting others chart her future, accepts a job as second steward aboard Almost Paradise. But when she finds the captain dead before the charter even begins, her plans seem to capsize. Jimmy James Gamble senses something vulnerable and slightly naive about Kenzie when he finds her on the docks. Realizing danger may still be lingering close, he uses his hidden skills to earn a place on the charter. But being there causes him to risk everything—especially as more suspicious incidents occur. As they set out to sea, Kenzie and Jimmy James both wonder if they're in over their heads. They must figure out how to stop a killer before anyone onboard is hurt . . . otherwise, both their futures might just run aground.

Dead Reckoning

A yachtie fears for her life when she's the only witness to a murder . . . Kenzie Anderson knows what she saw at the harbor—a woman strangled and pushed overboard. But there's no proof of a crime . . . only her word. Jimmy James Gamble believes Kenzie, even if no one else does. As he senses the danger in the air, all he wants is to keep her away from any more trouble—especially after their last charter. Either Kenzie or the yacht they're working on seem to be a magnet for murder and mayhem. Someone is willing to kill to get what he wants—and will do so again if necessary. Can Jimmy James and Kenzie navigate these unfamiliar waters? Or will relying on dead reckoning lead them to their deaths?

Tipping Point

Awakening in a boat surrounded by nothing but water, a yachtie has no doubt someone wants her dead. Kenzie Anderson is determined not to let anyone scare her away from completing the charter season—even with the threats on her life. The only person she can trust is Captain Jimmy James Gamble, despite their tumultuous relationship. Kenzie and Jimmy James both suspect turbulent currents rush beneath the tranquil surface aboard the luxury yacht Almost Paradise. Secrets seem to abound, each one increasing the tension aboard the boat. As answers rise to the surface, neither Kenzie nor Jimmy James is prepared for what they find. Have they both reached their tipping points? Their adversaries want nothing more than to make Kenzie disappear . . . forever. It may be too late for a mayday call.

LANTERN BEACH CHRISTMAS

Silent Night

Catch up with your favorite Lantern Beach characters as they come together to help the town's beloved police chief. On the night before Christmas Eve, as she begins her maternity leave, Lantern Beach Police Chief Cassidy Chambers disappears. Suspecting foul play, law enforcement officers combine forces with the Blackout Security team and island residents to find her. Despite a snowstorm in his path, Cassidy's husband, Ty, desperately tries to return home in time to save her. With his wife's and baby's lives on the line, he needs a Christmas miracle. Will the tightknit community of Lantern Beach be able to rescue their beloved police chief in time? Or will Cassidy's cries for help be met only with silence?

LANTERN BEACH BLACKOUT: DANGER RISING

Brandon

Physically he's protecting her. But emotionally she's never felt more exposed. The last person tech heiress Finley Cooper ever wanted to see again was Brandon

Hale. Two years ago, Brandon shattered her heart. Now Finley needs protection, and, against her wishes, Brandon is assigned the job. Even worse, they must pretend to be a couple in order to find answers. Brandon, a former Navy SEAL, met Finley while on an undercover assignment in Ecuador. But he broke her trust, and now he doesn't blame Finley for hating him. As a new Blackout operative, Brandon's first assignment throws him into Finley's life 24/7. Someone wants her dead, and it's clear this person won't stop until that mission is accomplished. To keep her safe, Brandon must regain Finley's trust. Can he convince her she's more than a job to him? Or will peril permanently silence them?

Dylan

His job is to protect her. The trouble is . . . she doesn't want protection. Former Navy SEAL Dylan Granger's new assignment requires him to use both his tactical abilities and his acting skills. Hired by Katie Logan's father, his job is to protect the gutsy university professor while concealing his identity. To maintain his cover, he takes the unassuming role of her new assistant. Katie—a disgraced reporter—has stumbled upon a lead she can't ignore. Now it's clear someone is targeting her, but she refuses to back down. Her handsome new assistant is a welcome distraction from the chaos. But Dylan's skillset goes way beyond his job description, and Katie begins to suspect there's more to Dylan than he's letting on. Dylan's mission can't be disclosed—not if he wants to keep Katie safe. But as his feelings for her grow and the danger increases, keeping his secret becomes more of a challenge than he ever imagined. With innocent lives on the line, Dylan must choose between protecting Katie or savings others.

Maddox

He's on the case . . . and she's his prime suspect. Classified technology is missing, a delivery driver is dead, and former Navy SEAL Maddox King must find the culprits before a dangerous plan is enacted. To find answers, the Blackout agent must go undercover as a maintenance man at millionaire Seymore Whitlock's estate. While there, he sets his sights on Whitlock's personal assistant, Taryn Parsons, a woman who has everything to gain and nothing to lose. Six months ago, Whitlock plucked Taryn out of obscurity to become his caretaker. But with deadly incidents haunting the estate, Taryn doesn't know who she can trust—including the new maintenance man who is both intriguing . . . and unnerving. The stakes continue to escalate, and Maddox is running out of time to find answers. With the body count rising along with his list of suspects, this assignment may be his most challenging yet . . . for both his skillset and his heart.

Titus

She shattered his heart once. Can he set her betrayal aside for the sake of his country? The last person Titus Armstrong wants to join forces with is the woman who dumped him for his brother, Alex. But Presley Lennox is Blackout's best chance at infiltrating a dangerous organization known as The System and finding out more about their deadly plans. Presley Lennox wants out—of both an abusive relationship and the radical group she's become entangled with because of Alex. When Titus reappears in her life, he's like an answer to prayer—until he asks her to dive deeper into the very life she's been trying to escape. A dangerous plan is brewing that could destroy thousands of lives. Titus and Presley may be the only ones who can stop what's about to be unleashed. Failure would mean certain chaos . . . not only for them but for their nation.

**BEACH BOUND BOOKS AND BEANS
MYSTERIES**

Bound by Murder

When widow Talitha Robinson buys an old store on the boardwalk in Lantern Beach, North Carolina, she's in for a surprise . . . or several. She plans to renovate the space and open Beach Bound Books and Beans, but never expects to find a decades-old skeleton hidden inside one of the walls. As word of the discovery spreads across the island, strange occurrences begin to occur around her. It soon becomes clear someone still knows something about the dead person—something they don't want discovered. Thankfully, former police chief and current mayor Mac MacArthur seems just as eager to unravel the mystery behind the skeletal remains as Tali. But as the two bind together to solve the case, a devastating secret is revealed. Will their newfound friendship come unglued before they find the answers to the past? Or will their blooming relationship die like the man hidden in the wall?Bound by Murder is book 1 in a four book series of novellas. Though the main mystery is resolved, there are threads that will continue throughout the entire series.

Bound by Disaster

Talitha Robinson is knee-deep in renovations as she prepares to open her new bookstore when a body washes ashore on Lantern Beach. While news of the suspicious death surges across the island, a stranger comes knocking on Tali's door, begging her to endorse his unfinished suspense novel. Unable to dissuade the author, Tali is left holding his manuscript in her hands. But she has no idea of the peril written on its pages. Mac MacArthur has kept his distance from Tali since they uncovered a shocking connection about their pasts. But when someone begins to act out the murderous scenes from the book, one victim at a time, Mac's protective instincts override his decision to stay away. As danger escalates, Mac and Tali must manage their conflicting feelings as they work together to stop this killer . . . before the last chapter is written.

Bound by Mystery

Talitha Robinson is well on her way to completing renovations for her new bookstore, Beach Bound Books and Beans, in Lantern Beach, North Carolina. But when she hosts a friendly meet-and-greet with bookstore owners from nearby islands, the progress she's making comes to a deadly end. Someone is backstabbed—literally—right under Tali's nose. To make matters worse, Tali's finger-prints are all over the murder weapon and a neighbor claims to have seen Tali commit the crime. Mac MacArthur knows Tali isn't the type to hurt anyone, but it doesn't take a former police chief to figure out things don't look good for her. The two work together to read between the lines and decipher the truth before Tali gets locked away for crimes she didn't commit. As more evidence stacks up, it becomes clear that someone wants to take Tali out of the story. For good.

Bound by Trouble

With the grand opening of Beach Bound Books and Beans, Tali Robinson's dreams are finally coming true. She hopes to now put the past behind her and start a new chapter. When a suspicious stranger mysteriously shows up at her celebration, her hopes disappear faster than a bestseller at a book signing.Mac MacArthur is ready to solidify his relationship with Tali. But mending their differences is easier said than done. Then someone sets their sights on Tali—and wants to put her out of print . . . permanently. With trouble brewing, Tali and Mac have no choice but to dive into the chaos of the past. However, as more answers are revealed, the danger increases. The truth will come at a great cost . . . one that will bind them together or drive them apart.

Bound by Mayhem

As cast and crew members prepare for Lantern Beach's first annual Christmas play, catastrophe strikes. Abby Mendez, the director and brainchild behind the play, never shows up for a dress rehearsal. Threats emerge, and it becomes clear that not everyone on the island feels the Christmas spirit. With dangerous encounters and ghostly disappearing acts threatening not only the play but also the safety of Lantern Beach residents, former police chief Mac MacArthur and Abby's friend Tali Robinson jump in to help. The stakes rise as the perpetrator continues to haunt Abby's past, torment her present, and threaten her future. When it seems all hope is nearly lost, can the people of Lantern Beach work together to save the play? Or will this phantom scrooge steal the final act?

COMPLETE BOOK LIST

Squeaky Clean Mysteries:

#1 Hazardous Duty

Half Witted (Squeaky Clean In Between Mysteries Book 1, novella)

#2 Suspicious Minds

#2.5 It Came Upon a Midnight Crime (novella)

#3 Organized Grime

#4 Dirty Deeds

#5 The Scum of All Fears

#6 To Love, Honor and Perish

#7 Mucky Streak

#8 Foul Play

#9 Broom & Gloom

#10 Dust and Obey

#11 Thrill Squeaker

#11.5 Swept Away (novella)

#12 Cunning Attractions

#13 Cold Case: Clean Getaway

#14 Cold Case: Clean Sweep

#15 Cold Case: Clean Break

#16 Cleans to an End

While You Were Sweeping, A Riley Thomas Spinoff

The Sierra Files:

#1 Pounced

#2 Hunted

#3 Pranced

#4 Rattled

The Gabby St. Claire Diaries (a Tween Mystery series):

#1 The Curtain Call Caper

#2 The Disappearing Dog Dilemma

#3 The Bungled Bike Burglaries

The Worst Detective Ever

#1 Ready to Fumble

#2 Reign of Error

#3 Safety in Blunders

#4 Join the Flub

#5 Blooper Freak

#6 Flaw Abiding Citizen

#7 Gaffe Out Loud

#8 Joke and Dagger

#9 Wreck the Halls

#10 Glitch and Famous

#11 Not on My Botch

Raven Remington

Relentless

Holly Anna Paladin Mysteries:

#1 Random Acts of Murder

#2 Random Acts of Deceit

#2.5 Random Acts of Scrooge

#3 Random Acts of Malice

#4 Random Acts of Greed

#5 Random Acts of Fraud

#6 Random Acts of Outrage

#7 Random Acts of Iniquity

Lantern Beach Mysteries

#1 Hidden Currents

#2 Flood Watch

#3 Storm Surge

#4 Dangerous Waters

#5 Perilous Riptide

#6 Deadly Undertow

Lantern Beach Romantic Suspense

#1 Tides of Deception

#2 Shadow of Intrigue

#3 Storm of Doubt

#4 Winds of Danger

#5 Rains of Remorse

#6 Torrents of Fear

Lantern Beach P.D.

#1 On the Lookout

#2 Attempt to Locate

#3 First Degree Murder

#4 Dead on Arrival

#5 Plan of Action

Lantern Beach Escape

Afterglow (a novelette)

Lantern Beach Blackout

#1 Dark Water

#2 Safe Harbor

#3 Ripple Effect

#4 Rising Tide

Lantern Beach Guardians

#1 Hide and Seek

#2 Shock and Awe

#3 Safe and Sound

Lantern Beach Blackout: The New Recruits

#1 Rocco

#2 Axel

#3 Beckett

#4 Gabe

Lantern Beach Mayday

#1 Run Aground

#2 Dead Reckoning

#3 Tipping Point

Lantern Beach Blackout: Danger Rising

#1 Brandon

#2 Dylan

#3 Maddox

#4 Titus

Lantern Beach Christmas

Silent Night

Crime á la Mode

#1 Dead Man's Float

#2 Milkshake Up

#3 Bomb Pop Threat

#4 Banana Split Personalities

Beach Bound Books and Beans Mysteries

#1 Bound by Murder

#2 Bound by Disaster

#4 Seagrass Secrets

#5 Driftwood Danger

#6 Unwavering Security

Beach House Mysteries

#1 The Cottage on Ghost Lane

#2 The Inn on Hanging Hill

#3 The House on Dagger Point

School of Hard Rocks Mysteries

#1 The Treble with Murder

#2 Crime Strikes a Chord

#3 Tone Death

Carolina Moon Series

#1 Home Before Dark

#2 Gone By Dark

#3 Wait Until Dark

#4 Light the Dark

#5 Taken By Dark

Suburban Sleuth Mysteries:

Death of the Couch Potato's Wife

Fog Lake Suspense:

#1 Edge of Peril

#2 Margin of Error

#3 Brink of Danger

#4 Line of Duty

#5 Legacy of Lies

#6 Secrets of Shame

#7 Refuge of Redemption

Cape Thomas Series:

#1 Dubiosity

#2 Disillusioned

#3 Distorted

Standalone Romantic Mystery:

The Good Girl

Suspense:

Imperfect

The Wrecking

Sweet Christmas Novella:

Home to Chestnut Grove

Standalone Romantic-Suspense:

Keeping Guard

The Last Target

Race Against Time

Ricochet

Key Witness

Lifeline

High-Stakes Holiday Reunion

Desperate Measures

Hidden Agenda

Mountain Hideaway

Dark Harbor

Shadow of Suspicion

The Baby Assignment

The Cradle Conspiracy

Trained to Defend

Mountain Survival

Dangerous Mountain Rescue

Nonfiction:

Characters in the Kitchen

Changed: True Stories of Finding God through Christian Music (out of print)

The Novel in Me: The Beginner's Guide to Writing and Publishing a Novel (out of print)

ABOUT THE AUTHOR

USA Today has called Christy Barritt's books "scary, funny, passionate, and quirky."

Christy writes both mystery and romantic suspense novels that are clean with underlying messages of faith. Her books have sold more than three million copies and have won the Daphne du Maurier Award for Excellence in Suspense and Mystery, have been twice nominated for the Romantic Times Reviewers' Choice Award, and have finaled for both a Carol Award and Foreword Magazine's Book of the Year.

She is married to her Prince Charming, a man who thinks she's hilarious—but only when she's not trying to be. Christy is a self-proclaimed klutz, an avid music lover who's known for spontaneously bursting into song, and a road trip aficionado.

When she's not working or spending time with her family, she enjoys singing, playing the guitar, and exploring small, unsuspecting towns where people have no idea how accident-prone she is.

Find Christy online at:
www.christybarritt.com
www.facebook.com/christybarritt
www.twitter.com/cbarritt

Sign up for Christy's newsletter to get information on all of her latest releases here: **www.christybarritt. com/newsletter-sign-up/**

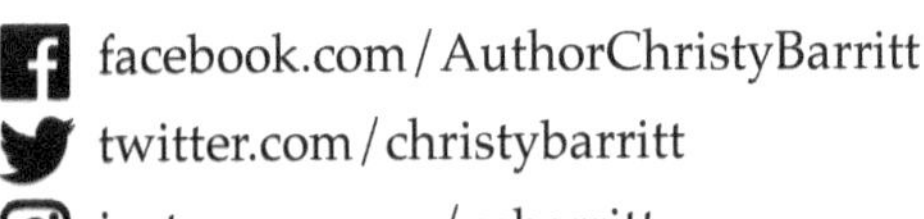

facebook.com / AuthorChristyBarritt
twitter.com / christybarritt
instagram.com / cebarritt

www.ingramcontent.com/pod-product-compliance
Lightning Source LLC
Chambersburg PA
CBHW031953150726
47990CB00005B/1690